SNOWY PEAK SERIES

Cloud
Nine

INTERNATIONAL BESTSELLING AUTHOR
AMANDA SINATRA

CLOUD NINE

Amanda Sinatra

authoramandasinatra@gmail.com

Cover Design: Liz Parkes

Developmental/Copy Edits: Marni MacRae

Proof Edits: Lunar Rose Services

First Edition Paperback February 2026

ISBN: 979-8-9931318-3-2

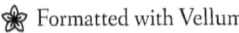 Formatted with Vellum

*For my sister, who has been my best friend and biggest supporter,
this story would cease to exist if it wasn't for you pushing me to
do my very best.
I love you.*

- **Alley-Oop:** when a rider rotates 180 degrees or more in the uphill direction.
- **Double Cork 1260:** is an aerial maneuver in snowboarding and freestyle skiing that involves two off-axis rotations (corks) and a total of three and a half rotations (1260 degrees) while in the air.
- **Air to fakie:** Any trick in the halfpipe where the wall is approached riding forward, no rotation is made, and the boarder lands riding backward.
- **Nose-Roll 180:** Start a toe or heel side turn, and once you get on edge, lift the tail of your board, keeping the nose on the ground. Then, spin the board to land switch.
- **Double McTwist 1260:** combing two front flips (double cork) with three-and-a-half (1260 degrees) rotations in a single aerial maneuver.
- **Frontside 180:** rotate your body and board 180 degrees with your front, facing downhill while performing the spin, starting regular and landing switch (backwards).

- **Frontside 360:** a full 360 degree spin, where the riders front rotates in a downhill direction, initiating with a toeside carve.
- **Twisties:** is a mental block occurs when an athlete loses their sense of space and direction while performing mid-air twists and flips
- **Crippler:** an inverted 540-degree spin, combining a backflip with a 360-rotation.

TRIGGER WARNINGS

This story contains graphic sex scenes, minor flashback scenes of mental abuse, PSTD from mental abuse, anxiety, PCOS (Poly Cystic Ovarian Syndrome) representation along with scenes describing PCOS.

If any of these triggers are too much please stop right here and close the book.

DEAR HANNAH,

Thank you so much for taking your time with our family, especially little Jonah. The photos came out great, and they're hung up in our living room. We get so many compliments from friends and family, and we recommend your services.

The reason I'm emailing you again is because I was wondering: do you offer private sessions? Your technique is hard to find, and I would love it if you could do some nude—

Deleting emails from the fathers of the family photos I take who ask for nudes never gets old. In three out of the six sessions, the men decide to email me, straight up asking for explicit content. Emails usually start with a thank-you, compliments on my work, and a note that they've recommended me to others, praising my skills. Then they dive right in, asking if I offer other expertise. One guy showed up in just a bathrobe, and I never ran so fast in my life.

If you checked the trash tab on my email, you'd find countless more.

Maya suggests I post them anonymously on Reddit to get a good laugh, but I'm afraid it'll somehow trace back to me.

It's disgusting and not at all surprising at this point.

Unfortunately, I lost clientele, had to ghost previous wives because I couldn't tell them their husbands were ruthless pigs.

And now I sit cross-legged on my black, leather sofa, eating hot Chinese food from my local restaurant down the street while I upload today's work on my laptop. Keeping my phone propped up, I listen to my best friend ramble on about her shitty date from last night.

"And then, oh my god, Hannah, he pulled out a gift card from his wallet!" she shrieks, the phone's speaker crackling.

I drag files across the screen, organize them by date, then start to upload the photos in Photoshop. "How much was on it?" Nothing revs Maya's engine more than a man paying the whole meal with a gift card, especially on a first date.

"It paid for the whole meal!" Bingo. Guy number...six? I lost count at this point. I swear, these types of men have a radar out for Maya. It's quite comical. Maya cares for the wads of hundreds he can carry in his wallet, but the minute he busts out a gift card, Hell freezes over, and she instantly gets the ick.

"Maybe Tinder isn't your app," I tease, tagging photos my client had asked me to edit.

"Nobody uses Tinder anymore," she states.

I shrug. "Then how are you finding them?"

"Hinge."

I laugh, then take another bite of my pork fried rice. When one app dies of popularity, you bet Maya will find the next hot thing to catch some male attention.

"Ugh! It's so annoying! I swear I have a tattoo on my forehead that says 'cheap.'" A loud purr echoes through the speaker as her giant orange tabby, Simon, makes his appearance, loud and proud. Then a cork pops, and a red wine is poured into one of Maya's ever-growing collection of wine glasses. "Thank God for this." Her glass is about empty when she pours herself another.

"Slow down, you're going to wake up with a hangover again," I advise.

She snorts, another chug down her throat. "After last night, I'm surprised I didn't drink more."

"I'm sure it wasn't that bad."

"Says you."

I'm careful not to over-edit, smoothing out harsh lines, adjusting each layer accordingly. The process is tedious, but I do love it. Each photo takes some time to edit, but I finish the first batch while Maya pours herself a third glass of red wine.

At least she's enjoying herself.

Another loud purr catches my attention, and Maya smooshes her face against his fur, then he lovingly licks her nose. "So, what about you?"

I internally groan. I love Maya with all my heart, and she means well, but I can't date right now, not after how things ended last time. Instead, I choose to fuck with her. "I did have a date last night."

Her face covers most of the screen. "Shut up!"

"Yeah, I mean, if he was honest with me from the beginning, I wouldn't have cared," I fib. I use my best convincing voice to really pull this off. "If he's hiding a bald spot, odds are he's hiding more skeletons in his closet."

She raises her glass, then sips it. "Like what? Dead bodies?"

"Dead exes. Tax evasion. Maybe he's secretly a part of the mafia?" I raise my eyebrows for dramatic effect. "We went to Chili's and he was balling on a budget when it came to the three for 11.99 deal."

Her silence has me checking my phone screen.

Maya flips me off when I look. "You're a lying sack of shit, Hannah Rose St. Pierre."

I'm trying my best not to laugh as I start fussing with the exposure and contrast. Once I get the perfect balance, I crop it to what the client specifications. "And you ate it right up."

I hear Simon meow-yelp, finding Maya giving me a look, the orange tabby nowhere in sight. "Girl, it's been two years."

Here we go again. "And?"

"And?! Don't let that stupid fuck—"

"Maya, I'm not NOT dating because of him." Well, sort of.

"Oh, please, you can't even say his name!"

"Yes, I can."

"Prove it."

Damn, this pill is going to be hard to swallow. "Liam, see?" I feel it getting stuck halfway down my esophagus. Even with therapy, saying his name is like tasting a hot, steamy, pile of garbage that's been sitting out in the August heat.

Curse her for being right.

Maya smirks, catching me in my lie. "That sounded painful."

I flip her off, continuing to sift through different layers of the photo before moving on to another set. "If our friendship didn't span over thirteen years, I might've killed you already."

She touches her chest dramatically. "I'm wounded."

"If you only called me to talk about dating..." I love her dearly and enjoy all our conversations, but I'm piled under with work, and my deadlines are creeping up faster by the minute. The first week of November is always chaotic when it comes to last-minute Christmas photos.

"Yes, actually, I have one more thing to ask you. My parents' ski resort is looking for new photos for their website. Want to shine with your expertise and take them?" Maya folds her hands like she's about to pray—mostly to a god she never believed in—hoping I say yes.

I stop editing, tapping some of the keys on my keyboard,

looking everywhere but at her. A place I love so dearly—yet I skipped last year because of him. Things ended before our trip, but is it so wrong to go back to a place I considered a second home? He never set foot on the property. I still have a claim to it.

"When?"

"Yes!" she cheers.

"Well, give me a date." I go back to my editing.

"First weekend of December, okay with you?"

Of course, it's okay, she knows that. I know that. So, why the hell am I hesitating?

"I can see the wheels turning in your head," she comments.

I give her a dirty look. Maya holds up her hands, backing away from view.

Glancing at my shelf, I take in my snowboarding trophies, letting my eyes drift to the picture frames. Some gold, others black, where memories are encased forever in a set of four by six frames. One of my mom and me at high school graduation, another of Maya at my eleventh birthday party, sticking two fingers above my head. But my favorite is the family portrait in front of Snowy Peak resort—the very last photo with my dad. They gave him four months to live, and he demanded we take him one last time. I know he wants me to go and stop making excuses.

I need to get out of this rut.

"Yes, that works perfectly."

Maya dances back on screen, shaking her hips, drinking her wine.

"All right, bye!" I end the call, watching her dive for her phone before it goes back to the home screen.

Taking my last bite of dinner, I work another two hours on edits, making sure I've checked off everything on my client's list, then upload them into a gallery, emailing her a link to access it.

Blowing air from my lips, I shut my laptop and prepare

myself for a nice hot shower. In my shoebox apartment in Boston, I scour through an overflowing hamper, half-dirty, half-clean clothes, sniffing every pair of underwear until one gives off a floral scent. Ah, yes, clean! Score!

My room is starting to showcase signs of being a possible candidate for a feature on *Hoarders*. Usually, it's around this time when I get my act together and clean before my mother drops in unexpectedly.

One time, it happened, and she nearly had a stroke. Then she hired a cleaning service for the day, and they were paid double just to endure the smell of rotting pizza I accidentally left under my bed.

Can I blame her? No, but I also have the habits of someone who is barely home but also gets overwhelmed if my tasks pile up too quickly.

I stand in front of my bathroom mirror, shower running at the hottest temperature, creating steam that wafts past the curtain. I hold my midsection, staring at faded stretch marks and the slight stubble of a two-day-old shave below my belly button. The area that, even after losing forty pounds, still won't disappear. My scale mocks me from underneath the sink, even with the door shut; it laughs at my weight, having hit a rough plateau.

It's been two years since my diagnosis of PCOS. A diagnosis I had a hard time accepting until it was everywhere on social media, with people trying to sell supplements. Because nothing makes it more legitimate than Poly Cystic Ovarian Syndrome being added to your health history on your medical records, laughing at you. From skipped periods to painful ones, along with an unexplained, extreme thirst for water, right down to excessive body hair, it all makes sense after a series of blood tests were run two summers ago.

It's also been two years since I told my ex that there was a chance of my getting pregnant, might be difficult or nonexistent.

It's been two years since we left each other's lives, and some of his words still stain my thoughts.

I never break, but lately, inside, a crumbling weight of wanting perfection is starting to show.

The tips of my fingers graze along my chin, finding a few hairs coming back in their stubborn spots. Other hairs barely pierce the skin, creating dark specks. If anyone looked closely, they would see only a portion of what I struggle with.

Stepping into the hot shower, scalding water hits my skin, and I lean my head back so it soaks my red hair. I hate this part of my shower. The part where I run my fingers through my thick waves to make sure every strand is wet, only to pull out what amounts to chunks, sticking them to the shower wall to gather after I'm done. Although I'm lucky to inherit thick hair, it didn't take away the side effects of PCOS showing near my temples.

After my forty-minute everything-shower, I wrap myself securely in a thick towel, leaving my hair dripping wet down my back, and stalk off to my bedroom. Kicking my sneakers out of the way, I pull out a purple suitcase that was tucked in the back of the closet and covered in a mound of sweatshirts.

I really need to clean out my closet; otherwise, a tsunami of sweatshirts is going to bury me alive.

My phone buzzes where I left it in the living room, right next to the empty Chinese takeout container. Maya sent me a string of messages with tons of exclamation points, instructing me to pack my sexiest dresses and heels.

I text her back with the middle finger emoji, and she responds minutes later.

> Maya: We're finally single at the same time.
> Pack your best shit, or I'm forcing you to go
> shopping when you arrive.

Me: I never agreed to date while I'm there.

Maya: Doesn't mean you can't flirt?

Me: Ew, I'll pass.

Maya: Buzz kill. 👍

Me: Horndog. 👍

She sends me a GIF of Robert Downey Jr. rolling his eyes. I laugh and throw my phone on the couch, shaking my head.

I love my best friend.

ONE YEAR AGO...

The paper on the exam table crinkles every time I shift my weight, a nervous habit whenever I'm sitting at the doctor's. My legs bounce, counting the seconds until they turn into minutes, picking at my already holey jeans on my knee.

I'm here to see an endocrinologist because my gynecologist suggested my results were better suited to someone who has expertise in women's health, specifically someone with PCOS.

A slight knock pulls my attention to the door, and a woman in a white coat peeks through. "Hi, Hannah, I'm Dr. Ghoshel. How are you?" She smiles sweetly at me, her long, dark hair braided away from her tawny, pixie-like face. She shuts the door behind her as she reaches forward to shake my hand. Her eyes are a caramel brown; quite stunning to look at, her fingers warm against my clammy ones.

"Hi, and I'm okay, I guess. I'm a little nervous." She has no idea I'm on the verge of shitting my pants waiting for her arrival.

"Understandable." Dr. Ghoshel pulls a pen from her breast pocket, marking something down on a piece of paper left on her portable desk. "But I'm here to help you understand your results and talk about options."

"Yeah, my gynecologist said she was going to forward it all to you." I pick even more at my jeans, feeling pieces of them unravel.

She nods, takes a seat, and begins to type. "I took a look at your files, and I can see your A_1C levels are high, along with your testosterone, which puts you in the pre-diabetic category, along with your insulin levels. You have insulin resistance on top of it. With these results, we like to classify this as metabolic dysfunction."

I let her words sink in slowly, and numbly say, "So... PCOS?"

"When did you notice your symptoms?"

I swallow hard. "Four months ago. I skipped two periods."

She types away, and I can't handle the sound of silence between us, so I start to blab about other symptoms. "Sometimes I get acne all over my chin, and hair fallout happens...like a lot... in the shower.

"What are your periods like?"

"Heavy the first day, makes me achy, and then it's light for the rest. It's usually around four days. That's if it doesn't just get skipped."

Dr. Ghoshel clicks one more time, signaling her printer to spit out a few pages. She reaches for them and staples them together, handing them to me. "I've printed out some information about foods to avoid. Your biggest enemy, Hannah, is sugar."

I look down at the packet she hands me, reading the bold letters PCOS, that mock me. "Sugar?"

"Yes."

There's no way.

No way I'm diagnosed.

Barely looking up, I ask, "What are my options?"

"Are you looking to get pregnant?"

I blink, mouth going dry. "Pregnant?"

"Yes. Then we can determine which path to take when it comes to medication. It'll be difficult to conceive if your PCOS isn't controlled." Dr. Ghoshel puts on latex gloves.

"Medication?" It's an out-of-body experience having your doctor nonchalantly tell you your health is in jeopardy, along with the possibility of having trouble conceiving your own child.

"Metformin is an option we recommend first."

So many emotions come at me, I might topple from the weight of it all. "Is it forever?"

"Temporary. Until it's under control."

Have I become out of control...with my health? "What's the dosage?"

"I'll start you off in small doses to make sure it doesn't affect your stomach. It's all your choice, of course. If not, we can go another route."

I think back to her previous statement. "You said it can be difficult to conceive if not controlled." She nods, waiting. "But how do I cure it?"

Dr. Ghoshel's face is neutral. "There is no cure, Hannah. It can be genetics, hormonal imbalance, anything. What we can do is try to lessen your symptoms and get some of your blood work done to aim toward improving your levels."

I'm numb from head to toe, trying to comprehend her words, watching her watch me with a puzzled expression. I grip the edge of the examination bed, my fingernails digging into parts of the foam pad. How can I decide what path to take when I'm not even sure of my own future?

CHAPTER 3

HANNAH

MY HEAD LEANS against the pane of cold glass in the back seat of the taxi. I'm exhausted after having procrastinated the night before to pack all my shit. Time flies when you forget your best friend gave you a month's notice.

We finally got off the highway thirty minutes ago, and the populated areas became thin, civilization weeding out until neighbors are few and far between. Roads are getting tighter to maneuver, but that just means we're reaching my favorite part of the drive.

I catch my driver, Glenn, peeking through his rearview mirror and smile. "We're only five minutes away, Miss."

"Thank you, Glenn," I say, smiling back.

His gray, handlebar mustache twitches as his smile lights up his whole face. "It's perfect timing that I picked you up. I have grandkids not too far from where you are."

"Oh, really?"

"Yes! I plan to surprise them, maybe take them out to dinner."

"That sounds wonderful! What are their names?"

Glenn digs in his coat pocket, pulling out a worn-out, brown leather wallet. With one hand controlling the steering wheel, he flips it open. I reach for it and see a picture of two brunette girls smiling ear to ear, holding a chocolate lab puppy.

"Oh, Glenn, they're adorable!"

"The one on the right is Annette, and the one on the left is Beatrice. Twins, only a minute apart." He flips the wallet back and tosses it onto the passenger seat.

We talk about them for a few minutes, what their hobbies are, and how they're freshmen in high school. It's a nice conversation, one that isn't centered around me or my health.

Glenn drives carefully through dirt roads covered in freshly fallen snow, winding around patches of forests, coating bare branches, and creating a winter wonderland. It's our climb to my favorite place, heart fluttering with each turn.

My leg bounces, thinking back to my first time on the slopes as a kid, how my love for them led me to meeting my best friend in the entire world. Throughout high school together, we did it competitively, more so me in the end, resulting in awards and recognition, but my love for photography took center stage shortly after.

It may have taken the back seat for a while, but it'll be nice to return, especially here.

I take a deep breath, lean my head back against the seat, and continue watching the landscape change as we drive higher in into the mountains, the sun reflecting off the ice-covered branches making them shimmer as we drive by. Glenn hums to the radio, a jazz station that I quite enjoyed for the ride. I cross my arms over my chest, warm inside my pink winter jacket.

Glenn takes one last sharp turn, revealing a familiar sign, its wooden structure weathered by years, its words reading Snowy Peak Resort. Beyond the tree line widens as he circles us around to the front. Christmas decorations are already on display, gold garland strings along railings and the front porch.

I give Glenn a nice tip, thanking him for driving me out.

"It was my pleasure, Hannah. This place is beautiful. I might have to bring my granddaughters here sometime!" He opens the car door for me and starts to unload the trunk of my belongings.

"I think that's a wonderful idea, Glenn." Readjusting my blue winter hat, I hear Maya's voice calling my name and turn to see her running down the steps, her curly, dark hair tamed by a yellow winter hat and a black coat. Her boots skid to a stop, only for her to tackle me to the ground, hugging like she's convinced I'll disappear forever if she lets go.

Our bodies land in a pile of snow, our laughter an infectious sound that fills my heart with joy. Her hugs are like a warm blanket wrapped around my body after a long night in the cold; reassuring and comforting, something I'd needed for a long time.

She starts to squeeze me tighter, her weight pushing me down into the snow.

"Maya, you're crushing me!" I complain, feeling my body sinking like quicksand.

She sighs with contempt. "Good, because it's been too long without seeing my best friend."

"My funeral is going to arrive real quick if you don't give me some air!"

"Dying by my hands is quite climactic."

I try to throw her off, but she keeps a firm grip. "Maya, I'm freezing!"

"All right, you whiny baby." She rolls off of me, but not before hitting my arm. "Want to make snow angels?"

I snort, hitting her back. "Maybe after the snow dries inside my pants."

Maya gets up and offers me a hand, pulling me to my feet. She smirks, then grabs my face with her leather gloves, pinching my cheeks. "Stop hermitting, I missed you too much."

Maya's face is red from the winter air, dark curls wild, peeking from underneath her winter hat. "I missed you, too."

Our fifteen years of friendship remain unbreakable, no matter the distance, and it fills me with elation to know it will always stand the test of time.

She releases me from her grasp and slings my duffel bag over her shoulder. "Get your snowboard, girlie, I made sure Mom and Pops gave you the cabin across from me."

"Oh? We're not sharing this time?" I take my snowboard from Glenn and wish him a good day.

"You missed the arrival of delicious men. A bachelor party. I need room to get exercise, if you know what I mean." Her wink has me rolling my eyes. Leave it to Maya to find the nearest pack of horny, drunk men ready to make mistakes.

I wave Glenn off as he honks away from the resort, then follow Maya up the steps to the entrance of Snowy Peak Resort. Maya's parents, Jill and Anthony, have owned it for over twenty years, and it has always been a place I find myself coming back to whenever the holidays roll around, except when I dated Liam. He never wanted to go.

More gold garlands drape the reception desk and banisters, with lights strung around columns that hold up the foundation. Guests gather in clusters, some by the fireplace. Children laugh, playing a game of checkers on the coffee table while their parents converse with one another. A fully decorated Christmas tree is displayed by the bay window, presents tucked just beneath its branches.

The smell of fresh coffee and pastries is just too intoxicating to ignore.

We give each other a knowing look and beeline toward the table by the fireplace. Maya pours us each a cup of coffee as I inhale a chocolate doughnut, moaning from the taste alone.

"Cream and three sugars?" Maya asks, holding up a blue porcelain creamer.

"Just cream," I correct, wiping my mouth on the back of my hand. She smiles, understanding my need to control my sugar intake. The doughnut was pushing it.

Stupid PCOS.

I take a sip of my warm coffee. It coats my throat and pushes the chill out of my body. "Fuck, this is a good cup of coffee."

Maya laughs. "I forced my parents to switch brands. Let's see if I can swindle my way into other things."

"Like?"

Maya blows on her coffee. "Iced coffees."

"Yes, because coming in from a chilly day on the slopes, someone is dying for an iced beverage." I take another sip, instant warmth heating my veins. I wiggle my toes in my boots.

Maya eyes me over her cup. "Shut up and stop wiggling your toes."

I stick out my tongue. "Don't be a brat."

Suddenly, I hear my childhood nickname coming from upstairs. "Hannah banana!"

I wave enthusiastically at Jill. She greets us at the bottom of the steps, embracing me in a soft hug. I hear another round of footsteps descending and peek over her shoulder to see Maya's dad in a blue sweater and khakis. It's not hard to see how Maya is the spitting image of her father, tan skin, dark wavy hair, but his eyes are a striking blue, something that completely skipped over his daughter. Jill's eyes are stunning, deep brown, naturally blonde hair, and fair skin. "Is that Hannah banana I see?" He waits for Jill to step back before giving me a bear hug, nearly crushing my lungs.

"Easy, hun, you're going to knock the wind out of her," warns Jill.

He takes a step back, checking me over. I catch my breath,

still smiling from their love. Maya's dad, Anthony, stepped in when my father passed away from cancer when I was sixteen, becoming the rock I needed during difficult times. I will be forever thankful to him for teaching me how to drive and making sure Maya and I were brought home from any party we got invited to.

My mother worked long nights to keep a roof over our heads, and Maya's family was always there for after-school activities and ceremonious moments when my mom couldn't be. No fault to her, she just had to work hard to prevent us from being homeless.

My dad had been the breadwinner.

It was more than just friendship; they had become family over the years.

"Anthony and Jill! I love what you've done with the place!" I beam, giving the new lounge space another look.

"Thank you, Hannah! I'm so glad you like it! Make yourself comfortable for the rest of the day, we'll work on all the technical stuff tomorrow." Jill maternally brushes my arm, reminding me to call my own mother once I'm alone in my cabin.

"And," Anthony adds, "it's pot roast tonight in the dining hall. Make sure your bellies are empty, and be prepared for a round of charades." Anthony pats my shoulder and leads Jill over to the front desk, collecting a key. "At Maya's request, here is cabin eighteen, next to nineteen."

Maya snags them, twirling them in her hand. "Thank you, parentals, see ya later!" She grabs my bag and forces my snowboard into my hands.

I wave sheepishly at her parents and follow Maya out the door. "Do you have fire ants in your pants or something?"

Maya gives me a quick look over her shoulder. "I have some

tea to share, and I didn't want my parents to overhear or be anywhere in the vicinity."

That piques my interest while we make our way over to cabin eighteen. Maya unlocks the door, tossing my duffel bag on the bed. I prop up my snowboard on the nearest wall, joining her. "Alright, what happened?"

Maya fiddles with the thermostat and sits on the small sofa near the fireplace. Draping a blanket across her body, she dives into her story. "Remember that guy I went out on a date with a month ago?"

I nod, unsure where she's going with this. "Gift card dude?"

Maya stares up at the ceiling, embarrassed to even look at me when she says, "He's here."

"What!?" I gasp.

She groans. "He. Is. Here."

"Purely a coincidence? Right?"

Maya keeps quiet, finally looking at me.

"RIGHT?"

"No, because my dumb ass told him about my family's ski resort and that he should check it out!"

"Maya! You didn't! Even after he used the gift card?"

"It was before! Gosh, we were having a good time, and then he pulled it out, waving it around like he was made of a million bucks. Now he's in the lobby with his family, and I had to get out of there before he cornered me into another date!" She sinks low into the couch, groaning.

I bite my bottom lip. "And we have the pot roast dinner in the dining hall. How are you going to avoid him? Your dad always makes you start charades."

"I decided I'm not going." Maya's face resembles a toddler throwing a tantrum.

Covering my mouth, I swallow my laugh, trying my best to compose myself. Maya, however, doesn't find it funny and throws a pillow at my head. It hits me square in the face, knocking an obnoxious giggle out of me.

Eventually, she breaks her stern expression and joins me on the bed, laughing, her shoulders shaking as she settles next to me, wrapping an arm around my shoulders. "If I fake being sick, will you cover for me?"

"And miss the gift card dude, trying to get your attention? Never."

She groans and falls backward on the bed. I follow suit, resting my head against hers. "Maybe he won't show?"

"Maybe."

"What does he look like? You know, so I can warn you or tip him off that you're here."

She pulls my hair hard enough that I let out a yelp. "I'm sorry! It was hard to resist."

"Right, anyway, he's kind of stocky, short-cropped, black hair. Big, brown eyes. It's sad because he's quite handsome."

"And you can't get past his gift card usage?"

"Not for a first date...or ever. I am the best liquor on that damn shelf. I deserve someone who *can* afford it."

Maya never thinks less of herself; she is always putting herself on a pedestal, and only the worthiest of men are allowed to step up and try to prove it. I wish I were more like her.

"Well, let's hope he doesn't show up," I say reassuringly.

"Or magically gets run over by a reindeer."

But he does, in fact, show up, and Maya nearly trips one of the kitchen staff members trying to avoid charades, almost knocking over the dessert table, leaving me in a fit of giggles and her parents shocked and confused by her sudden departure.

It feels so good to be home.

MORNING LIGHT FILTERS through one of the nearby windows as I open my eyelids. Snugged nice and tight under the many blankets Snowy Peak provides for their guests, my mind and body are calm for the first time in I don't know how long. I wiggle my toes and wipe the crust from the corners of my eyes, stretching my arms high above my head.

I text Maya, asking if she's awake, but I only get crickets in response. There's a good chance she stole a bottle of wine from the kitchen after she hightailed it out of there, trying to avoid Gift Card Dude during charades. She most likely drank the whole bottle. Can I blame her? No, but replaying how it happened still results in uncontrollable laughter as I finish my stretch.

Slapping my forehead, I remember I forgot to call my mom and send her a quick text to let her know I'll catch up with her later, then hop out of bed, my stomach rumbling for some breakfast.

Taking a quick shower, I check every inch of my body for possible hair growth. I swear it's growing faster by the minute, constantly removing pesky hairs from my chin, now a couple on my neck, to make sure I'm not walking outside in werewolf form.

I toss clothes out of my suitcase like a madwoman, finding my favorite pair of black leggings and my favorite cream turtleneck. I need to stop packing my favorite outfits at the bottom; I'm just setting myself up to ruin perfectly folded clothes.

A dab of concealer, a couple of strokes of mascara, and I'm good to go. I can't wait to start taking photos of my favorite place.

Nothing smells more heavenly than the freshly fallen snow when I open my door. I inhale deeply, enjoying the notes of pine that come my way, and look up to find clear skies as I walk along the snowy path. New footprints made in the snow bring my mood way up, and I'm smiling as my boots crunch, a satisfying sound with every step.

As I make my way to the main building, I'm already getting hit with the scent of pancakes and delicious bacon, making my mouth water as I enter.

Some guests are already awake, sitting by the fire, reading or keeping cozy. A line has started to form by the dark, oak double doors to the dining hall, and the lights strung along the banister and checkout desk, woven into garlands, shine bright and colorful. Even the coffee table has a red table runner and green candles placed in silver holders.

Jill comes downstairs moments after I enter, carrying a small black box. "Hannah, I was wondering if you would like to add this ornament to the tree." She opens the lid, and my heart swells three sizes.

"The Maya and Hannah forever ornament," comments Jill.

I smile. "I can't believe you still have this." I can still see the smudged paint on the end of my name when Maya bumped into me. We were thirteen and a little hysterical back then.

"It's a classic piece. I couldn't let it go." She hands it over while we walk together to her Christmas tree. I place it next to a round, red ornament, admiring its place.

"It's good to know it'll always have a home." The bell to the dining hall chimes a second time, reminding stragglers that breakfast is being served.

Jill places the empty box on the coffee table. "Go eat, and when you're done, you can meet me outside."

I nod, making my way to the line and pushing through the double wooden doors, where I'm hit with the warmth and the smell of maple syrup and crispy bacon.

The line inches along a buffet-style setup, people loading up on a variety of foods. I pile my plate with a couple of blueberry pancakes, some bacon, and fruit. A dollop of syrup and a cup of orange juice round out the meal. I'm about to exit the line when someone creeps up beside me.

I almost drop my food, jumping when Maya, hiding behind sunglasses and a baseball cap, appears.

"What are you doing?"

She ignores me and scopes out the scene. "Is he here?"

It takes me a second to register, and we make our way over to an empty table with her up my ass, trying to use me as coverage. "Gift card dude?"

"No, Sasquatch. Yes, Gift Card Dude!" She drags a chair, pushing it against mine until we're touching knee caps. "I haven't seen him yet, but that doesn't mean the slimy bastard didn't slip through the cracks."

I chew on some bacon. "It might be easier if you just, oh, I don't know, tell him the truth and move on?"

Maya steals my other piece of bacon, a look of horror on her face. "So he can sweet-talk his way back in? Absolutely not!"

"For someone so quick to cut people off—"

She waves her hands in my face. "Usually, I never see them again!" Her voice reaches several octaves higher than usual as she pulls her hat lower to cover her eyes, fidgeting in her seat.

Surrounding tables filled with families stop mid-bite to watch Maya's semi breakdown.

She gives them dirty looks. "What? Never seen a girl lose her shit before?"

"Oh my god, Maya, you have to relax." I try to apologize for her behavior, getting some dirty looks in return, along with one woman commenting on her inappropriate language in front of children.

Ignoring me, she proceeds to take fruit off my plate. "Great batch today."

I try to playfully stab her with my fork. "So, go get your own, you heathen."

Maya pops a blueberry in her mouth and almost chokes. "Shit." I smack her back while she heaves, trying to get the fruit down. Eventually, it passes, and she breathes heavily over the table, gasping for air. "He's here!"

I look around, trying to spot Gift Card Dude, but Maya has already rushed out the back, leaving a smoke trail in her haste. The girl is insane, but I love her.

Shaking my head, I toss my plate in the trash and go look for Jill, locating her outside, standing next to a man on a ladder while she hands him a section of white lights. "I figure we can start inside since we've finished with the decorations. I was also wondering if you could take a couple of night shots with everything lit up?"

"Yeah! No problem! I'll take some test shots inside first before I begin," patting my camera bag with pride. I love my job.

"Awesome, and if you need to adjust objects or the lighting, you have my full permission." Jill finishes handing over the line of lights, and they move on to another section of the roof.

I sent Maya a text, giving her my location.

> Me: I'm about to take photos in the front lobby if you need me.

Maya: Okay, I'm currently stalking the bachelor party by the ski lift.

> Me: Wow, you move fast.

Maya: I don't like to waste time ;)

> Me: Are any of them cute?

Maya: Two, the others are definitely married, besides the groom.

I knew my next text would put her into a panic state, but I couldn't resist.

> Me: What if...omg they use gift cards? Lol.

Maya: If you curse me, I will shave your head while you sleep.

> Me: Love you too.

Maya: Bye, bitch.

I shake my head, laughing, and slip my phone back into my coat pocket. Unzipping my camera bag, I pull out my Nikon Z5, wiping the 35mm lens with a microfiber cloth to make sure it's clear and clean before I begin any test shots.

With the strap around my neck, I move through the room in different positions, taking pictures in the best light. Some of the kids pose by the couch, giggling as I get down on my knees to take close-ups, making silly faces. I take photos of couples on the couch, cozying up and enjoying the small fire, then move to the front desk, catching Joan, the receptionist, handing a set of keys to a couple, snapping the exchange from a distance.

As the shutter sounds and I capture more and more of this beloved resort, I start to envision what Jill and Anthony's new website could look like, and I can't wait to share with them how they could market this place even better.

Smiling to myself, I continue taking photos, even some of their dining hall, where people linger by the buffet table, looking for leftovers from breakfast. Once I have a good collection of the interior, I pull out my phone and make notes on which areas I need to tackle next and which ones I've already done, checking if Jill and Anthony want me to retake anything or add more.

I'm about to make my way over when I collide with a hard body. "Oh, I'm sorry!"

"No, my apologies, Miss." A man, all but five feet tall in a thick winter coat, helps me keep my balance. He seems strangely out of place for how he's dressed. He's wearing a green scarf wrapped tightly around his neck, and he carries a black briefcase, brown leather gloves gripping the handle. His hair is white as the snow, with a beard to match.

"I'm looking for Mr. and Mrs. Gomez. You wouldn't happen to know them?" he asks, adjusting his jacket.

"Yes, actually. Jill is over by the cabins. I think she was by cabin five," I explain.

He nods in appreciation. "Thank you. Have a good rest of your day," then walks off without a response, following the old footprints in the snow.

Strange, never seen him before.

After twenty minutes of test shots, with a frozen nose, I decide to take a break and look for some hot chocolate, praying someone brought the cart out.

What I find is an empty lounge, and the coffee counter is nowhere to be seen. Maybe there's some in the dining hall.

Usually, they leave a cart out before the snack bar is replenished.

A freshly stocked hot chocolate station catches my attention, and I make my way over with a little more pep in my step.

Hushed whispers pull my attention from the warmth of my freshly poured hot chocolate, and I recognize Jill and Anthony conversing with another man. I tiptoe closer, leaving my mug behind, and duck behind the stainless steel counter, where the chef's door is ajar.

Anthony is sitting behind a desk, Jill perched on the edge, and the white haired man from earlier sits across from them, his back toward me.

"The numbers don't lie, you're underperforming," he says, handing a stack of papers over to Anthony.

Jill purses her lips. "Are you sure? Not even the sales from last year helped?"

He shakes his head. "I recounted several times. The revenue has decreased over time, but your profit dropped drastically once other neighboring ski resorts came into play."

Anthony skims through the papers, jaw flexing. "It looks like this is our last season."

"You have until February, maybe, if you're lucky. I suggest finding a buyer sooner rather than later."

Jill runs her hands down her face, frustration coating her words. "If we're lucky?"

It registers then that his man is their accountant. *Holy shit. I'm eavesdropping on something serious. I can't be here.*

I'm about to take my leave when the next words out of their accountant's mouth halt me in place.

"You guys had an excellent twenty-five-year run, not a lot of places survive that long. Maybe it's time to move on while you can."

I slowly back away from the hot chocolate cart, my steaming

cup left behind. Once I'm out of earshot, I run as fast as I can to find Maya—dashing between tables, weaving past other guests, nearly knocking over a little kid, trying to dodge a family heading toward the exit.

No, no, this can't happen. Not now. Not when I finally stopped making stupid excuses and came back. To lose my second home would be like losing my dad all over again. My lungs burn the harder my legs pump, and everyone catches sight of the girl running like a crazy person with a mission to complete.

Because there's no way Snowy Peak Resort is closing.

CHAPTER 5
NOAH

MY HANDS GRIP her dark hair as she continues to suck on my dick, her tongue working in tandem with her mouth. I lean my head back, closing my eyes, focusing as she moves her plump lips to the very tip of my cock.

We're inside my suite, the lights dim, curtains drawn for privacy. I'm up against a wall, and she's on her knees before me. The sight is fucking beautiful.

"Fuck," I breathe. She isn't naive when it comes to a blowjob, that's for sure.

She flicks her tongue like a snake, then her lips suction on the side of my shaft, probably trying to give me a hickey.

Her hands play with my balls a little too roughly, forcing me to slow her down to a stop. "Easy."

She hums in understanding, taking her time once again.

My phone buzzes in my pocket, but I ignore it, trying to hold on and not lose my focus.

It's been a while since I got off with someone other than my right hand, and I refuse to ruin this moment because the guys want to harass me tonight. I've fucked plenty of times, fingered, and tasted a lot of pussy from here to goddamn Cabo, but these days, cumming by a plethora of different women has been... difficult.

Squeezing my eyes tighter, I let her continue to blow me, her fingernails dragging down my thighs as she takes me all the way in, almost down to my balls.

I lean my head back against the wall, hoping I can come in her mouth so I'm not so goddamn stressed.

My phone vibrates again, along with her teeth scraping underneath.

Hard knocks and my teammates' voices start to make my dick go limp.

"Stop, stop!" I demand, losing my grip on her hair.

She pops my cock out of her mouth. "What's your problem?"

She's already standing, adjusting her skin-tight, black dress, wiping her mouth with the back of her hand. Loose, dark curls fan around her long, narrow face, eyes dark and smoky, red lipstick smudged down her chin.

"Let's go, Hart! It's party time!" Taylor shouts.

I grind my teeth. Fucking cock blockers.

"Well?" She taps her foot, arms crossed, a permanent scowl on her face.

I shove my dick inside my pants, cursing under my breath. "You gotta go."

She laughs, shaking her head. "Wow, the famous Noah Hart, two-time gold medal Olympian, likes to waste a girl's time."

The doorknob jingles, the guys hollering like idiots on the other side.

"That's not it." I'm already cleaning up, putting my shirt back on. "I'm sorry, but you have to go."

She's already strapping on her heels, rolling her eyes. "And you probably don't remember my name."

Damn, I know it's close to Megan, or maybe it's Samantha?
"Uhhh…"

She stops, hand hovering over the doorknob. "Lauren? It's Lauren. Yeah, you're a waste of time." She swings the door open. Mark, Cody, and Taylor are all casually lounging outside, trying to hide their smiles.

"Excuse me," she says.

They all back away, watching her walk down the hall out of sight.

Mark enters first, laughing. "Sorry for interrupting." He rubs the back of his freshly buzzed head. "At least you got some—"

"God, no." I walk over to the window and draw back the curtains, looking out at the soft glow of Aspen, Colorado. "It was hard because of you fucking clowns fooling around outside my door."

Cody and Taylor take it upon themselves to get comfortable on my bed, rearranging the pillows like they're ready for a sleepover.

"Hey, how were we supposed to know you had a beautiful lady over?" says Cody.

"Was my ignoring your texts and phone calls not enough of a hint?" I need to do better at hiding my whereabouts.

Mark leans against the bedside table, arms crossed. "Maybe it's time to slow down for a bit. You've been with a new chick every night since—"

"I'm not talking about this right now." They may care, and they're like brothers to me, but it's also none of their business how I cope with shit.

Taylor rests back against the headboard, arms behind his head. "By all means, get as much head as you need. We just want to make sure you understand we're here for you." He crosses his legs, wiggling his eyebrows. "Might I suggest a three-some? Preferably another male with a larger penis?"

I look up at the ceiling, sighing. "No, Taylor. I will not have sex with you and another male."

He smirks, pleased with himself. "Never say never."

I run my hands through my dark, curly hair, trying not to pull it out of my scalp. "Is that why you fuckers decided to show up here? To check up on me? I told you I'm fine."

"Are you though?" questions Cody.

"'Cause, lately you've been all over the place," adds Mark.

"If I wanted therapy, I would've paid for it." This is a never-ending discussion about my personal endeavors and how I handle even the slightest inconvenience. I know what I'm doing. I know who I'm doing it with.

Mark rolls his eyes. "Right, well, you're the king of avoidance, so..."

I ignore his comment and step into my shoes, grabbing my black puffer jacket. "Are we going out or not? Since you interrupted me." Plucking a white beanie from my suitcase on the floor, I adjust it on my head.

We're about to head out when Mark stops me at the door. "You know we're not judging you, right? That was never our intention."

I gesture for him to exit with me. "I know. I just wish you all would understand it doesn't need to be discussed. What's done is done." I pat his back, and he gives me a small smile.

Locking the door behind us, we run to catch up with the guys, hoping tonight I can let off some steam, letting the memories of her fade away.

CHAPTER 6

HANNAH

"UGH, every time a man goes ape shit, a tear drips down my leg." Maya moves her dark sunglasses to the bridge of her nose, eyeing, quite possibly drooling over the pack of men in front of us.

"Your brain needs to be studied." Area 51 sounds like a good place to test the unusual workings of her brain.

"They'll find copious amounts of sexual thoughts and desires."

"Maybe a couple of screws loose, too."

Lucky for me, Maya is found watching the bachelor party bicker over what they want to do next. She sips gingerly from her coffee mug, smirking as she pushes those dark sunglasses back over her eyes. "I love when men get feral over activities."

"You also go crazy when they take out the trash."

She waves my comment away. "It's the simple things, really."

I grip her arm, forcing her to look at me. "I didn't come over here to ogle, I came here to tell you something I overheard."

I have her attention from the tone I use. She pulls her

sunglasses off, eyes searching my face for danger. "What happened?"

"Let's go somewhere more private."

I lead her back to my cabin, the once-happy Christmas wreath reminding me of a downfall that is sure to transpire in the next month. I hate knowing this before Maya and having to tell her...

She begins to pace. "All right, spit it out."

I shut the door behind me and lean against it. Anxiety ripples through my body, making my legs shake. "Your parents' accountant showed up when I was taking test shots this morning."

"Dennis, yeah, he's been with my family since the beginning. What did he want?" Maya bites her lip, waiting, her body swaying as she crosses her arms.

"I ended up in the kitchen looking for the hot chocolate cart and..." I swallow hard, fingers clammy, bracing myself for impact. "...I overheard a very private conversation. He said the place has lost revenue."

She huffs out a clear breath of relief. "Yeah, we fluctuate before the winter season kicks off. It's normal." With a shrug, she lets out a breathy laugh, but as I watch her fingers twist on the sleeves of her winter jacket, I know it's all a show. "For a second, you had me thinking the place was going to close or something."

I blink several times at her, and my silence stops Maya's cold, shaking hands. How do you tell your best friend that your childhood wonderland is going under? How do you tell her that everyone is going to lose their jobs and that a place once filled with hope, dreams, and beautiful memories is going to close before the season even starts?

She swallows, and I can hear it from where I stand. "Hannah...what did you hear?"

Her doe-like eyes kill me, forcing the worst to come from my mouth. I can barely speak above a whisper, my heart ripping right down the middle. "They're not going to make it this season. February at most, maybe."

Maya sinks to the floor, crestfallen from the news. I reach her in seconds, curling next to her on the floor, hugging her shoulders.

She tries to breathe, rocking back and forth. "My parents..."

"Probably didn't want to worry you," I mention, hoping this is the case, but the moment the words left my mouth, I knew it wasn't.

"This is the place where we escape, our home away from home," she mumbles, tears streaming down her cheeks.

I swipe them away with my sleeve, my own tears falling, dripping down my chin. If we lose Snowy Peak, we lose a piece of our childhood—the memories, the last place before my dad...

We cry together on the floor for a while, holding each other as our lives depend on it. I can't believe this is happening, and there's nothing we can do to stop it.

For a while, we sit in silence after our crying session, legs crossed, picking at the carpet. My head pounds, eyes sore. What had been a great morning had quickly turned into a shitty day.

"I think you should talk to them, get the truth from them," I suggest.

"Will you come with me?" she whispers.

I still. "Maybe that's not such a good idea."

Maya looks up, giving me her best puppy dog look. "It's as much your place as it is ours. We grew up here. I know you feel the same way as I do. Please?"

I sigh, nodding. "Sure."

She gives me another squeeze before standing, taking me with her.

I want to reassure her we'll find a way, but the hope I once had trickles away as we get closer to the main building. Because what if we're too late?

One of my favorite dishes of the night suddenly tastes like cardboard. Maya barely looks up from her plate, picking at charred pepperoni slices, her mind is most likely where mine is —in negative land.

I try to finish what I can, but it's the cumulonimbus cloud that hangs over our heads, threatening to drown us out, and my anxiety keeps coming, knocking the wind out of my lungs.

After make-your-own-personal-pizza-night, Maya asks her parents to speak with us privately. We follow them to the main suites, leading us into their room. Decorated with Christmas-style curtains and lights, right down to the comforter, Jill encourages us to sit, while she and her husband stand, waiting for us to begin.

I swallow a hard lump in my throat, unsure how to proceed, when Maya starts to ramble, clearly upset, skipping straight to pissed off.

"So, when were you going to tell me the resort was going under?" The accusation is clear in her tone, her eyes bouncing between her parents.

Her parents exchange a look before responding. "And where did you hear this?" Jill questions, her expression blank, arms crossed.

Maya snorts, not impressed by her mother's deflection. "Come on, Mom. I want the truth, please."

My gaze drops to my lap as my hands fidget, and I chew on

the inside of my cheek, trying not to draw attention to myself as Maya's anger rises further. The room starts to shrink, suffocating me with all the words being left unsaid.

Anthony speaks instead, watching us intensely from where he stands. "I want to make it perfectly clear that we tried our best to keep this place up and running as long as we could. Our plan was never to sell, but we hoped we could pass it to you, Maya, when we were ready to retire."

Maya narrows her eyes at her parents. "Go on."

They both nod, then Jill says, "Believe us when we say we're truly devastated, and we exhausted all our resources to try and save it. Which is one of the many reasons I asked you to invite Hannah." She then turns to me, her eyes glossy. "We were hoping that with new photos and a better website with ads, we could try to at least break even before the winter season ended."

My heart contracts, sadness seeping into my bones at their attempts. "I'll do it for free, and we can still try to run the ads and the new website."

Anthony wraps a protective arm around Jill's shoulders. "No, Hannah, that's not fair to you. We will still pay you for your time. We're just glad you got to spend one last season with Maya before it closes."

Maya is at the door before I realize she's not by my side anymore.

"Maya!" I call after her.

Anthony runs his hand down his face as his shoulders sag in defeat over his only daughter's devastation. "We tried, honey."

"Yeah, well, not hard enough." Maya storms out of the room, leaving me with her parents, her steps running down the staircase.

I'm about to follow her when Jill stops me in my tracks. "I'm sorry, Hannah. If anything, we're glad you came. We just wanted one last family moment here, even if it's a bittersweet ending." She cups my cheek before exiting the room.

Anthony remains by the fireplace, leaning against it. "If it's not too much to ask, can you talk Maya down from that ledge? You're the only one who can."

I nod. "I'll try my best."

The problem is, I want to join her.

CHAPTER 7
HANNAH

EVENTUALLY, I find Maya sitting in an empty ski lift chair, the lift stationary, and take a seat next to her, waiting for her to speak first.

An owl hoots somewhere in the distance, and the trees create shadows from the moon above, looking like monsters across snow banks. It's beautiful how everything remains still, as if the whole world has stopped for just a moment, giving us a chance to catch our breath.

Maya swings her legs back and forth, sighing. "I know, I know—storming off like that wasn't the best way to handle things."

I shrug. "Well, in your defense, they kept it from you."

"Yeah, but I could have reacted better. Gosh, I cringed the whole way up here at myself for it. Hit me next time, please?" She turns to me, smirking.

"Whatever keeps you in line," I laugh, copying her movements.

Her smile fades, and her legs slow their swinging.

I flex my fingers, my black gloves keeping them warm. "I'm sorry I was the one who found out first."

She gives me a half smile. "I would rather it be you than some stranger."

"What about Gift Card Dude?" I tease, nudging her shoulder.

"I swear to GOD you mention him one more time, I'm going to dump hot dog water all over you outside so you freeze with the smell clinging to your body." She nudges my shoulder, and I smile when, suddenly, I hear Maya's chest shaking, barely controlling her laughter. At least we still have our sense of humor.

"We should go out with a bang, maybe create a winter wonderland event or something," I suggest, watching stars twinkle above.

Maya grabs my face, noses touching, brown eyes wild. "What are you doing, Maya?"

She kisses my forehead. "Hannah Banana, you're a fucking genius!" she shouts, rocking our seat back and forth.

Thank God the lift is stationary.

"How? What did I say?"

"We're not getting any new revenue, so maybe an event can change that? How the hell did my parents not think of this before!"

"Maybe they did, and because of the lack of revenue, couldn't afford it?"

"Maybe, but there has to be a way around it to at least try!"

My mind starts to grind like rusty gears, formulating an idea. "Okay, so what kind of event should we aim for? We have to try and get not only returning customers but new ones."

She taps her chin, formulating a deep-rooted plan. "All right, we're known to have the best slopes, regardless of the neighboring competition." She pulls out her phone. "I'm just going to see what the others are offering."

"I wonder if they do events, too. Maybe that's why they're

able to keep afloat." I can see the website coming together, with new photos showcasing the brand-new events and what Snowy Peak offers. I smile to myself while Maya types vigorously on her phone.

"No harm in getting inspiration from others," she comments, smiling devilishly, then says, "I see bake-offs for Christmas cookies, kind of boring. Craft centers, book clubs for winter romance books, snooze fest. Kids' karaoke night. Jeesh, how are they making bucks off of these cheesy-ass events?"

Giggling, I suggest, "You know Snowy Peak is known for slopes? Why not make an event out of that, maybe a competition?"

Maya rocks the cart again. "Hannah Banana!"

"I'm going to kill you!"

"Not after the idea you just gave me, you won't."

"Better be a goddamn good one, otherwise you're about to eat yellow snow," I threaten, trying to stop the cart from swaying more.

"We can have snowboarders come and do the event! Give them a platform and exposure, along with their families and friends who come to support them!" She smiles, clasping her hands together.

"Creating more revenue," I say, tapping my chin. "Maybe offer a prize? Make it into an actual competition?" I add. "Would your parents be cool with it?"

"Only one way to find out. I don't think any neighboring ski resorts offer such inclusive activities. This could be huge, Hannah." Maya beams.

"I can take pictures of them, hyping up the event!" Man, I hope her parents say yes. "Run the ads and revamp the website. Maybe call the local newspaper to run an article for it?"

She hugs me tight. "Okay, let's take the night to refresh and use tomorrow to create our pitch and present it to my parents after dinner, sound good?"

"Good to me. I'm freezing my ass off anyway."

"If we hurry, the hot chocolate station should still be open."

I nearly trip when Maya hops off the seat first, kicking snow in my face. "You did that on purpose!"

"Can't prove it!" she yells, running down the hill, sliding with her snow boots on.

The night sky up in Vermont, away from city lights, is clear —stars shining bright overhead. I can see the Big Dipper and Little Dipper, clearly visible, unlike a typical night in Boston. The air is fresher up here, calming. It's never this quiet at home; my life is filled with noise. My mind is constantly replaying the what-ifs, the roar of my insecurities that have drowned out everything since my diagnosis.

But Maya needs me, her family needs me. If this is the final season here at Snowy Peak, we'd better make it a fucking good one.

MAYA TEXTS ME EARLY, asking if I want to join her on the slopes today. It's been a while since we snowboarded together, and it'll be nice to do something other than take pictures all day.

Taking a quick body shower and removing any extra hairs on my chin and mustache line, because PCOS symptoms stop for no one. I throw on my favorite snow gear and braid my wavy, red hair. I'm about to add my favorite blue beanie when my phone begins to buzz on the bedside table, my mother's face flashing on the screen.

Shit, I forgot to call her!

Picking it up, I answer with a cheerful, "Hello, Mom!"

"Hey, sweetheart! I haven't heard from you yet. Is everything okay?" Her voice, a sing-song of childhood memories, warms my heart.

"Yes. I'm sorry I didn't call you sooner. Things got a little hectic up here." I start to pick at the little hole I found on my knee. Great, hopefully this pair holds out for the week.

"Oh, is everything okay with Maya and her parents?" she asks in a concerned voice. Leave it to Mom to figure out that something is wrong in under ten seconds.

I take a deep breath and begin the story of why I'm here, how I overheard their accountant, right down to a possible plan Maya and I might have conjured up last night on the ski lift. I still have to work out some kinks, but I'm hoping tonight her parents will try at least one more time to save their second home.

"Gosh, you would go every winter break after Christmas to that place. I can't imagine it shutting down after so long." Mom hasn't been here since my dad's death. It's hard for her, even after all these years, to come back to a place where my dad was so heavily involved.

Both Maya and my family would travel during February break, spending time with kids our age while the adults had their time with late-night dinners and dancing. Days were spent skiing or snowboarding together. Now, my dad is gone, my mother works forty hours a week at a well-paying job she hates, and the Gomezes are about to lose a family business that brings people together.

My heart feels heavy at the thought of a possible reality if we can't convince her parents to try our idea.

I'm not ready to give up just yet.

Mom pulls my focus back with her next question. "How are you feeling?" The question she poses really means, 'Hey, I know your PCOS sucks, but please tell me you're following your doctor's orders.'

I shrug like she can see it through the phone. "All right. Less headaches, better sleep. I'm still struggling to lose weight in my midsection." Flashbacks of Liam and me tangled in bed sheets, my shirt hanging loosely over my chest as I ride him. Hurt hits me hard at the memory, making my hands shake, trying to keep my phone steady against my ear.

It was never for comfort; it hid my insecurities. Eventually, not even a regular bathing suit seemed comfortable enough to wear in public.

Shaking the memory away, breathing deeply in and out through my nose, I continue to pick at the hole in my snow pants.

"How is your blood work?"

I groan internally. Because she's a good mother, I can't fault her for asking all the questions about my physical health, but it's a battle only I can face alone. "I go in two weeks for a follow-up. I'll find out soon if my levels dropped."

Rapid knocks are heard outside my cabin door, and I silently thank a higher power for the interruption. "Hey, Mom, I gotta go. I'll keep you posted when the results come in, okay?"

Our brief exchange ends with I love you. She cares deeply, and I'm thankful for that.

I open the door to find Maya in brand new, neon-pink snow gear, gripping her white snowboard, smiling from ear to ear. "Morning, sunshine!"

I snort. "What's with the new clothes?" She looks like a beacon for one of those starlets on the Las Vegas strip.

"My new, optimistic mood needed a makeover."

"So, looking like a life-size Barbie was the only option?" I loved Barbie growing up, but this is so out of character for Maya.

"It looks really expensive."

"The perks of working as a PA for a female social media influencer, sweet cheeks."

"You got her left overs, didn't you?"

"No judging. Let's hit the slopes before I trip you in a snow mound."

"I feeeeeeel the love." Grabbing my black snowboard with various stickers stuck on over the years, we make our way to the ski lift, trudging through a fresh layer of snow.

She throws her arm over my shoulder and squeezes. I'm forever grateful to have her by my side.

We head in line for the lift; some small groups are ahead of us, young teens in their snow gear, excited to join the morning ride. The sun begins to rise above the mountains, creating a warm, yellowish glow across the horizon. The smell of cold snow and the brisk air touching my face like an icy kiss keep my anxiety at bay. To think, Snowy Peak Resort can disappear in the blink of an eye if we can't convince her parents to try one more time.

Simultaneously, we sit on the next seat, rising up the mountainside. "How are we going to present this idea to your parents?"

Maya looks over her shoulder, watching the next pair take their seats. "I was thinking of just word vomiting the pl—"

She freezes, her eyes bulging from her eye sockets. "Fuck!'

I whip around, trying to spot who she's staring at. The two males who took the seat behind us are a little further back, talking to one another, completely unaware of Maya hiding behind me.

"Who's that?"

"Gift card dude! AH! He's fucking EVERYWHERE!"

Maya rocks the seat as I cling to the bar for dear life. After the swaying stops, I take a deep breath, making sure we stay put. "I mean, he's staying here, so…"

Maya sinks further in her seat. I have to keep her from slipping out to her death by gripping the collar of her jacket.

She faces the front again, forcing me to throw my arm over her shoulder for extra coverage. "As long as I'm off and down the hill before him, I can escape without being seen. I should be in the clear."

I try to get my arm back, but she tugs tighter. "Or you can just confront him now and move on quicker?"

A look of horror paints her face. "And expose myself to a possible second date?"

"You can say no, you know?" But we both know Maya doesn't have a mean bone in her body. She would say yes to a third and fourth date to avoid hurting anyone's feelings.

The alternative is to hide...exactly what she's doing right now.

"Just keep looking forward, I don't think he knows it's me." Maya peeks around us one more time, then shivers. "Gosh, I can't believe this."

"All right, can we return to our scheduled program?"

She waves me aside. "Yeah, yeah, let's continue."

"I was thinking we would showcase a PowerPoint? Compile all the reasons we should have the event and how it can benefit the resort. I started it last night," I say with a hopeful smile.

Maya shakes my body, once again rocking not only me but our seat. "I swear, without you here—"

"Stop shaking the seat!" I interrupt, barely keeping my mind occupied from how high we are rising. "Are you trying to make me shit my pants?"

"Wouldn't be the first time you did that."

"At least mine wasn't diarrhea."

She holds up her hands in surrender. "You win."

Our stop is approaching, and Maya, suddenly antsy, swings her legs back and forth. "Okay, so, PowerPoint, check. Can we meet before dinner to finalize it?"

Inches separate us from the landing. "Yes, it would be good to give a presentation to your parents, give them a visual that it could work."

A staff member approaches our seat, ready to usher us off safely. Maya wastes no time and hits the ground running, knocking the staff member into the snow. "See you at the bottom!" she screams while strapping her snowboard to her feet.

Meanwhile, I help the poor soul who got clotheslined by Maya's body.

She's gone by the time I help the staff member up, and Gift Card Dude jumps down with his friend, completely oblivious to what transpired moments ago.

I shake my head—not at all surprised by her theatrics—and make my way over to the beginning of an intermediate trail, the Jigsaw, strapping myself securely to my snowboard and adjusting my goggles over my eyes. I let the course take me to a faraway place, where my anxiety is nonexistent, my PCOS dormant, and Snowy Peak Resort is safe.

Just before dinner, Maya is sprawled out on my bed as I sit on the couch, going over the finer details of our neatly organized PowerPoint. When I say neatly, I mean I organized all her chaotic thoughts. Funny, how I can't keep up with my room back at home, but a PowerPoint? No problem.

We add pictures of possible event ideas and what Snowy Peak can offer for food and refreshments. Maya suggests a thorough bullet-point system, so that her parents don't ask a million questions and derail them from our actual pitch.

"Do you think this will work?" she asks, biting her lip.

I blow a loose strand of hair away from my face. "If we are persuasive enough and make sure they understand it's not the end, then yeah, I think this could work."

"I don't think I can eat," Maya admits.

"You can't avoid the dining hall forever. Eventually, you and Gift Card Dude are going to run into each other."

"It's not that. I'm worried, Hannah. What if my parents toss this whole pitch out the window? What if they already have buyers lined up and we just wasted our time?" Her bottom lip quivers, tears pooling in her big, brown eyes.

Closing my laptop, I force her to scoot over and join her on the bed. "It won't happen because we're going to convince them, and let the record show that we have done exceptionally well in the past in convincing your parents of crazy ideas."

She smiles. "Remember when we convinced them to get our belly buttons pierced at the same time, and your mother nearly had a stroke because it got infected?"

"Yeah, and then I had to get rushed to the ER, while yours got stuck in your drawstrings and ripped out, and you were bleeding everywhere? Only later did we find out our rooms were right next to each other."

We stared at each other for a moment, soaking it in, then laughed like it wasn't the most traumatic event we shared.

"All because they took us to Martha's Vineyard that one time over summer break. You convinced my parents so easily that your mother was already okay with it. I realized then my parents loved you so much they would believe anything that came out of your mouth," Maya adds, coming down from our laughing fit.

I smile at the memory, knowing we have matching scars on our belly buttons. "So, when I say we can convince them?"

Maya sighs in defeat. "Then we can convince them."

We make her parents sit in their room while we set up the PowerPoint after dinner.

Maya sits bouncing her legs on one of the lodge chairs, eyes darting back and forth between her parents and me. Her anxiety is making it hard to focus. Front and center for everyone's attention, I use my computer to sift through slides, explaining our reasoning for trying new event ideas. "I think after some thought, Maya and I believe we can bring in more revenue by planning a special event," another click, and our first slide details possible ideas, neatly organized. "With some research of neighboring resorts, the common factor is they all host events, whether it be paint night with wine, crafts for kids, or even a karaoke night. Although the slopes are the main attraction, we see that offering other activities entices more people to attend. People like variety. Why not give it to them?"

Maya stops bouncing, leaning forward, elbows on knees, biting her nails.

I start. "Here are some possible ideas for added events that could help bring in new and returning customers." I watch Jill and Anthony read the list, catching eyes with Maya, giving her a hopeful smile.

She surprises me by jumping to her feet, coming to stand beside me. "Mom, Dad," she addresses them in a formal tone that makes them laugh. "This place means everything to me, to us, the whole family. It would be a terrible idea not to give it one more try and save a place that has been a second home not only to us but also to others. Please, let us try these events, or some of them?"

At least she waited til after I handled presenting our Power-Point before blurting out a desperate plea. Even more shocking is that Maya sounds coherent rather than a hot mess.

Anthony looks at his wife, silently exchanging some weird mental thought between the two, and says, "You're right, Maya. We didn't try hard enough."

I hold my breath, gauging Maya's reaction.

She freezes all movement. "I was?"

Jill lets Anthony take the floor to explain. "We gave up too easily, and that's not who we are, and that's not how we raised you. So, I made a phone call to a friend, and I think we found a way to hopefully save this place after all."

My eyes widen, mouth agape. "Are you serious?"

Jill nods, smiling. "Twenty-five years in the business, we sometimes forget the people we meet along the way if we ever need a favor..."

"And to not hesitate and give them a call," Anthony finishes, then adds, "so, we called up our friend Tommy Jones."

"Holy shit," I exclaim, excitement radiating through my body. "He's one of the youngest Olympic male coaches in North America."

"Lucky for us, he came here with his daughters for vacation, and we asked if they could fit one more spot on their tour." Anthony drapes his arms around Jill, squeezing her shoulder.

"That would mean..." Maya pauses, calculating the idea in her head. "We can ticket the event, set up ads, and gather more crowd attraction?"

She takes the words right out of everyone's mouth as Anthony nods, confirming. "Precisely. People don't have to stay at the resort, either, to attend the event; it can be ticketed to outsiders as well."

Jill beams from where she sits. "And, lucky for us, we have other great contacts from local vendors who owe us a few favors."

Holy shit, this might work.

Maya is barreling toward her parents, squeezing the crap out of them. "Whatever you need us to do, we're here to help!"

Jill looks over at me, smiling from ear to ear. "As long as Hannah stays."

My heart swells as I join them for a group hug.

For once, something might actually work out for the better.

CHAPTER 9

COACH JONES HAS us at Catinas restaurant in the center of Aspen. Freshly poured beers and warm bread are served to us while we put in our orders for dinner. We're all dressed casually, enjoying the second-to-last night of our time in such a welcoming place.

It's been almost a year since our participation in the Winter Olympics, and we're finally at the last stop of our tour from visiting other states across America to thank and meet the ones who supported us back home.

I've had my fair share of fun, met one beauty after another, but I'm happy to end the tour on a high note and get my ass home.

The restaurant is low-key, with dim lights and soft classical music playing while waiters and waitresses tend to neighboring tables. The place boasts black satin tablecloths, and shiny silverware is arranged for each course, though I'll probably use one fork.

I'm already halfway through my first beer when Coach drops the bomb.

"How would you feel if we added one more stop to our

tour?" He clasps his hands on the table, a hopeful smile on his face.

We groan in unison, Taylor lowering his head, mumbling, "The old bastard can't let us rest."

"This old bastard is not much older than you." He takes a hearty sip of his beer.

"The only difference is that our bones don't crack when we get out of bed," jokes Mark.

Coach chokes, and Cody has to smack his back to get him to stop. "I'm only thirty-five!"

"That's pretty old if you ask me," I tease. I butter a warm piece of bread, then shove it all inside my mouth, trying to smile between big bites.

Tommy Jones is the youngest in history to coach the Olympic snowboarding team. With twin daughters of his own, his passion for snowboarding started at the age of ten and blossomed as the years went by.

Unfortunately, he sustained an injury that cost him to lose a chance at his spot on the team, but he had the opportunity to work under the last coach and now has to wrestle us around as the lead.

And I know he loves every second of it.

Steamy, hot plates grace our table. From filets to salmon, with sides of broccoli and mashed potatoes, we all dive in. Every bite of the filet is like butter, melting the minute it hits my tongue.

I moan, enjoying my meal, when Taylor comments, "Funny, that was the sound you were making last night when"— I kick him hard in the shin. Taylor hollers, and people around us stop mid-meal to check out our table.

Coach closes his eyes and sighs. "Please, not at the dinner table."

"Fucking Christ, Noah. Could you kick a little harder?" Taylor's halfway under the table, rubbing his leg.

I side-eye him while shoving a big piece of meat in my mouth.

"We're still sorry about that," Cody apologizes.

Cody will always be the sensible one in the group, and for that, I'm grateful. I nod in his direction, silently acknowledging his attempt to derail the conversation.

"Who's 'we'?" Mark waves his fork around, a piece of salmon hanging on for dear life. "'Cause, last time I checked, Noah is the only one who can't keep his dick in his pants."

"I don't want to talk about anyone's extracurricular activities at dinner, please, I want to keep my food down for once," complains Coach, running his hands down his face.

The bastard isn't much older than us; hell, he'd had his girls when he was barely nineteen.

Cody changes the subject for us. "Let's go back to the topic of possibly extending our stay?"

"Yes, right, well, good news is—we are!" Coach dives back into his mashed potatoes, definitely preparing for our reactions.

Why the hell am I not surprised he pulls something like this? Last minute, too. Yeah, typical Coach Jones for you. I swear he finds the thrill of sharing shitty surprises.

I grind my teeth, pushing my empty plate aside. "Can I skip?" Any longer on the road with these fucks, and I might actually put myself through therapy.

"Dinner? Or our new stop on the tour? Cause I'm going to say no to both." Coach takes another bite of his salmon, eyeing me down to challenge his authority.

I grab Cody's hand, securing it around my neck, pretending he's choking me. "Put me out of my misery."

"It's only one more stop. That's it." Coach pulls out a trifold pamphlet, tossing it in the center of the table. "Snowy Peak in

Burlington, Vermont. I know the owners, and they asked for a favor, so now we're heading there tomorrow morning."

Mark snags the pamphlet, flipping through its contents. "It's family-owned since the early 2000s and accommodates wheelchairs...hmm...oh, they have impeccable slopes."

Taylor rips it out of his hands. "I love the little cabins." He smiles, his eyebrows rise. "There's a sauna and a jacuzzi, too? Sign me the fuck up."

"I don't mind if it's to help others," Cody states.

"I'll see if Sophia wants to come. Maybe make it a little vacation for us," Mark comments, taking back the pamphlet.

"So, you weren't going to wait for our answer? You just did it anyway?" I snipe. Because god-for-fucking-bid we get a decent break.

Coach slides his empty plate aside, wiping his mouth with the black cloth napkin. "I'm sorry, but when a friend calls in for help, I come to support. That also means you *all* come with me."

"I didn't know I was shackled," I mutter.

"You've already made a commitment for this tour, and that includes dates added at the last minute."

"That's fucking bullshit.

Silence hushes over our table, and Cody nudges me, probably wondering if I'm okay.

I haven't been okay in months.

CHAPTER 10

ONE YEAR AGO...

Sean finishes his Double Cork 1260, skidding down to the finish line of the halfpipe, all of us hopping over the barrier, running to bear hug Sean. Mark screams in victory, Cody cries, and Taylor jumps on his shoulders. The high of his win finally happened all at the same time. My heart might burst from my chest with all the happiness and tears.

Cody, being the youngest, experiencing history being made; Mark, the oldest, getting the recognition he deserves; and Taylor, overcoming an injury to see it all through. Sean, completing his run without any hiccups, is the icing on the cake.

Cameras are flashing while reporters lean over the barriers, trying to get someone to speak with them about our victory. Nothing else matters.

I grab the lucky son of a bitch by his face. "You did it, you crazy fuck!"

He kisses my head. "We did it, you bastard!"

Sean's score is announced, giving him an eighty-five out of a hundred.

He's getting his first silver medal, and tomorrow, I'll be competing for first place.

It's kismet.

Coach Jones comes barreling down, pushing his way through the crowd, gripping Sean's shoulders, shaking him. "I knew you could do it!"

We cheer, arms around each other's shoulders, jumping together and chanting our team mantra.

We're taking the party back to our rooms.

"Noah!" Olivia waves her hands above her head, dark hair and eyes striking against the snow. I maneuver my way to her, picking her up and swinging her around, kissing that red, lipstick mouth.

She giggles, ruffling my hair. "I'm so proud of you!"

I kiss her again, deeply, not giving a shit that the crowd around us can see me shove my tongue into her mouth. She returns the kiss with just as much force, our bodies pressed tightly together.

Coming up for air, I scoop her in my arms, while she laughs and swats at my chest. "Noah! What are you doing!"

I smile down at her, her lipstick ruined, knowing most of it is on my face. "We're celebrating, baby! Party back at our place!"

She snuggles her face in my neck as we make our way back to the suites, getting ready for a night of celebration and good company with my girl by my side.

I'm pretty fucking drunk, and somehow I've managed to remain standing, high-fiving anyone who cheers my name. The euphoria of winning resulted in Sean and me doing a keg stand, then playing flip cup. At some point, I stumble upon Coach asleep outside on a patio chair. The old fart takes one shot and falls right to sleep. I guess being thirty-four years old and dealing with us does that to you.

The guys are scattered around our suite, talking it up with friends and other members of our team. Olivia is nowhere to be found, having gotten a drink maybe an hour ago and never returned.

My drunk ass decides to make it my mission to find my girl-friend and make love to her.

Fuck, I love her.

I check my bedroom first, only to find it empty. Frowning, I mosey my way over to Sean's room, seeing him not too long ago enter, wondering if maybe he's seen her.

My hand grasps his doorknob, and being drunk, I barely get it open, stumbling inside.

"Heyyyyy, Sean, have you seen—" My heart drops, the beer bottle I'm holding falling from my hands and hitting the floor, beer splashing at my shins, soaking my jeans.

Long, dark hair cascades down her back, her hands splay across his chest as she rides him, moaning his name with each thrust. Sean grips her ass, moving her faster.

Beer threatens to come up as I stumble back, hitting my shoulder against the door, knocking shit over.

Olivia turns around, eyes wide, and halts her movements. "Shit, fuck, Noah."

Sean peeks around, pushing her off. "Goddamnit!"

I'm already out, trying to get away from them, pushing through teammates, hands shaking, my mind replaying it over and over again.

"Noah!" Sean calls. I keep moving toward the front door, swallowing back excessive saliva so I don't puke.

This can't be fucking happening.

I'm almost there, inches from escaping, when Sean slides to block the door. "Noah, please listen."

My steps retreat, bumping into someone. "No, Sean, fuck off right now."

"Noah." Goddamn Olivia. Her quiet voice shreds another piece of my heart, until scraps are left, barely enough to repair.

She broke me in those few moments of giving herself to Sean, and there's nothing either of them can say to fix the damage they caused.

I barely give her a glance, Sean pushing me back into the room. Music starts to die, it's quiet, all eyes on us, while I try not to lose my shit.

Sean holds up his hands. "Noah, we can explain."

"How? Did she trip and fall on your dick?" I scoff. "She cheated, and it had to be with my best fucking friend!"

I'm seeing red, my fists clenched at my sides. He takes another step closer. I'll knock him out. To hell with the repercussions.

"We've wanted to tell you for a while." He's inching closer, hands still raised in defense.

"When? Before or after you fucked her god fucking knows how many times?" My words are harsh, venomous, striking out to hit him where it hurts.

"It's wrong, and I'm drunk, and it's no excuse for how you found out, and I should've told you sooner." Sean tries to reach for me, but Olivia comes into view, blocking his path, and it takes every part of me not to break down and fall to my knees. Because I love—loved her, so goddamn much.

Tears fall from her dark eyes, and her bottom lip quivers as she hugs herself. "Noah, I'm so sorry."

How can I go on when the two people I loved the most ripped out my beating heart?

FOR THE NEXT FEW DAYS, my main priority is revamping Snowy Peak's website and creating a few sample ads for Jill and Anthony to look over. I've been sending them mockups of what it could look like, getting back what they like and don't. It's nice to help people I care about.

My stomach flutters at the possibility this might work.

All staff members at Snowy Peak have begun preparations for the event. They ordered a giant Christmas tree to be placed in the center and planned to host a lighting ceremony after the team's arrival. My job is to capture every event from here on out.

I take a quick shower, braid my thick, red hair back, put on my favorite blue beanie, comfortable snow gear, and grab my camera as I head to the main building.

I spot Maya in the foyer, pacing behind the front desk and giving Joan instructions on what to do and how to do it. I can tell Joan's trying not to interrupt or offer any suggestions. Once Maya is in planning mode, there's no stopping the avalanche tumbling down the mountain.

Lucky for everyone else, I know how to stop it.

Not caring about her loud protest, I drag her the hell out of the reception area, get a quiet thank-you from Joan, and force her to sit. "You have to relax, your face is starting to show blotchy red patches."

She touches her cheeks on instinct. "I'm just nervous, okay? They're coming in less than," she pauses, checking her watch, "ten minutes, and I need to make sure their first impression is a good one."

Looking around, noticing a few subtle changes from when I first arrived, most likely Maya's doing, I know the coach and his team are going to appreciate the homey feel of this place and hopefully enjoy themselves. "Everything is perfect and going to be fine. Now, please, relax before you pass out."

She fans herself, watching the front entrance, most likely counting down the minutes, driving herself crazy. I shake my head and laugh, while Maya gives me a dirty look, knowing I can tell what she's thinking. "Go stand somewhere else, I need to spiral alone."

"And miss an epic show? No thanks." Taking out my Nikon, I clean the lens, preparing for when the Olympic team walks through the door. It'll be a great shot for the resort's social media accounts, announcing their arrival.

Jill gave me their log-in information last night, now it's connected to my apps, so I can easily switch between accounts to do live updates.

Maya flips me off and proceeds to stare straight ahead, trying to avoid my presence. Her dark, curly hair hangs down her back, a light, beige cashmere sweater complementing her warm complexion.

The foyer is quiet; most of the guests are still sleeping. The coach had told Anthony their arrival would be bright and early, probably to avoid possible chaos if people recognized them, only to bombard them with autograph requests.

I haven't kept up with any current members of the Olympic team, but I know they have one who won back-to-back gold medals in the halfpipe. Luckily, the Gomezes have one built further on the property for kids who are training to compete for a spot.

Voices are heard just on the other side of the double doors, which swing open as a man leads the pack, sporting a black winter jacket with his title in gold stitching stating "Coach" on the breast pocket. I get my camera ready, taking shots of every interaction, Anthony coming into focus as he greets him with a hug.

Members of the Olympic team start to pile in, and they're quite an attractive bunch.

One has deep-brown hair in a bun, a full beard, and dark eyes. A black, spiral tattoo curls up his neck, disappearing in the collar of his jacket.

The one in the middle—blond, clean cut, with striking green eyes—keeps his focus on the conversation between Anthony and his coach.

And on his other side, the final team member has dark skin, light eyes, a short haircut, and is a few inches shorter than his teammates.

"Well, they're not so bad," I comment, taking another shot of the male snowboarders watching their coach and Anthony converse.

"It's intimidating to see an Olympic medalist in the flesh," she says, watching them move around.

"Hmm, I guess." I zoom in to get a group shot. "The only difference is they have medals, we don't."

"You could've, if you kept going."

I shake my camera at her. "My love for this contraption took over."

"Girls," calls Anthony, motioning for us to join him.

I have to drag Maya, pulling her out of the trance she put herself in from all the testosterone in the air.

She stumbles off her seat and comes with me, where her dad introduces us.

"Girls, this is Tommy Jones, coach for the men's Olympic snowboard team. And over there," he points to blonde twins who somehow slipped past us and are laughing by the coffee station, "are his daughters, Elise and Ella, both seniors in high school. Tommy, this is Maya, my daughter, and her best friend, Hannah, who will be taking photos of the event."

We shake his big hand and exchange pleasantries. Coach Jones points to the trio of men behind him. "Man bun over here is Cody Smith, middle man is Taylor Reed, and our big air legend is Mark Coleman." All three men shake our hands, excitement radiating through my bones at everything finally coming together.

"And..." Coach Jones pauses, looking around. "Where the heck is Hart?"

Man bun Cody shakes his head. "Some girls recognized him outside, so he's signing autographs."

Taylor, in the middle, rolls his eyes. "Can't ignore his admirers."

Mark slaps him on the back. "'Cause he's a man whore."

Coach Jones spins around. "Keep the crude comments to yourselves; we are in the presence of young ladies."

All three men hold up their hands in defense.

Eventually, they all migrate to the lounge area, where Anthony talks Coach Jones' ear off.

I linger back, taking more photos, when I hear a door swing open behind me, making me collide with something hard.

Big, gloved hands keep me steady as I turn to see a tall man with tawny skin and swept-back, dark, curly hair hiding behind sunglasses. He wears the same matching gear as the other

Olympians, with a dark beauty mark on his left cheek. He pulls his sunglasses down to assess me, light brown eyes catching me off guard.

"I'm sorry, I didn't see you come in." I apologize.

He gives me a quick look up and down and says, "Clearly." His eyes watch my every move, making me squirm. But his attitude is something I won't tolerate. Remembering his hands are touching me, I shrug him off, putting space between us.

"As I said, I'm sorry." Crossing my arms, I let my camera hang off my neck.

He taps the lens with his gloved finger. "Nikon Z 5?"

"Uhh...yeah?"

"I hope you know how to use it."

Who the hell does he think he is, questioning me about how I operate a camera? "I do." *Keep your cool, Hannah. Don't say anything rude.*

He smirks, slowly pushes his sunglasses back on, those piercing brown eyes hidden once more, and stalks off, joining his teammates by the fire.

"There's Noah!" calls Taylor, greeting him with a fist bump.

Maya catches my attention, quickly noticing the sour look on my face. Before she can reach me, Anthony calls me over. Plastering on a fake smile, I make my way to where Maya stands, utterly aware of his presence, and find him ignoring mine.

What the fuck is with this guy?

Coach Jones smiles at me. "Now that Noah has finally made his way inside, I wanted to suggest to you, Hannah, that while we practice, maybe you can join us and take some behind-the-scenes shots? Whatever Gomez over here pays you, I'll give you extra."

His offer takes me by surprise. "Really?"

"Of course. I plan on using the material for their portfolios."

Maya pinches my side, encouraging me to take the offer. "Uh, yeah, sure, thank you for the opportunity!" The idea of my work taking up space in their portfolios is a huge boost for my career. Mark, Taylor, and Cody give me a thumbs-up, while Noah ignores the conversation, typing on his phone.

Anthony claps his hands together. "After dinner, we'll go over the dates for the event. Please, in the meantime, make yourselves comfortable and go explore our resort!"

Joan comes over and hands each of them their cabin keys. Coach Jones and Anthony leave us to talk privately, while the twins get a tour from one of the staff members, the men talk about the autographs Noah signed outside.

"Kids, or...?" Mark edges.

"In their early twenties, one gave me her number." Noah holds up a folded piece of paper, waving it around. "Might call her later if I get bored."

Taylor snorts. "You're always bored. What number is this? Fifteen?"

Noah shrugs, unbothered. "Maybe ten, I lost count when that other girl gave me a blow job in my suite in Aspen last week."

The men snicker, making my stomach turn. My eyes lock onto Noah's, and a sly smile appears, mocking me from afar.

I grab Maya and pull her away from their gross comments. "What the hell is wrong with them?"

"Well, for starters, nothing, they're quite delectable," she purrs, eyeing Mark.

I snap my fingers in front of her face. "Focus, Maya. They're pigs."

"Just Noah, the others have decent pasts. I looked them up before they arrived." She pulls out her phone and shows me a recent article about Noah's relationship status. "I guess he's on the market again."

"Whatever. I'm already not a fan of his attitude, but as long as he performs for the event, he can do whatever he wants."

They eventually leave, most likely checking out the resort. I watch Noah like a hawk, disapproving of his rude remarks and drilling my eyes into his back. He stops, looking over his shoulder one more time, and smirks at us before leaving.

"Whoa," whispers Maya.

I cross my arms, irritated to say the least. "Whoa, what?"

"I think he caught the vibe that you're not a fan," she guesses.

"So? Sucks that not everyone wants his attention."

"By the smile he just gave you, he just might give you his, and not in the way you think."

I roll my eyes. As long as he does what he's supposed to do for Maya's parents, then I won't have to kick his ass.

Stunning red hair and wide, blue eyes take me off guard the minute she turns around. My breath catches far too quickly, almost knocking the wind out of me.

Freckles kiss her cheeks and scatter across her petite nose, and her lips are full and lush. I wonder what it might feel like to take my teeth and pull that bottom lip, what kind of noises she might make.

She bumps into me, and my jackass self knows it isn't intentional. I stop her before she stumbles any further.

"I'm sorry, I didn't see you come in," she apologizes, her voice a sing-song of notes so delicate it's like relaxing under the Tuscan sun after a cool swim.

And how do I keep my composure? By coming off like an asshole.

I give her a quick look up and down and say, "Clearly." I push my sunglasses down my nose, my eyes watching her every move.

She shrugs off my touch, creating space between us. If looks could kill, I'd gladly fall into an early grave if she were the one to strike the final blow.

"As I said, I'm sorry."

I'm never caught off guard, ever, and somehow she's disarmed me in just a couple of minutes with our exchange. My approach is nonchalant, arrogant, and it takes her only a second to catch on that I'm the worst possible person who has ever graced her presence.

It heightens my need to toy with her, watching this little mouse run away from the big bad cat.

A camera hangs from her neck, and I tap the lens with a gloved finger. "Nikon Z 5?"

She lifts her eyebrows. "Uhh...yeah?"

"I hope you know how to use it."

"I do," I smirk, slowly pushing my sunglasses back on. If I stay any longer in her presence, I might do something stupid.

I'm with the guys now by the fireplace inside the main building at Snowy Peak, and she's grilling me from across the room, arms crossed, camera hanging from her neck.

She's on the shorter side, not as short as her friend with the wild, curly hair, but short enough that she can be tucked safely under someone's arms.

And I can't stop staring.

And I don't want to try.

"Kids, or...?" Mark edges, drawing my attention back.

She pivots her body to where she's in earshot, trying but failing at looking discreet. Oh, she's something else. Let's see how long I can play this game.

"In their early twenties, one gave me her number." I hold up a folded piece of paper, waving it around. "Might call her later if I get bored."

Taylor snorts. "You're always bored. What number is this? Fifteen?"

I shrug. "Maybe ten, I lost count when that other girl gave me a blow job in my suite in Aspen last week."

It doesn't take long before she sneers in my direction, eyes narrow. Her lips slightly curl in disgust as she turns away from us, her red hair in some type of braid, where all I want is to unravel it with my fingers and run my hands through it. God, she is breathtaking.

Fuck, I need to get myself under control.

She grabs her friend and leaves, while I stare hungrily at her backside.

She's a force to be reckoned with, and I'm not afraid to shift the tide to get what I want.

A staff member had already handed us each a cabin key, instructing us to leave our bags, and someone would carry them to our rooms shortly.

The resort is quite quaint, with plush maroon couches and Christmas lights strung along banisters, twined around railings. Cody and Taylor help themselves to an array of donuts, double fisting a few jelly-filled.

Coach Jones comes back around, clapping his hands at us. "All right, let's get settled in, and tomorrow we can work out a practice schedule."

Social media is a blessing and a curse. A blessing because it keeps me updated on world news and what my family members are up to, especially Mom and my kid brother Cameron, who are home in Utah. Phone calls are one thing, but it's nice to *see* what they're doing. I try to call them here and there, but my schedule makes it difficult. At least my brother is doing well in school and keeps up with my stats to keep Mom informed. Maybe one day my brother and I can travel together when he makes the team.

A curse because I get hit with a photo of Olivia and Sean on vacation because I can't seem to unfollow her. No matter how hard I try, I'm addicted to wanting to know where she is and if she's still with him, and sure as shit, they're all cozied up near a fireplace. Her hair is just as striking as her eyes, nothing out of place with her smile.

My heart is ripped bare-handed from my chest while hers is placed gently in Sean's hands.

I swiped out of the app and tossed my phone aside, trying my best not to spiral back down into my depressive state. It's comfortable, but the guys had to pull their hardest to get me back to the surface.

Now I just sleep with who I want and when I want because it's easier to mask rather than let anyone get close to my battered heart again.

And this time, I have my sights set on the color red.

"Are you okay?" Henry side-eyes me in the back seat.

It's the millionth time he's asked, making me want to jump out of our Uber at high speed to end my misery. "I'm fine."

"He's not," comments Mark, looking over his shoulder. "He just loves masking because he enjoys suffering."

I'm two seconds away from choking him out when Taylor chimes in, "In Noah's defense, he wasn't expecting them both to be there."

I bang my head against the window. "Can we stop talking about this, please?" There's nothing left to discuss, or analyze, or even give a shit about. What's done is done.

"You've come a long way, I don't want you to shut down

again." Mark's concern is warranted but it's not what I need right now.

"Sounding a lot like Cody." I close my eyes, picturing freckles like it's the constellations in the sky. Eyes as blue as sapphire, and pale skin looking soft to touch. She has no idea she's become my anchor in those mere seconds of seeing two people I thought meant everything to me.

"Sorry if I'm concerned for not only my teammate but my best friend."

He's pissed because I know he wants what's best for me but what's best for me right now is to stop talking about my goddamn emotions like a therapist.

I play with my gold watch. "It doesn't matter."

"At least Cody was smart enough to take another vehicle," huffs Mark, giving up.

"Noah, why don't you ask Hannah out?" suggests Taylor, pushing the light above his seat on and fixing his hair through the camera app.

"Because Hannah is too good for him." Mark is getting on my last goddamn nerve.

"Or she's just right," adds Taylor.

I don't say anything because deep down, once you get past the barbed wire around my heart, you'll find broken pieces that maybe not everyone wants to deal with.

My phone chimes, checking my messages to find a new thread with Henry.

Henry: It's okay, you know.

Me: I don't know what you're talking about.

Henry: It's okay that the idea of someone new can scare you.

Instead of giving in to his attempt at trying to talk through my emotions, I play the dumb card.

Me: Scared? Scared of who?

Henry: I don't know, you tell me.

Her sweet face comes to me like a leaf dancing in the wind, gliding towards me without the troubles of my past. Once again, anchoring me down, keeping me still so I don't crash and burn.

Red.

THE DAY GOES ON AS normal. Maya is nowhere to be found inside the main building when Gift Card Guy catches wind that the Olympic snowboarding team occupies the lounge in the afternoon. He tries to flirt with the twins, only to get shut down when he discovers both are under the age of eighteen. I tell Maya that little tidbit, and she sends me a voice memo of her cackling like a witch brewing a potion.

Someone new shows up in a pristine blue suit, blond hair trimmed short on the sides, and a silver phone plastered to his ear. Apparently, Noah invited his personal assistant to the event, wanting to keep track of the publicity that will be pouring in, in just a few days after the ads. At least he's giving us the traction we need to bring in more revenue.

Otherwise, I find him repulsive.

I end up taking photos of two of his teammates, chatting it up with Mark, and finding out he's married and that his wife, Sophia, is pregnant with their first baby.

"What are you having?" I ask.

He smiles big, lighting up like the Christmas tree behind

him. "A girl, and we're naming her Lily, after Sophia's grandmother."

"Aw, that's so nice!" I smile in return, already a big fan of how kind and conversational Mark is. We chat more about our families and my history with Snowy Peak.

He leans casually against a wall while sunlight filters through the window. "It's a really nice place they have here. I hope our event saves it. I would love to bring my family here when it's not on business terms."

I ask him if I can take a picture of him posing casually by the window. He agrees, keeping his posture relaxed but still as I take a couple of shots. "It's been my second home since I was twelve. We have to save it."

Taylor is next, and I learn he swings for the opposite team and prefers rugged men chopping wood. The man is an open book, not afraid to broadcast his likes and dislikes. "I like an ideal lumberjack, you catch my drift?"

Shaking my head with a laugh, I have him pose in a chair, closer to the Christmas tree, lounging without a care in the world. "I can't say I want the same, but I get the vision."

He laughs, pushing his blond hair away from his forehead. "The world is our oyster, no point in wasting time. Experimenting is fun." He ends our conversation with a wink and leaves me standing alone, staring dumbfounded at my camera.

What an interesting individual.

Cody is nowhere to be found.

So, that leaves me with Noah.

And I have no interest in doing a solo portrait of him...unless he keeps his mouth shut.

Instead, I take photos of Mark and Taylor speaking with other guests, laughing, and somehow, Noah catches my eye, watching every move I make.

He makes me grind my teeth.

Girls either sit next to him or on him, laughing as they twirl his hair, teasing or taking turns whispering in each other's ears. This family place has turned into a goddamn nightclub, pissing me off even more.

Noah catches my stare, smirking like he's a little kid caught in the act of drawing all over someone's living room walls with a Sharpie. His eyes, a deep, rich brown, are haunting in a way; they send chills running through my body, keeping tabs on me as I weave in between groups of guests, kids running up to the snowboarders, asking for autographs. Noah isn't afraid to make his laser focus on me blatantly obvious, and that's another irritating factor about him.

If I can just blend in with the rest of the crowd, then I'm in the clear to escape.

"Excuse me?"

His voice, smooth like butter, gives me an odd chill down my spine.

"When were you going to take my photo?" His manners are sickly sweet, leaving a gross taste in my mouth.

I cock an eyebrow, only giving him half my attention. "When you're alone and not smothered in a female pack of hyenas."

He pretends he's wounded, holding a hand to his heart, then moves smoothly across the floor until he blocks my view, taking over my personal space. "How about now?"

Gosh...he is...overwhelming.

I look up, following his feet to his face, swallowing back a tickle in my throat. Our eyes lock, and heat rises up my neck to my cheeks. His smile reminds me of a Cheshire cat, sneaky yet charming, his dark curls inviting to touch. The idea that someone so...attractive can exist right in front of me...

"I can be shirtless if you like?" he offers, clearly impressed with himself.

The perfect image of him tarnishes in seconds after his gross comment. Then again, why did I ever think he was? "Find me when you get knocked down off your imaginary pedestal, k?"

Pushing past him, he chuckles like I told the funniest joke.

He's so fucking arrogant.

I make it my mission for the rest of the evening to avoid Noah, and the girls gathered around his shit circle, while I stab aggressively at my salad, judging. I have to remind myself he's here to help Maya's parents, and after that, he'll be gone.

The others are digestible, and it surprises me that Mark and Taylor join me for dinner.

Instead of letting Noah get to me, I brush off what I can't control and engage in lighthearted conversation with them.

"Tell me, Hannah, are you a skier or a boarder?" asks Mark, eyeing me over his plate of spaghetti.

Taylor leans in, completely enthralled, waiting for my answer.

"Snowboarder born and raised," I declare, getting a high five from both men.

Mark twirls his spaghetti and says, "Single or taken?"

Taylor's eyebrows raise, his eyes flickering back and forth between us.

I laugh, not quite sure where he's going with this twenty-question game. "Single."

Mark hangs his head low, and Taylor celebrates, smacking his teammate's shoulder. "You owe me twenty!"

I backpedal. "Did you bet on my relationship status?!"

Mark pulls a crisp twenty out of his back pocket, tossing it at Taylor. "In my defense, and I am a married man, mind you, I thought someone as nice and pretty as you was taken."

Taylor waves the bill away, tucking it under his plate. "From the way you've been grilling the shit out of Noah since his arrival, I assumed you hated the male species and thought you were against penises."

I frown. Clearly, it's no fault of their own for not having any idea of my dating history, but damn, am I that obvious in my hatred for the man? "Well, glad that was such a hot topic for you both."

Taylor takes a deep sip of his water. "Hannah, it's all in good fun. Speaking of fun, where's your spunky friend, Maya?"

Appetite gone, I push my half-eaten meal aside. "Hiding out from Gift Card Dude."

"Who?" they say in unison.

"Some guy she went on a first date with decided to use a gift card." Now my stomach is twisted in knots.

Taylor nearly chokes on his spaghetti, tears streaming down his face from laughing. Mark has to smack his back to control his fits.

They both get dessert, but I decline, remembering I already had my sugar for the day, while envying everyone who orders dessert, because they're the best here.

Mark and Taylor devour a skillet chocolate-chip cookie, polishing it off in minutes, then relax in their seats.

Taylor rubs his stomach. "I'm gonna have to hit the gym later tonight to burn this off."

Mark rolls his eyes. "God forbid you enjoy a dessert every once in a while."

"This body is built to perfection; I must maintain it." Taylor lifts his shirt up to show us his well-sculpted abs.

Mark smacks them.

I snort. At least they're entertaining. They seem more like brothers than teammates, and it's nice to watch their exchange.

Eventually, they head out, wishing me a good night, leaving me in the dining hall until I'm kicked out by the kitchen staff.

Standing outside the dining room, across the lounge area,

Noah has a girl's back against the wall, his arm above her head, lips inches apart.

Heat rises up my neck as I try to sneak out, avoiding anything that'll make a sound, when I trip over my own two feet, stumbling towards the door, trying to get my footing.

Squeezing my eyes shut to block out the horror, I slam my side into the door, rattling it.

"Fuck," I hiss, rubbing my shoulder. That's going to be a huge bruise in the morning.

Silence follows after my tumble, and I look around to find Noah and the random girl gone.

Well, *she's* gone.

Noah stands behind me, looking down like I'm a cockroach and his foot is seconds away from squashing me to death. "Stumbling into people and doors? There should be a hazard sign around you at all times."

I get to my feet and brush myself off. "Girls straddling your lap at a family resort? That warrants an arrest."

He recoils, then recovers in seconds, resuming his nonchalant demeanor. "I'm only here to do one thing: perform at the event and get out. What I do in my downtime shouldn't be up for discussion."

Our bodies somehow gravitate toward one another, barely a couple of inches separating us as we stare one another down. "That's fine, but keep it behind closed doors. I'm trying not to barf every time I walk by the lounge."

"You're rather hyper-fixated on my extracurricular activities." His eyes dart down to my mouth, then back up.

Our height difference is staggering; he towers over me with ease, overtaking my space and making me a little nervous. But I refuse to cower. "As long as you do your job, then we're done here."

"Are we?" he moves a millimeter closer, our chests barely touching. His eyes smolder, trying to size me up.

I shake myself out of his trance, reminding myself this man is nothing but a playboy with a rude mouth. "Just stay out of my way, and I'll stay out of yours."

Noah reaches forward, moving a loose piece of my hair away from my face. My heart almost drops in my stomach. "Fine by me, Red."

CHAPTER 14
NOAH

RED. It's the perfect nickname for someone so fiery, especially the way she tries to ignore me. It's incredibly obvious when she does, and...oh shit, my cock fucking twitches because of it. She does something to me, a feeling so familiar yet new, I want to bury myself deep inside her. Her words come out venomous like mine, headstrong and resilient. I can picture us colliding in the bedroom.

And her presence is becoming easier to detect, even when I'm in the middle of making out with another woman.

But that mouth is going to get her in trouble, especially the way she questions every move I make or how I waste my time. She ruffles my feathers and has no idea she's doing it.

Now I lie in my bed, moonlight sneaking past the striped curtain, while I try to jerk myself off, thinking of Red, but even the image of her isn't enough to get me where I want to be. I go limp, huffing like I just ran a goddamn marathon.

The goal was to get myself off to help me sleep; now I'm just staring at the ceiling, contemplating hitting the gym to burn off steam or doom scroll through social media until the sun rises.

I pull up my gray sweats, then run both of my hands down

my face, dragging my skin like it's melting off my bones. My phone chimes somewhere in my room while I dig through my suitcase for a clean shirt. Back-to-back chimes can only mean one thing—the group chat is in conversation about something important.

Finding a clean, black, long-sleeved shirt, I throw it over my head, snagging my phone from the bedside table. Already, thirty messages have been sent between the guys, and I have to scroll up to find out where it starts.

> Mark: Coach wants us to run some practice drills.
>
> Cody: For how long?
>
> Mark: Couple of hours. He wants us warmed up before we go through the practice schedule leading up to the event.
>
> Taylor: You're going to have to give me some time. I have a guest in my bed.
>
> Mark: It hasn't been 24 hours yet, and you already found someone to sleep with?
>
> Taylor: I love a welcoming bachelor party.

Taylor sends a GIF of Mr. Bean's eyebrow wiggles.

I roll my eyes, scrolling further down, skipping all the mindless banter, and finding at the bottom of the text thread that Taylor shares a website called Luminous Lenses.

> Taylor: Our photographer's portfolio, if anyone is interested. Her stuff is quite impressive.
>
> Cody: I like her attention to detail. Our photos are going to come out great!

Cody hearts the link, forever the supportive guy.
I keep on reading.

Taylor: What's the owner's daughter's name again? Meghan?

Mark: Maya, you neanderthal. You asked Hannah about her at dinner, remember?

Taylor: Ah, shit, you're right. Sorry, that info was railed out of me tonight.

Mark: 😭😭

Taylor: But, Cody, get up on that!

Cody: stfu 🖕

The day Cody stops pinning over his situationship is the day Aliens will take over.

I click the link and find a simple logo appearing on the screen, a double L with swirls intertwined. I tap the drop-down menu, scanning for—bingo, the about me section. It's her face that greets me first, an up close shot, red hair framing her delicate face, lips pouty and pink. She's in a long-sleeved, green sweater, skin pale and dotted with freckles over her nose and the tops of her cheeks. A face so striking in looks, a mouth so tempestuous to touch, my dick twitches again.

Fuck.

Underneath her photo is a small paragraph describing who she is.

Hi! I'm Hannah! I'm a graduate from MassArt, I have a passion for baking, and I am a pizza enthusiast. I love to binge-watch 90s sitcoms, and I dream of going to Paris someday. Photography has been my passion since I was a little girl, and to have my own business and bring joy to families, couples, and even friends has always been special to me. Thank you for trusting me, and enjoy the samples in my gallery!

She links it at the bottom, and I click, mesmerized by landscapes, portraits of families, little kids, a high school senior gallery, and shots of flowers and wildlife. Every photo has her touch, making it unique only to her. Red's talent is evident, and it makes her even more irresistible, especially when it comes to her dedication to her craft.

And I'm certain she'll be attending today's practice.

> Me: Meet you fuckers out there bright and early. 🤙

CHAPTER 15

HANNAH

I BANG on Maya's cabin door, not caring who hears me. She opens on the fifth bang, almost hitting herself in the face, and looks at me like I've lost my mind. "Girl, are you trying to put a target on my back? What if Gift Card Dude sees me at this specific cabin!?"

I shoulder past her, not caring about her complaints. "Sorry, but Noah is insufferable."

Shutting the door, she takes one look at my face and forces me to stop pacing. "You're as red as a ripened tomato. What happened?"

"What happened? Maya, have you seen the girls basically dry humping him in the main building? In front of all the other guests? Kids can see that!" I throw my hands up, totally over him, everything, and everyone.

Maya keeps her hands on my shoulders. "I mean, yeah, it's a little inappropriate, but they're not straddling him and making out."

"Making out? I saw them minutes ago doing exactly that!" Why is she defending him!?

"Was anyone else there?"

"No, but—"

"Then, as long as the kids didn't see, I don't see an issue."

"How are you okay with this?"

Maya curls back into bed, patting the seat next to her. "Come here, my little cherub."

I roll my eyes, kicking off my shoes, and join her under the covers. "Seriously, he's so...gross and arro—"

"And a two-time Olympic gold medalist who can potentially save my family's business. If he makes out with a few chicks and the kids don't see, then, yeah, I'll be okay with it," she interjects, snuggling closer.

"What if a kid sees? What then?"

"Then I speak with my dad and Coach Jones, and we tell Noah to keep it in his goddamn pants."

I snort, shaking my head. Noah is allowed to do as he pleases, but he came here willingly to Snowy Peak. However, I refuse to let him walk around like a god who can get away with anything. "He's just...ugh!"

"You had maybe one interaction with him?" Then she pauses, watching my face change, catching on. "Oh, you spoke to him again? When?"

"Before I sounded the alarm at your door."

"And?" she encourages, waving her hands at me.

"I tried to leave the foyer quietly, but tripped on the rug. We got into a heated exchange, and I told him to stay away from me," I say in a rush.

Maya bursts out laughing, almost choking.

I smack her in the face with a pillow. "Stop laughing!"

She wipes her tears away. "I'm sorry!" Eventually, she gets herself to calm down, catching her breath. "I don't know what's funnier," a few giggles slip out as I give her my dirtiest look, "Are you tripping or did you tell him to stay away from you?"

"How is this funny?!"

"Because you have to be around him for pictures!"

"I don't have to take his photos..."

"Hannah, he's basically the lead of the event."

"So? He has other teammates!"

"Are you going to take weird photos from afar, then?" She waits for my response, but I just roll my eyes. "That's what I thought."

I groan and pull the covers closer to my chin. "There's something about him, Maya. I'm not a fan."

She eyes me. "Hannah, I'm actually surprised by your early judgment of someone. Are you sure you're not basing it on the crap Liam put you through?"

Her words sting, and I know she isn't bringing him up to cause harm, but I hate how she just knows what runs through my chaotic head. "Maybe."

She pats my cheek. "It's okay. I just want you to know you're worth more than that bogus bastard who hurt you, and it's okay to feel a little guarded of men."

"As long as you remind me to ease up?" I gently kick her in the shin.

"Ouch! Yes, you little gremlin. Life is too short."

"Speaking of life being too short, when are you going to stop hiding from Gift Card Dude and become part of civilization again?"

Maya gives me a dirty look. "When hell freezes over."

"Don't make me drag you out of here by your hair. I'm not afraid to make a scene." I tug at a chunk of her beautiful, dark curls.

"Do that again, and I'll put Nair in your shampoo bottle."

"Very mature, Maya."

I can feel something vibrate underneath my butt, and Maya retrieves her phone by pushing me over to the other side, almost off the bed. "Hey! I almost fell!"

"Your thick booty would've cushioned the fall." She types a response to whoever's on the receiving end. "Okay, tomorrow morning, you meet with Coach Jones and my dad, they want you at their practice to take behind-the-scenes pictures."

"Are you coming with me?"

She stiffens up. "Maybe."

"Maya," I whine, shaking her body. "If I'm not allowed to sulk in my past, then you're not allowed to hide from yours."

"Way to throw my own logic back in my face."

"You love me for it."

"Fine! I'm starving anyway, let's go to the dining hall."

"It's closed."

"You're forgetting my parents own this place."

I jump out of bed. "Really? You sure?" I dramatically clutch my heart, getting a few pillows tossed my way. I try not to laugh but fail miserably.

"I'm tempted to infest your cabin with bed bugs," she threatens.

Maya stands next to me by the half-pipe, while I adjust my camera, deciding on the best position to catch the sun blazing overhead. Although it's winter, the sun can still be an eyesore, and I dread not bringing my extra equipment to counteract the brightness.

Maya becomes my personal assistant, having the crowd join in on some photos, hyping them up, or simply asking one of the guys, especially Mark or Cody, to pose with fans or sign autographs.

We're all having fun, and I even got some of Coach Jones fooling around with some of his guys.

I walk around, zooming in on more wholesome interactions, kids smiling, faces tilted up the slope as they watch the guys' early practice, getting a glimpse of what they can expect during the live event. Keeping a steady hand, I pan up, zooming in on the halfpipe, and find Noah adjusting his goggles, licking his lips. Distracted, I watch through my lens; his concentration depicts someone who is about to take the most important test of their life. He rolls his shoulders, stretches his legs, and listens to, most likely, a pep talk from Coach. His jaw set, a muscle pulsating along his neck, he's focused and ready.

Noah begins with no hesitation, effortlessly performing an Alley-Oop with ease, enticing loud cheers from the crowd watching. With the shutter set, I end up capturing a shot of him in the air, then transitioning into the Crippler. The execution is smooth, and I'm in awe as he continues his routine, snapping more photos when he lands the Double Mctwist, remembering how I had struggled when I was first introduced to it during my snowboarding days. Noah makes it look natural, as if he were born to be one with the snowboard.

Something I can appreciate, regardless of his indecent behavior.

I can see why he's a two-time gold medalist.

The rest of the men take their turns, showing off their skills to the crowd, hearing some of the kids shout their last names in encouragement. I make sure I get wider shots and eventually make my way up to the top, taking a photo of Mark's back as he looks down at the halfpipe.

Noah stands close; I can feel his eyes on my back, most likely judging me for something. Maya is too busy chatting it up with Cody, asking all types of questions about their sponsorship to the tour they just finished up in Aspen a week ago.

I, however, became a victim of Noah's presence. "Enjoying the view?"

I swallow, rolling my shoulders back. "Yeah, it's nice to see the view from the snowboarder's perspective." Now, please leave me alone, is what I should've said right after.

"It's one of my favorite views," he mentions.

"Didn't know someone like you appreciates nice views."

He's leaning over my shoulder, looking at the screen on my camera, and reaches forward with a gloved finger, pointing. His body barely touches mine through our thick layers of snow gear, but damn, I feel the heat. "Here, where Mark is facing forward, you know he cares about what he's doing."

"You got all of that from one picture?" I'm afraid to look over my shoulder to see how close his mouth is.

"It's all in his stance."

I cave, taking the tiniest of peeks, and find his eyes unmasked, staring right at me. His lips, slightly pouty, are at eye level until I look up. Warm brown eyes with flecks of gold keep me grounded for the briefest of moments, until the crowd cheers after Mark's run.

Snapping out of it, we step back from one another. "Right, well, I have a job to do, and you're distracting me."

"As long as you get my good side," he comments.

I snort, trying to hold back a laugh, but fail. Then again, I really didn't try to hide the humor at his cocky attitude. "I don't think you have a good side."

Noah gets close, and I panic that he might see a chin hair if I missed any from this morning's pluck-fest. My insecurities creep in the closer he gets, then he moves his lips to the shell of my ear, a hint of cockiness laced in his words. I want to step away, to hide, but he has me ensnared with his heated stare. "If I'm being honest, I prefer my girls good, Red."

A shiver runs down my spine when he steps back.

"Don't call me that."

"Call you what?" He brushes past me.

Anthony surprises us by coming up with Coach Jones. "Hey, Hannah Banana! Taking some good photos?"

I want to die, right here, right now. My childhood nickname makes Noah do a double-take, then a sly smile creeps up his face, knowing he can use it to his advantage.

My heart rushes up my neck, flaming my cheeks. Fuck me.

"Hannah Banana?" He's laughing, a dark eyebrow rises.

"Don't call me that either, or I'll kick your teeth in." I'm done playing nice.

"Oh, don't worry." He walks around me, only to stop to move my hair aside. "I like Red better."

He leaves me with his haunting laugh, joining his teammates.

I have half a mind to turn around and swing, hoping to damage that pretty face of his, but remember, he has more than a few inches on me, and I'd just end up hitting his chest.

Maya comes my way. "Ready for l—whoa, what's with the sour face?"

"Nothing. Just hungry, let's go."

Maya stops me. "You sure?"

I take one more look back at Noah, and he winks in my direction, making my ears burn underneath my knitted hat. "Just a dog not knowing his place, that's all."

Maya has convinced every Olympian to sit with us during lunch, talking their ears off about how she grew up here with me. Noah's PA surprises us and takes an empty seat next to Mark, glued to his phone, typing vigorously while sitting in his crisp business suit. His blond hair is slicked on the sides, his nose straight, looking down.

Maya eyes him from her seat. "Who are you?"

He looks up briefly. "Who are you?"

Oh, boy. He has no idea what he has just started.

"Maya Gomez, daughter of the owners who run this establishment." Her words are clipped.

He smirks. "Henry. I'm Noah's personal assistant." He has no intention of extending a hand; instead, he looks back down at his phone, typing away.

"Why does he need his assistant here?" Maya leans forward, trying to get his attention.

He barely looks up and says, "Because a twenty-six-year-old man can't function without someone running his errands, that's why."

"Oof, harsh, Henry." Noah arrives, his arm slung over a pretty blonde's shoulder, guiding her directly to our table. I try to remain focused on my measly salad, moving cherry tomatoes around on my plate, when the fucker decides to sit directly across from me.

"You hired me for my expertise, not for being nice." But they playfully nudge each other.

"There's the shithead," comments Mark, sliding down a bottle of water.

Noah catches it before it topples over, unscrewing the cap and taking a swing. Focusing hard on my food, I know he's grilling me over the bottle in his mouth.

I peek, watching him take a few big gulps, his Adam's apple moving up and down, then crush it with his bare hands. "Thanks, man."

Henry must've gone to grab him some food, cause I hear a ceramic plate slide in front of him, my eyes catching a glimpse of a silver fork and knife in his big hands. "Thanks."

"Hannah, when do you think we can see the photos from

today's practice?" asks Cody, forcing me to join the conversation.

I grind my teeth and make sure my eyes land solely on Cody,

"Soon. Another day's worth and they'll be added to the new website and ad by the end of this week."

"I bet you got some sick shots," adds Mark.

"I actually looked you up the other night, and I must say, you have impressive work," Taylor compliments.

I blush. "Thank you."

Noah leans forward when I keep my eyes trained to look everywhere but at his intense stare. "It's good we hired someone with experience, then. A true professional."

I clench my hands under the table. He's mocking me from earlier. Don't you dare cave, Hannah.

He continues. "But it's interesting. I have yet to experience her work firsthand. Tell me, Red, when is it my turn to pose for you?"

I snap, the pressure of his words cutting my twig of restraint in half. I unleash my death stare, finding an amused Noah smirking at me. "Depends, when you're done sticking your tongue down every girl's throat."

Our eyes connect, his beautiful chocolate-brown eyes sizzling my skin from his unrelenting stare.

He smiles, a contagious sight, enjoying this little one-sided game way too much. "Jealous, it's not you?"

"Of being another notch on your belt? I'll pass."

Henry freezes mid-text, eyes darting between us. "Is there something I should know about?"

Maya lightly touches my arm, silently asking if I'm okay.

Noah ignores Henry. "I don't plan on changing my ways, so get used to it, Red." The girl next to him slithers her arms across his chest, like a cat in heat.

That does it. "Then you're out of luck for your shots." I lean back, crossing my arms.

Everyone at the table goes silent. I can hear Maya swallow, all eyes darting from Noah's face to mine.

But he only smiles, shaking his head, and cuddles closer to the mysterious blonde, tickling her ear with his nose. I'm gripping my fork so hard, Maya has a hard time prying it from my hands.

It's all a game to him that he thinks he can get away with because he's helping out. He's relaxing back in his chair, playing with the mysterious blonde's hair.

I wish I could hit something.

Ella and Elise arrive, smiling from ear to ear, waving a spiral notebook at us.

"Ladies, it's nice that you finally joined us," states Taylor.

"Yeah, we practiced on the halfpipe today, very smooth. Nailed all my jumps," boasts Cody.

Ella smiles at Cody, her cheeks flush. Ah, to be seventeen again and have a crush.

They both sit in unison. "Our father had us on a mission these past couple of days, and we're actually here to speak with Maya and Hannah...alone." Elise eyes the men, forcing them to remove themselves.

Noah is the first to leave, taking his blonde with him, ignoring all but his PA, who talks to him in hushed tones.

Ella leans forward, smirking. "It's nice to see Noah get challenged by someone, especially a woman."

I stab my salad, hearing the fork grind against the plate. "I didn't ask for it. He just won't take the hint."

Elise laughs. "You're his new fascination."

I'm about to leave my food and dip when Ella stops me. "Please stay. We're sorry if the topic of Noah irks you. It's actually good you're both here." She pulls out a notebook, thumbing through the pages until she finds the right spot. "Your dad, Maya, and ours had us on a little excursion. We decided to speak with neighboring resorts' guests, ask them if they would be interested in our little event."

Ella slides the notebook toward us and points to a quick sketch of a bar graph.

Elise finishes for her sister. "And let's just say, the results are quite in your favor, that's if all members, including dearest Noah, participate according to plan."

Our hearts must've burst at the same time, because Maya reaches for me.

The twins compiled a survey from the surrounding resorts, along with a quick breakdown of potential revenue from the event alone.

As Elise said, if everything goes according to plan, Snowy Peaks could survive after all.

MY LIPS ARE ALREADY on the blonde's neck the minute we enter my cabin, kicking the door shut behind me. She's unbuttoning my pants while we step out of our shoes. I take the hem of her shirt and pull it over her head, going back to her neck, sucking it hard.

She moans as she guides me further into the room, pulling me down on my bed, hovering over her body. I snake my hand toward her back, unclasping her black bra and tossing it halfway across the room.

I pull back, and the cool air makes her nipples peak as I dive mouth-first, flicking and sucking on one and then the other. Her moans are loud, echoing through the room, and her fingers glide through my hair, nails scraping my scalp as I continue to tug on her nipple. She reaches for my collar, trying to pull it up. I break away for a second, removing it and throwing it behind my back.

She smirks, then catches my mouth with hers, except... My mind imagines Red and her plush lips, wishing it were her hands and body against mine, that I was the one privileged to devour her. To take her to new heights and hear breathy moans come from her.

This kiss is flat. No fireworks. No desire to tug her underwear off. I start to slow my movements while she picks up speed, her fingers digging inside my boxer briefs.

She stalls, then pulls back. "You're not even hard."

I shut my eyes, because how do you tell a pretty girl who's basically half naked in your bed she doesn't do it for you? Because you're wishing the smart-mouth redhead was under you instead.

She crawls out from under me, probably gathering her belongings. "I should've known the minute you got into that argument with the redhead."

I open my eyes and roll on my back, staring up at the ceiling, afraid to even look her in the eye. "I'm sorry." I've never been so flaccid in my entire life. What a joke.

"Oh no, don't apologize to me." She comes over, obstructing my view, leaning over me. "But you should tell her how you feel. Maybe she can help with your problem."

"You're too nice," I mumble.

She gives me a half smile. "See you around, Noah." She leaves me with my embarrassment and thoughts of Red. It's the first time since my ex that someone else has taken up residency in my head.

And it scares me.

I'm up the next morning, having made the decision last night to hide in my cabin, putting my phone on silent and trying to get her out of my head. Whatever effect she has on me is something I wasn't prepared for. Granted, she makes my dick twitch, and her smart mouth pushes my buttons, but for her to infiltrate my mind while I'm trying to hook up with someone else? Absolutely diabolical.

It's completely out of left field.

Mark, Cody, Taylor, and I are at the top, waiting for maintenance to smooth out the half pipe. The air is frigid, the sun bright and blinding, the only warmth to kiss my cheeks. Closing my eyes, I breathe deeply, cold air coating my throat, lighting my muscles up, and keeping my focus sharp.

"Where did you go last night?" asks Cody.

I open my eyes, finding him staring at me with concern. "I stayed inside, wanting a night to myself."

His eyes squint slightly, definitely not taking the bait but accepting my answer regardless.

Cody is the only member of our team who doesn't pry into others' business but will lend a listening ear if needed. A calm presence through a storm, a solid friend overall. And yet he's the youngest in our group. He's a good kid. I wish he weren't so hellbent on his on-and-off-again girlfriend.

Henry approaches us, bundled up in sleek snow gear, taking a picture of Cody and me. "For the gram."

"Do we have any idea if they started to sell tickets?" asks Mark, joining us.

"I tried to ask the owner's daughter, but she just gives me attitude," Henry says, typing on his phone.

"Did you say something to her?" questions Cody. His tone is rather accusatory. Weird.

He barely looks up from his phone and says, "I bumped into her at the coffee station. She argued with me about not paying attention. I told her if she knew I wasn't, then why didn't she move out of the way before we collided? I tried changing the subject, asking about ticket sales, and she just blew me off."

"They're both so feisty, I love it," comments Taylor, sliding his goggles down to cover his eyes. He takes his place, strapping his snow boots, and starts his run, shouting, "Let's gooo!"

"Both?" Henry gives us a confused look.

"I'm assuming he means Hannah and Maya. Quite the duo." Mark lines up next, watching Taylor perform below.

"They're best friends, right? I get why they act defensive, especially to us outsiders. They're putting all their trust in us to save their favorite place. I'd be on edge too," comments Cody, following behind Mark.

I blink. "You're quite team Hannah and Maya this morning."

Cody looks over his shoulder and shrugs. "They're not bad people."

"Then again, I'm not the one fighting my sexual tension with one of them," Mark adds, chuckling.

I flip him off behind his back as he starts his run, hands up in the air like the cocky bastard he is.

Henry comes over, flashing me his phone. "Got another sponsor lined up. Are you interested?"

But I'm too busy staring ahead, where Red comes into view, climbing up with her best friend.

My eyes are hidden behind tinted goggles, watching every move she makes, right down to her facial expression. Even now, her nose scrunches as she talks to Maya, one of her arms moving with animation to whatever they're discussing. Her hair is fiery like her personality, and I can't help but let myself indulge in inappropriate thoughts of how feisty she could be in the bedroom. What words and moans I can get those sinful lips to release, or how my hands could roam all her curves while I'm buried deep inside her, admiring who and what she is.

It would be an honor to have her sit on my face and ride it until she begs me to stop.

That's the real tragedy here. Coming off arrogant and rude

is not my usual demeanor, but when someone takes a baseball bat to your heart, it's hard to repair the damage and let someone else in. Red just does something to me that I put up walls to protect myself. Even if I want to feel her hot mouth on me, it's wrong to rile her up, but the faces she makes and her quick comebacks are too entertaining.

And I won't let up, because I don't think I want off this train, and I haven't even touched her—yet.

That's the real tragedy here.

CHAPTER 17

HANNAH

THE NEXT MORNING, after a sluggish start and oversleeping, I awoke to Maya pounding on my cabin door. I stand once again by the halfpipe, adjusting the lens to take photos of Cody. He performs a Double Cork, flawlessly, I might add.

I put the setting on burst and watch as he spins into his landing, his hands rising in the air, a couple of guests cheering.

Moving my camera around, I catch Coach Jones speaking with Henry, pointing to the halfpipe behind him.

I'm about to snap their interaction when something black covers my view. Peeking over my lens, Noah stands with his snowboard against his chest. "Red." He removes his goggles, an outline indented in his face. Noah's tawny skin shines in the winter sun, his dark mole lifting when he smiles, a set of pearly white teeth blinding me.

Hoping to ignore him, I turn around, but am met with his chest once again blocking my view. "I'm trying to work."

"I know, that's why I'm here. I'm ready for those pics you owe me."

"I'll pass."

He mirrors my steps. "Don't you think the captain of the team deserves to be included in the pictures?"

"Captain?" I scoff. "Gosh, why am I not surprised?"

'Now, Red—"

Getting in his face by standing on tiptoes, I point a finger at him. "Listen, I don't care who you are or your title, as long as you keep your promise to save the resort and compete in the event, then I'll snap a few photos of you and your adoring fans. As for the portrait, you can shove it up your ass, and also, stop calling me Red."

"My, do you have a temper?" he teases.

I flex my fingers inside my gloves. "You're doing this on purpose."

"Pissing you off? I mean, it's easy, but no, not on purpose." He steps closer, removing his winter hat. Hair the color of onyx, curls thick and bouncing, is hard not to admire.

I shake my head. "I swear you have a monkey in your head banging symbols."

"You want to get inside my head, Red?"

"And suffocate from your egotism? I'll pass."

He pushes his hair back, not moving but staring, like he's trying to see inside my head.

My eye starts to twitch. "Then why can't you leave me alone?"

He pauses and licks his bottom lip. "Because I can't."

I'm the first to move, stepping back to create space. I don't want to be part of his little game; these back-and-forth mind tricks are just to humiliate me. "If it entertains you to mess with me, then you can go fuck yourself."

I'm already turning away, not bothering to wait for his stupid reply. I need to get out of here, create more space between us. I'd never met someone who could so easily get under my skin.

Why the hell does it have to be Noah?

I catch sight of Maya and the twins sitting at a picnic table, talking and sipping from Styrofoam cups. They catch sight of my frown and don't hesitate to ask what's wrong.

"Noah Hart, that's what," I snap, taking an empty seat next to Maya.

"Yeah, he has that effect on people," states Ella, taking a swig of her drink.

Elise adds, "For us, he's like a big brother, so we're used to his jokes."

Except, I don't think he's joking with me. "Ever since he arrived, he's done nothing but piss me off."

"Probably thinks you're cute," Elise theorizes, taking a bite of her cinnamon roll.

"Isn't that kind of high school?" Seriously, we're adults, picking on a girl because you think she's cute is ridiculous.

"Well, considering we're both in high school," Elise says, smirking.

Both girls give each other looks and laugh. "That's all we know," adds Elise.

"Right." I keep forgetting how much younger they are.

"They were also just finishing up telling me about the latest gossip of your least favorite person." Maya wiggles her eyebrows. "And it is quite juicy."

Do I really want to know more details about that unbearable man? A quick look over my shoulder, and I see the arrogant ass setting up at the top, waving at a group of fans at the bottom.

Yeah, maybe some inside gossip might help throw him off my back. "All right, spill it."

Ella commands the floor. "Before the boys went on their tour, Noah was in a committed three-year relationship."

Elise looks at her sister. "Guy was head over heels for her."

"Just before tour, she ends up breaking it off, stating it was her, not him, and she needed to," Ella pauses and uses air quotes for emphasis, "figure herself out."

Elise rolls her eyes. "Now, Hannah, I know you didn't think anything of it when we first arrived, but have you noticed only four male members were participating in the event?"

I shrug. "It never crossed my mind...why?" I've barely researched them, as it really wasn't on my to-do list before their arrival.

"Sean ended up taking a medical leave. We think he had something to do with the breakup, but we just can't prove it." Ella finishes off her drink, tossing it in a nearby trash can.

"And how did you find this out?"

Sly smiles creep up on both their faces. "Our inside sources must stay a secret." They both say in unison. Quite impressive.

"Now, this doesn't excuse his behavior, but it does explain why he's acting like a meanie." Elise takes out her phone and types.

Perfect. Noah Hart gets dumped by the love of his life... might have caught his teammate screwing around with her... maybe. Not a hundred percent confirmed, just a theory in my head, but for some reason, I trust the girls' sources. "Were they close? Noah and Sean?"

"They were like brothers," Ella mumbles.

All our attention returns to Noah. He takes his position, goggles covering those intense eyes. On instinct, I get my camera ready and make my way over to the barrier, trying to get a clear shot of his routine.

He starts with similar moves from yesterday, except he adds in a new move, something I'm unfamiliar with, as he gains air, spinning not once or twice but three times. Using burst, I catch his move when he loses his hold.

Noah flails in the air, losing his board as he tumbles face-first into the side of the halfpipe, going still. My breath catches, taking a step forward, when Coach Jones and the others rush to his limp body. The blood rushes from my face, and I feel the presence of Maya, Elise, and Ella by my side.

I watch as Maya's parents arrive next, ambulance sirens going off in the distance. Henry is running over, his coat barely zipped.

Everything happens so fast, by the time the EMTs arrive and put him on the stretcher, stating he's breathing, reality finally sets in.

Noah almost got severely injured, and although he's a thorn in my side, nobody deserves to get hurt doing a sport they love.

CHAPTER 18
NOAH

ONE YEAR AGO...

I stare down at the newly groomed walls of the halfpipe, my right hand sore and bruised, tucking it safely in my pocket. My gloves create a safe cushion, but I can still picture and feel Sean's nose where my fist connected, hearing a crunch as I broke it.

It does little to ease the tension in my shoulders; Olivia is most likely waiting at the bottom, regardless of whether I told her to leave last night or not.

Nothing will change what she's done, what *they've* done.

Tinted goggles block my eyes while I scan the crowd, knowing Sean is also out there watching, probably waiting for me to fuck up.

How do you move on from the two people you loved who hurt you the most? It's like a black and white film playing over and over, all color lost from my life. Empty and numb, cold air stings my cheeks, my chapped lips crack, and I taste blood on my tongue.

I'm a walking mess.

Coach is aware of what happened, waking up just as I

knocked Sean to the ground. Except he took the blame for my outburst. How fucking noble of him.

Doesn't change all the damage that ensued.

Seconds tick by, and my countdown begins. Rolling my shoulders, I inhale a shaky breath and begin my run when a snap echoes out.

I'm gaining speed at the right time, easing myself into my first trick, sticking a McTwist, then Nose Grab, hearing shouts of excitement over the roaring in my ears. Wind whips past, stinging my cheeks, my stomach in knots, kickstarting my anxiety.

Olivia's face flashes in my mind, replaying all of our moments, our secrets, right down to the quiet times of comfort and stability. She is—was my anchor, my reason for getting my shit together. The engagement ring hides inside my underwear drawer at home. Christmas would've been our time.

Now it's lost to lies and betrayal, and it fucking hurts.

My knuckle throbs when I complete a Trail Grab, landing not quite right, but it doesn't derail me from sliding further down, where I amp up for my last set of complex moves.

The landing might cost me a point or two, but I'm still projected to win gold.

People are chanting my name, the crowd in sheer pandemonium. I'm gearing up for my last sequence of tricks, knowing I'm pulling a new one out of my pocket just before the finish line.

My body shakes, but I persevere, catching air, my nerves shot as I start my first spin, higher than intended.

Every ounce of my being suddenly halts, my limbs locking in place. My brainwaves short-circuit as my body flails, losing all sense of control. All I can do is close my eyes.

Olivia's face flashes behind my eyes, then screams pierce my ears as everything goes black.

Present day

A soft beep continuously fills my headspace, pounding behind my eyes, resulting in me groaning. Nothing hurts, but being awake is something else entirely. It means I have to face what happened.

"There's the poor bastard." Mark's voice makes me nauseous.

"Why is he acting like that? Didn't the doctor say he's okay?" Cody's concern takes pity on me.

I crack my eyes open, catching sight of all three of the guys staring at me. "It's like I'm in an episode of *Grey's Anatomy*."

Taylor shakes his head, sitting comfortably at the end of the bed. "You got so lucky."

"Really? Cause my head is pounding," I complain, wiggling my toes. Nothing feels out of place, nothing severely broken. Shit, he's right.

Coach Jones comes waltzing in, face red, sweating, dripping down his temples. "Trying to get a nurse in this god-forsaken place is ridiculous."

"Is that why you're sweating like a pig?" I point out. For someone who's not that much older than us, it's like he's never worked out in his life.

His eyes find me sitting up, and he sighs with relief. "I'm in layers, you jackass." Coach comes closer, getting a good look at me. "Since you don't have any injuries, I was trying to track the nurse down so we can get the discharge papers going."

My stomach drops, panic rising in the back of my throat. I can't go back. He can't force me to participate after that. He knows what transpired out there. We all fucking do.

The guys share looks with one another, proving my point—it's over.

"I'm done."

Tommy Jones is a man of many things: a father, a coach, someone's uncle or brother, but he's never been someone who loses their cool. I guess today is that day. "You have got to be fucking kidding me, Hart."

"Not this time. You know what's happening again, face it. It's over, and I'm done." God, my fucking head is killing me. I reach for the call button, buzzing the shit out of it to hopefully get some pain meds. There's a good chance I have a slight concussion.

"You're just gonna give up?" Now he's pissing me off. Coach is right by my side now, and the guys are watching, anticipating an intense verbal argument. Unfortunately, I don't have it in me.

"I. Am. Done." I press the buzzer harder, hoping she comes quickly to buffer this wack conversation. My head throbs, making it harder to focus. It's like someone ran over my skull with spiked tires.

He runs his hands down his sweaty face, cursing under his breath. "Please don't tell me it's what I think it is..."

I don't say anything, and he hangs his head, backing into the seat behind him. "This changes...everything."

He's right.

It changes my life.

I SIT ALONE in my cabin, legs bouncing with anxiety. There's been no word of Noah's condition. I keep checking my phone in between staring at the door, waiting for Maya with any type of news. She left a couple of hours ago to talk with her parents, trying to get some information, yet the silence of not knowing is killing me.

Noah is a condescending douche, but to get hurt, especially to the point of knocking oneself out, is scary and might lead to other complications. And I wouldn't wish that on my worst enemy.

Time ticks on, my stomach jumbled with knots, when finally Maya lets herself in, her face an ashen mess.

"It's not bad, but it was a close call," she says, sagging to the nearest chair.

Sweet lord. "What did they say?"

"Mild concussion, no sprain. He got very lucky, Hannah." She runs her hands down her face. "The question is, will he participate after he's healed up?"

"I'm sure he would...right?" Crap, even I'm nervous about the unknown.

She rolls her neck, then her shoulders. "Right now, he's stable and resting. The doctor says it'll be a couple of days for recovery, but if he continues resting, we have a solid chance of him returning right before the event."

I blow out a long breath, releasing some of the nerves, causing my stomach to flip. "Well, that's good. I hate to say this, and don't quote me on it, either, but having Noah and his talent in the event is going to help save the resort."

"Oh, I will most definitely quote you on it. He was recommended to stay off screens, too. After that, he should be good to go."

I sigh with relief, anxiety exiting my body in one big whoosh.

Maya doesn't say anything else, just stares off into space, biting her lip. She looks like she's encountered her first ghost.

I tap her knee with my foot. "Maya?"

"I ran into Gift Card Dude." Her tone sounds like she just witnessed a murder.

"And?"

Her face falls into her hands. "We have a date."

I try my best not to laugh, but the sound slips out of me before I can cover my tracks.

Maya peeks through her fingers, a threatening look in her eyes. "It's not funny."

"Come on, it is a little bit. How did your worlds collide again?" Even though it was inevitable because he's staying at her family resort, which she mentioned on their last date, I find immense satisfaction in teasing her about it.

"Right outside YOUR cabin, that's how!"

I burst out laughing, finding the odds against her hilarious, when she's tried so hard up to this point in hiding from the poor guy.

"You find too much joy in my suffering," she mutters.

"Forgive me, but I am enjoying the free entertainment."

She tosses her dark curls aside and flips me off. "Now that I've given you the best stand-up of your life, can we go eat? I'm starving."

"Sure, sure." I throw on my pink puffer jacket and blue winter hat as Maya leads the way to the dining hall.

Jill stops us halfway up the steps. "Hey, girls, getting some lunch?"

"Yeah, is the sandwich station available?" asked Maya, lingering on the bottom step.

"Yes, it should still be open, but Maya, can I speak with you for a second?" Jill gives me a soft smile before Maya waves me off to go ahead, and she'll catch up shortly.

I bypass the stupid crowd of adoring fans that are hovering over Noah somewhere by the lounge, give a quick wave to his teammates, then help myself to making a small sandwich, taking the closest seat to the doors.

By the time I finish, Maya arrives, crestfallen, and slumps in the chair.

I barely have time to swallow and ask what's up when she blurts out the worst news imaginable. "He's out."

I almost choke on a bite of ham and cheese. "Excuse me, what?"

"Noah. Is. Out. Apparently, the injury was too much, and he's out until further notice."

"You have got to be fucking kidding me." Ironically, it's the same set of injuries I got before my competition back in high school, yet I had no problem competing.

The son of a bitch is definitely milking the attention.

"My dad spoke to Coach Jones, but he won't budge, not even his teammates can talk him back into it."

The sandwich doesn't settle right, my stomach swirling with anxiety. This can't be happening, not now, not after everything

Maya and her family have done to get this far, and now have it completely squashed by some arrogant piece of shit.

I'm already up and walking across the dining room, Maya on my heels, my half-eaten sandwich left behind.

"What are you doing?" she asks, trying to keep up with me.

"I'm going to remind Noah why the world doesn't revolve around him."

NOAH LOUNGES peacefully on one of the couches, leg propped up on two pillows, girls fawning over him and asking if he needs anything.

My blood begins to boil. Maya can sense my anger, and she grabs my arm, eyes pleading with me not to go over there. "Hannah, whatever you're about to do—"

"Maya, I love you very much, but I cannot sit back and watch him milk his non-existent injuries and refuse to participate." My body is shaking, my temper meter reaching its breaking point.

"Oh boy," mumbles Maya, as my arm slips from her hand.

I walk over, finding Noah has his arms behind his head, leaning back into a set of pillows, chatting and winking at those who hang over the couch, drooling.

I approach, waving them off. "Shoo, all of you."

"Excuse me?" one of them says.

"We're not dogs, you know," another says.

I snort. "Well, judging by how bad you're all drooling, I beg to differ."

A few gasps, one girl tries to step between Noah and me. "Can't you see he's hurt?"

"Can't you see I don't care? Now, go away, all of you, or I'll tell the owners you're loitering."

The sea of his pathetic fan club disperses, leaving just Noah and me staring at one another.

More like glowering.

"Is there a reason for your intrusion?" he asks, annoyed.

"Yeah, there is. For someone with barely a sprain and a slight concussion, you sure know how to milk your injuries," I snap.

Noah gives me a quick assessment, smirking. "Quite observant, Red. Although I am concerned about your obsessive habits. Might want to seek help for that."

I have to hold myself back from shouting. "You might want to seek help for your delusion, because for someone who has two gold medals, you act so fragile. It's pathetic."

He gets comfortable, putting his hands behind his head again, sighing like my presence isn't a bother. "Pathetic? That's new. Never met a woman with balls, Red. It's quite a turn on." His muscles flex, veins protruding from his tawny skin, and I try my best not to get distracted. He wears a white t-shirt and black sweats; only one foot has a sock on, the other is wrapped in a black brace. His dark curls are in disarray, and that stupid mole that lifts when he smiles has me boiling.

I shake my head, reminding myself of the reason I came over here. "You're a sad excuse for a snowboarder. For someone with your talent, it's a shame how it's going to waste."

Noah's eyes darken, and he loses his cocky smirk. "You know nothing about me."

I snort. "You're right, I don't. But I know when someone abuses his status. So, you either get off your ass, or you leave."

The air around us tightens, and Noah starts to lose his cool. "Sharp tongue you got there, Red. I'd watch yourself."

But I keep going, letting all my frustration and disappointment flood past my iron gates. "Anyone can replace you. The moves you perform are easy to imitate; a monkey could do it."

"And what do you know about snowboarding? What do you know about a sport that has shaped your childhood, following you into your adult life until it's all you consume?" His eyes pierce through my soul, holding me in place.

Before I can snipe back my retort, Maya jumps to my defense. "Actually, Hannah used to compete as a snowboarder back in the day."

Noah's eyes dart back and forth between us, looking baffled by the admission.

Maya clears her throat. "And if I think anyone is qualified for getting you back out there, Noah, it would be her."

Panic hits my chest, wondering where she's going with this.

Coach Jones makes a surprise appearance somewhere behind us, startling me. "I think that's a great idea, Maya."

Her smile is triumphant. "You think?"

My eyes widened. There is no way she set me up.

Noah has the same shocked expression, mouth silently agape. "Are you fucking kidding me?"

Coach Jones ignores his comment, looking over at me. "Hannah, Maya talks highly of you and happened to mention your amazing record as a snowboarder. I think it's a great idea for you to help Noah and remind him why we're all here in the first place." He shoots him a warning look not to argue.

But that doesn't stop the infamous Noah Hart. "You want some washed-up wannabe snowboarder to help me get back out there? I would rather swallow a bucket of nails than commit to something like that."

His words are harsh, forcing my will to blow up, exploding

through the dam of perfect composure. "And I would rather get stuck in an avalanche than ever waste my precious time on the likes of you."

Maya tugs at my arm. "Please, Hannah."

But I've had enough. Not giving them another chance for a rebuttal, I am the first to leave, moving past lingering guests, some of his fan club snickering as I walk back.

Retreating to my cabin is my first thought, but how quickly Maya can find me forces me to halt my mission of retreat and take a snowy trail to the first set of slopes on foot.

I wander, hearing kids squeal from the thrill of mastering the bunny slopes. Hugging myself, I curse my haste and for not bringing my jacket as frigid air bites at my cheeks, numbing the tip of my nose.

There is no way in hell I'm helping Noah readjust to snowboarding. Coach Jones is acting like he's some fragile little boy, and it's baffling how much he's coddled, when he barely got hurt.

Animosity toward Noah was warranted before his accident; now it's a monsoon of hate just by his choice of words alone.

He thinks swallowing a bucket of nails is better than being near me? It's almost laughable, and pride shines through me at my comeback.

No man will ever belittle me again.

I can hear my name called, wind whistling through ice-capped branches, muffling most of the noise. The trail breaks off, arrows pointing from left to right, indicating which path leads to a particular slope.

"Hannah, wait!" Maya's footsteps crunch heavily on the snow when I stop, huffing and puffing like she ran a marathon.

I turn to find my jacket clutched in her hands as she bends over to catch her breath.

"I can't believe you ran all this way," I say.

She holds up a finger, signaling for me to be quiet while she calms her pounding heart from the exertion of running. "Well..." she takes another breath, settling against a lamppost, "if you just waited a second, I could have explained."

"Oh, explain how you set me up? Why, Maya?" Here I am trying to cool off, and she just reminded me how betrayed I felt back there.

"Because, Hannah, I trust you to get his ass up. I trust you to make sure this resort is saved."

I throw my hands in the air. "How am I going to help save it when the fucker wants nothing to do with me!"

She throws my coat, hitting me square in the face. "The plan was set before I came into the dining hall. When my mother asked me to hang back, Coach Jones joined us and explained the situation. I was hoping to inform you before you went and attacked him verbally, which was iconic, might I add, and explain what we had in mind. I was just lucky Coach came by in time to help."

Part of me, and that part is a thin sliver, wants nothing to do with Noah and his fragile ego. But the other, where I put all my best efforts into saving Snowy Peak, forces my icy exterior to melt.

Unfortunately, my urge to save this place outweighs any con of working alongside the most insufferable human on the planet.

Fuck me.

I quickly put on my jacket, letting its warmth settle in my stiff bones, and rub my hands together to keep the blood flowing. Maya pleads with me with those doe-like eyes, forcing me into submission.

Little does she know, I already decided.

Sighing like the world is against me, I hold my arms open, a knowing look on her face that I caved, and she embraces me with the tightest hug.

"Thank you, Hannah. I wouldn't have asked you if I knew you couldn't do it," she mumbles in my hair.

It takes every ounce of willpower not to groan. Because she thinks so highly of me, it pains me to turn down any chance to help save what is such a staple of our childhood and lives.

We walk back, arms linked, steps in unison, hoping Noah hasn't moved from his spot on the couch. Odds are, he's still slumping against a plethora of pillows, adoring fans drooling over his physique. Not that I pay too much attention to it, but I am a human with two eyes, and I see the appeal, other than his rude mouth.

Maya leaves me to confront the brooding man on the couch, reading some type of magazine, dog-earing the page when he sees me approaching.

"Come back to gawk? A picture will help it last longer," he snickers, clearly pleased with himself. "Might I suggest a portrait?"

Usually, I approach situations with caution, rather than coming out guns blazing, but since Noah likes to think he's funny with his cocky persona, I might as well match his energy. At least I can get some enjoyment out of it.

I grab his ankle, wrapped in the black brace, and smile, flinging it off the couch. His foot lands with a hard thud, completely unbothered by the hit.

I knew that son of a bitch was milking it. "First, stop talking, your voice is grating on my eardrums. Second, I'm not here to coddle you like the rest of your adoring fans and teammates. I'm here to make sure you get off your ass and back on those slopes. I don't know why my involvement is necessary since you're more than capable of returning, but I'll be damned if your dumb ass ruins this for The Gomezes."

He cocks an eyebrow, no humor in his eyes. "Anything else?"

"Yeah, better be ready at seven tomorrow morning, otherwise a car will be ready to haul your ass out of here."

Noah gets up, showing he can walk, and nods. "Fine, Red."

I lift an eyebrow. "Never thought you'd give in that easily."

Noah takes a couple of steps forward, invading my personal space. "You're going to find out real quick what a waste of time it'll be."

He leaves me staring at his back, the muscles underneath his shirt tense as he pushes the dining hall doors open.

Feeling proud of my stance, I wander to a frost-covered window, peek out at the night sky, and give myself a little space before dinner.

Light snow begins to fall, kissing the ground, covering old footprints that mark the trails. Wood glows from an old flame inside the fireplace, the smell of cinnamon invading my nostrils.

I'm trying my best to see the bright side of this unfortunate situation, reminding myself in an endless loop that what I'm doing for Maya and her family, maybe even his team, can help save the resort and build something even greater.

Yet I can't shake this feeling that the can of worms I opened might've been infested with maggots.

CHAPTER 21
NOAH

I HOVER by the salad bar, piling my plate with various veggies, pouring dressing all over it while strenuously breathing in and out to keep my cool. She is...a firecracker. An absolute force to be reckoned with. I won't lie, her quick comebacks turned me the fuck on, had my dick twitching the whole time. But she has no idea what's going on.

No idea how truly fucked I am.

It's back, the infamous twisties—a goddamn omen of what will plague me for the rest of my life. It's as if your brain short circuits, causing every limb in your body to stop working. Like a fish out of water. Once is torture, a second time? Might as well order my casket. The cause? Unknown... I think. I'm a little fuzzy on the details since waking up, thanks to my slight concussion.

My career is being flushed down the toilet, and watching my teammates continue without me rips me apart inside. It twists the knife just right.

Red thinks she can fix me—heck, finding out she was a snowboarder in her high school days took me by surprise, and my reaction is nothing I'm proud of, but she'll be wasting her time. And as much as I'll thoroughly enjoy teasing her for it, I can't force her to participate in my already tragic ending.

But I'd be lying if I said watching her snowboard beside me wouldn't make my dick rock hard.

So, when she finally walks in for dinner, she barely looks my way, spotting Maya at her table, cozying up with my teammates. But I know she senses my presence, then our eyes meet, her mouth set in a half frown. She makes me want to brighten her mood, and I carry my plate over to their table, catching the thought and shoving it far down into the trenches of past heartbreaks.

No, I will not go there again. It's too dangerous. My wounds are mostly healed, but to think of anyone else as a potential girlfriend is something I steer clear of, now and forever.

I sit next to Taylor while he tells a story about his latest escapades, but I zone out, my eyes observing every detail of Red's face. She listens to him yap, nodding her head at the right places, resting her chin on her hand, and biting her bottom lip, which makes me want to roll my eyes to the back of my head.

It drives me crazy.

I grip the underside of the table as she turns to Maya, catching her attention for a second, that measly moment holding her stare while she licks her bottom lip.

Cody joins in, innocent fucking Cody.

"Hey, Noah." Cassy appears behind Red, her light-brown hair cascading down her shoulders, her eyes wide and delightful. A pretty girl, fit and smiley. But she's no Red. She's not a fire blazing through a rainstorm.

Red watches me like a hawk, waiting for me to respond.

I give her a smirk and look over her head and say, "Hey, what's up, Cassy?"

"Are you busy later?" she asks, twirling a piece of her hair.

"For you? Never," I flirt, knowing Red is trying her hardest not to watch our interaction. It does something to me, really gets me going, with her blatant jealousy. She wears it on her face, rolling her eyes like I'm the bane of her existence. Maybe Cassy can help fix my issue.

"Awesome! I'll meet you in the main building by the fireplace." She saunters off, and my eyes follow her ass for good measure until she's out of sight.

Red scoffs and gets up from her seat. Maya follows in tow.

Mark throws a dinner roll at my head. "Are you trying to piss these girls off?"

It bounces off, rolling away. "Who? Me?" Now I'm fucking with him, getting a nice middle finger from his end.

Taylor leans back in his seat, patting his stomach. "Why don't you ask Hannah out already and save us from this misery?"

"You know why I don't date," I remind him, pushing my uneaten salad aside. "But it is fun to mess with her. It's like watching a ticking time bomb."

"Except you've been eye fucking her since we arrived." Taylor gives me a look, already disapproving of my actions. "And we," he gestures to the three of them, "like Maya and Hannah."

I hold my hands up in defense. "Never said I didn't like them." I mean, I do enjoy our tryst, and she's not a bad person.

"You tease Hannah like you did Olivia before you started dating," mumbles Cody, staring down at his phone.

My hands flex on instinct, trying my hardest not to snap at innocent Cody. "Then she fucked my best friend. I'm trying not to let history repeat itself." Because with my luck, it's sure to continue on an endless loop.

"How do you know? Have you taken a second to actually get to know her?" Cody's defense for Hannah has me breathing hard through my nose, trying my best not to cause a scene or punch him. Why the hell am I getting so jealous?

"Why don't you get to know her since you're so ready to defend her?"

Taylor smacks the table, forcing Cody and me to recoil. "My god, man, you know Cody is dealing with his own shit."

"Noah, are you okay?" Mark asks, his concern making me more heated.

"I'm out of here." I'm out of my seat and already out the door before any of them can call after me.

Talking about my feelings with the guys is too much right now; I can't even have a civil conversation without someone bringing up Red and assuming there's more beneath the surface. For me to admit out loud to being aroused by Red is a whole other issue, one I don't think I'll be able to act on. She might stab me before I get too close.

And that also turns me on. I'm all over the place with my emotions; it's ridiculous.

Time to find Cassy.

CHAPTER 22

HANNAH

DRESSED from head to toe in my snow gear, I stand at the top of the halfpipe, looking down on the quiet resort. Sunrise takes its time, and branches coated in ice twinkle when the sun peeks over the horizon, creating a crystallized gleam. Snow falls in big puffs, looking like marshmallows, covering my knitted hat in minutes.

A few quiet chirps fill the vast silence, while a wintry chill nips at my nose and cheeks. Here, at Snowy Peak, the place I call my second home, memories of my childhood trickle in and spread warmth along my spine. How can a place so significant in my life cease to exist?

I watch for any sign of Noah, but he never shows. Seven has come and gone, and my patience has worn thin.

The bastard flaked.

Stepping into the bindings of my snowboard, I strap them in place and coast down, skidding toward the end, spraying snow.

A no-show from the notorious Playboy has me grinding my teeth all the way to the main building. I prop my snowboard outside and search for the little shit inside, most likely the girl at dinner, perched on his lap.

Pathetic.

Then I remember it's still early, and guests have yet to rise for today's activities, so I start to pace around the lounge.

Is he in his cabin sleeping?

I mean, if I have to burst his bubble and dump cold water on his head to wake him up, I won't pass on the opportunity.

Coach Jones comes in moments later, shaking off the snow from his jacket. He catches sight of my disheveled look. "Hannah?"

"Where's Noah?" I ask.

He pulls up his jacket sleeve, checking the time. "Um... I think he's at the gym with the rest of the—"

I don't let him finish, already heading back outside, making my way to the fitness building.

If he thinks blowing me off is going to stop us from practicing, he's dead wrong.

The fitness center is small, but it's open 24/7 for the night owls who can't sleep. Sitting at one of the benches, lifting weights, is Noah, except he's completely shirtless.

Arms sculpted likely from the years of training, flexing with each curl, Noah breathes through each rep he performs. Shoulders wide, torso dripping with sweat, making his abs glisten. He wears black shorts and white Nike shoes, a backward baseball cap to match. Music is blaring, while the rest of the team continues their rigorous workout routines.

All shirtless.

But I linger on Noah and how he moves about the gym, picking another set of weights. He has no idea I'm standing here gawking, mouth open, luckily not catching flies.

His muscles are defined and tempting me to come closer, just to feel how strong he really is.

I snap out of my stupor when Taylor calls my name, making the others turn in my direction.

I clear my throat and move past Cody and Mark running on the treadmill, stepping right in front of Noah.

He looks down at me, eyebrows rising in amusement. "What?"

"I told you to meet me. Did you forget?" I cross my arms, trying to keep eye contact and not wander down his perfect body.

Shit, he's...really good looking. No, Hannah, he's really good at being an ass.

Suddenly, my thick layers start to make me sweat.

Noah works on his triceps, giving me a look. "And?"

"And?"

Perspiration drips down his temple, eyes keeping hold of me, making it harder to breathe.

What the hell is wrong with me?!

Taylor comes over to pat the bench, signaling Noah to return the hand weights and lie back as he spots him. "Hannah, maybe come back later?"

Noah grunts with each lift. "Or not at all."

I swear, both men are asking to get slapped. "No, I think I'll stay so I can drag your ass out of here."

His grunts start to become deeper, ragged, like he's struggling to push the weight. "Red, some advice," he pauses, Taylor's hands hovering just in case, "kindly fuck off."

He...no, he did not just tell me to fuck off.

I stare, shock flushing through my body, my face aflame. I'm partly pissed and embarrassed, standing here in full gear, trying to get this douche to practice, and he couldn't give a fucking shit.

He finishes, then Taylor hands him a towel to wrap around his neck. He grips the ends and walks away, entirely over our conversation, weaving through the workout machines to the water station.

"Hey, asshole, I'm still here," I yell from where I stand.

Someone pauses the music at the exact moment I throw the insult his way. His teammates all give me worried looks. Mark whistles, shaking his head.

Noah chugs from his water bottle, crushes it, and tosses it in the nearest trash bin. "My, Red, you have my full attention now."

I gulp, hearing the others gather their things, whispering their condolences for my early funeral.

Noah stalks over, giving me barely any space to breathe. His stature towers over me, a body of pure perfection glistening with sweat under the lights. Some of his dark curls peek out from under his baseball cap, dark brown eyes dangerously cold, making me shiver. Every line and curve of his skin, right down to the muscles and chiseled jawline, this man is a work of art.

"Do you want to repeat what you called me?" It's not a threat, more of an invitation, and he knows what kind of trap he's set.

My stomach flips, causing my lower region to spike with pleasure like a stupid, hormonal teenager.

For fuck's sake, Hannah, pull yourself together! You swore off men, remember? Especially jerks like him!

No, I won't back down or cower. I'm not going to let Noah push me around like some rag doll. He may be hot and successful in his career, but he's nothing more than a player in this one-sided game of chess.

"I mean, it was pretty loud and clear from my end. But if you would like me to repeat, then sure, asshole."

His eyes are cast in darkness, knuckles flexing. "If Coach thinks he can force me to practice with some pretentious—"

"That's rich coming from the goddamn king of being such a pompous douche."

When did we get so close, our chests almost touching? I

have no idea, but I can spar all day with words if that's the game he wants to play.

He's not getting his slimy way out of this.

He's so close now, I can smell his breath, a minty scent wafting up my nose.

"Go away, Red. I'm not doing it."

If he ruins this for the Gomezes, I swear I'll make his life a living hell.

"You're going to show up tomorrow at seven, ready to practice. I don't care about your feelings. Get your shit together. It's pathetic."

"Forcing me back out there isn't doing anyone any good."

"You promised!"

"I never signed a contract!"

"I don't care! This place means everything to me, and you're going to destroy the one chance we've got to save it!"

Inches are what separate us; our lips close, dangerously too close. Chests rise and fall from our heated argument, neither one of us backing down.

He starts to shake, his hands flexing by his sides. "That's life, Red. Not everything you love can be saved."

"Why are you so heartless?"

He closes his eyes, taking deep breaths, exhaling it all before looking at me again, his false bravado cracking with each passing second. "I don't mean to be."

I'm too overheated and strung out from his close proximity, especially since he's shirtless.

I make the first move and retreat. "Tomorrow. At seven. If you're not there, I will burn your cabin to the ground."

"YOU PROMISED!"

"I never signed a contract!"

"I don't care! This place means everything to me, and you're going to destroy the one chance we got to save it!"

We're almost touching, it takes every ounce of my strength not to reach out, to stroke those porcelain cheeks with my fingers, wondering if they feel as soft as they look. God, she has me in a chokehold. What the hell is she doing to me? But she also pisses me off... It's infuriating. She's wasting her time with me, and yet she's so goddamn persistent. I don't want to yell at her, but she doesn't get it, and it's no fault of her own.

Fooling around with Cassy last night did me no good, not after my verbal battle with Red.

I'm taking deep breaths, closing my eyes to make sure I don't say another stupid thing. When I open them, her expression softens slightly, her blue eyes coax the next words from my mouth. "I don't mean to be."

Red blinks, somewhat stunned. She makes the first move, stepping back. "Tomorrow. At seven. If you're not there, I will burn your cabin to the ground." The door shuts tight behind her, my breathing ragged.

It's her threat while leaving that does it for me, because if she stayed any longer, her body would've been pinned to the wall, my lips all over her soft skin.

This back and forth of wanting to devour her, then to push her away, while wanting to be vulnerable, is enough to drive anyone insane.

What is she doing to me? The guys return minutes later, glancing around to see if she left. I'm back sitting on the bench, trying to calm my heart rate down. She makes me anxious, furious, and incredibly horny.

I hate it.

"Surprised you didn't trash the place," comments Taylor, coming to sit beside me.

"Hmph," I grunt, my heart rate not quite slowed down yet. "She is something else."

"I agree with her," announces Cody, and all of us turn to him, standing by one of the treadmills, adjusting his headphones. "We all let you accept your fate, but she's willing to help you back out there, regardless of her distaste for you."

"She was forced to," I remember.

"Nobody is forced to save something they love." Cody steps up, pressing start, and begins his warm-up walk.

Mark crosses his arms. "I support your decision, but I also agree with Cody. At least sleep on it?"

Picking up a fifty-pound weight, I start my reps again, getting a look from Mark. I roll my eyes, knowing he's waiting for an answer. "Yeah, yeah, I will."

He walks away without another word, taking the other treadmill beside Cody.

Taylor watches my reps, leaning forward with his elbows on

his knees, chin in his hands. "I mean, you have to admit, it's kind of hot that she used to snowboard competitively."

"She doesn't know how beautiful she is," I mumble, switching hands for another set of reps.

"What was that?" Taylor asks, leaning closer.

"Nothing." The concussion definitely messed with my rational thinking.

"Would it be so wrong to get to know her? You might actually enjoy her company." Taylor leaves me with his comment as he heads to the water station.

But I know there's more to her underneath that hard exterior, and if I peel back her complicated layers, I'm sure to find her heart.

The problem is, I can't show her mine.

CHAPTER 24

HANNAH

I STAND on the front steps of the main building, tapping my feet in frustration. Not only do I not want to be up this early, but coaxing Noah back onto the slopes just to save my best friend's family's resort is becoming more of a headache than a simple task.

And the bastard is late.

Again.

A few seconds away from heading back to my cabin and saying fuck it, a ginormous shiny black truck with flashy new rims pulls up to the front. The smell of exhaust tickles my nose, and I want to gag.

The driver's door swings open, and out comes Noah, adjusting his dark sunglasses, smiling like he just won the lottery. Wearing his signature all-black snowboard gear with some random logo on the front in white lettering, he makes his way over to the passenger side and helps his brunette friend, Cassy, from yesterday, out. They're both in a matching set.

What the actual fuck am I getting myself into?

I cross my arms, rolling my eyes. "You're late."

Noah makes his way around back to where I stand, his arm

draped causally over her shoulders. "Sorry, I had to take a little detour."

"To where? Mount Mansfield?" I scoff.

"Something like that." He winks at the woman next to him, who just laughs and squeezes the hand that hangs over her shoulder.

I have to clench my fists hard, my nails digging into my palms, most likely creating marks, just to hold back from punching him square in the face. "Well, enough fooling around. We need to be ready and back out there for the event. Let's go."

I move to get a better view of his ostentatious hunk of machinery and give a devilish smirk as I take a good, hard look at Noah, who shamelessly flirts with Cassy. "Nice truck, quite big, actually. Are you compensating for something, Noah?"

He stops mid-conversation, and his eyes squint. "Wouldn't you like to know, Red?"

I shrug. "It would probably be a disappointment anyway. Move your shit truck and come meet me at the top of the half pipe in five minutes; otherwise, you're on your own."

I walk away, satisfied with my comment, only my chest feels heavy, worry wrapping around my heart. If I can't get Noah back on the slopes in time for the event...it'll all be for nothing.

IF I HAD BET my entire life savings that Noah was still going to be late after I gave him a five-minute warning, I could've quit my job and hid out in a cabin deep in the woods for the rest of my life.

Odds were definitely in my favor today.

At the top of the hill, I stand at the beginning of the half-pipe, counting down the minutes for him to join me, and sure as shit, the snail is late.

Finding this a complete waste of my time, I'm just about to leave, when Noah startles me, clearing his throat.

"What the hell!" I yelp, almost dropping my snowboard.

Noah has a sour look on his face. "I've been standing here for five minutes wondering when you were going to look up from whatever the hell you were doing."

"I was counting, and you were almost late...again."

He simply strolls over to where I stand, looking down at me like a little kid. "Does it matter as long as I show up to your stupid lessons? I'm perfectly capable of getting back out there on my own."

I smirk. "All right, smart ass, prove it. Prove to your coach that you don't need a push, and I'll gladly leave you alone."

His cocky smile is shining bright today as he puts his goggles over his eyes and makes his way over to the starting line.

Well, this is going to be a lot easier than I thought. Maybe today will be the only day dealing with the bastard.

Noah sets himself up, rolling his shoulders before beginning his run, gracefully gliding like he's on air. His form is quite impressive as he performs his first move, the Alley-Oop.

Waiting for the landing, I notice a shake in his form, botching the move altogether, landing face-first in the snow. I take my snowboard, strap myself in quickly, and coast down, reaching him as he wipes snow off his goggles.

"That was smooth," I comment.

He rips off his goggles and tosses them aside. "I had it."

I can't lie when I say I'm enjoying this side of Noah, watching his feathers become ruffled.

"Really? Judging by your landing, I say otherwise." I smile big, not even fighting my sarcasm.

He wipes his nose with the back of his hand, removing the bindings from his boots. "You do it, then, if it's so easy."

An Alley-Oop I haven't performed since my high school days? Maybe it will get his ass into gear. "Sure, piece of cake."

He rolls his eyes and removes himself from the halfpipe, leading the way back to the top. Following with a little extra pep in my step, I set myself up, making sure my bindings were secure and my goggles were on correctly to prevent them from flying off my face.

"Alley-Oop?"

"Yes, Red."

I giggle, finding his annoyance a joy to experience.

"You're stalling," he mutters behind me.

I flip him off and say, "And my name's not Red, it's Hannah."

Ignoring whatever he's trying to yell at me as I start, I focus on gaining the right amount of speed, keeping focus on the lip of the pipe. I need to make sure my shoulders are turning uphill; otherwise, I'm going down and breaking a bone or two.

The motion is seamless, like riding a bike, the twist completing just before I hit the ground, my hands releasing from the board. Wind blows across my face from the acceleration, then I hit the ground in a flawless finish.

A rush of excitement runs through my body, feeling proud of myself for performing a move I haven't done in a few years.

Rolling with the high of my performance, Noah comes down on his board, shaking his head. "Your twist was too late."

I tear off my goggles. "Excuse me? That was perfect."

He moves his goggles down to hang around his neck. "No, it wasn't. Your turn was slow. Granted, your landing was good, but your turn needs work."

"I'm not arguing with a grown man who most likely uses a two-in-one shampoo," I snipe.

"And I'm not arguing with a grown woman who probably doesn't know what a dipstick is. Your twist was too late."

"Says the one who can't complete it!"

"I can!"

"THEN DO IT AGAIN!" My voice echoes off the mountain; I might've possibly woken every guest.

I try to calm myself down, pulling back the Velcro on my bindings, ignoring his judgmental stare, except I peek and find him already walking back up the hill.

Shit. Grabbing my snowboard in haste, I move aside, trying to reach the top before he starts. I barely make it when he sets off, mimicking the exact movement I just showcased, but his results aren't successful, once again landing face-first in the snow.

I barely move, watching him toss his goggles across the half-pipe, shouting, smacking the snow with his gloved hands. It takes me a minute to register the sinking feeling in my chest, the realization of what's happening right in front of me, to Noah himself.

There's only one other reason he can't do the Alley-Oop, and something tells me his team already knows why.

RED LEAVES before I get my ass up, wiping snow off my pants and backside, then my shoulders. I can take a wild guess as to where she's heading, and I can stop her, but I'm too defeated to care anymore that she's figured it out.

IF she's figured it out.

Most likely, she has.

At least Coach will face her wrath.

Making my way down to my cabin, I take one last look behind me, the sun creeping higher, shining bright, casting shadows off naked branches along glistening snow banks. It's rare for a quiet moment to present itself in my chaotic life, so I breathe in, letting cold air fill my lungs, keeping it inside until I exhale, trying to dissipate some of my anxieties.

Tilting my head back, I watch the first signs of snow floating down, pecking my cheeks and nose. It picks up, showering me until it starts to coat my clothing; maybe it'll bury me.

Because I'm a failure.

"No, you're not." Henry's voice pulls me back to reality.

I blink. "What?"

"You're not a failure," he reiterates, coming to my side. Snow covers some of his hat, his cheeks a rosy red.

"I didn't realize I said that out loud." I rub the back of my neck, my ears burning. Guess Henry now knows my depressing thoughts.

He bends down and scoops snow into his hands, molding it into a ball. "I didn't take you for someone to give up so easily." He chucks the snowball as far as it can go, then makes another.

I shrug, watching him make another perfect snowball. "Maybe I'm tired. Maybe I want to quit while I'm ahead."

"Or maybe," he throws it, almost landing where the first one does, "you're giving up because you think you'll never be good enough for anything or anyone."

Anxiety prickles my neck; his words are a little too spot on for someone who's just my personal assistant. "I didn't know I hired a therapist."

Henry smirks, making another snowball. "You didn't, but I am someone who cares. We call them friends."

Such a sarcastic son of a bitch. I love it. "Are you here to make sure I didn't hightail out of here?"

"Something like that." He throws one more snowball, a couple of inches further than the last two. "We have an interview soon. Coach is requesting you talk up the event."

I hang my head, sighing. "He's trying way too hard to sweep this under the rug."

"He has faith you'll bounce back. We all do." Henry is hopeful, like all the rest, except Red, who'd rather be anywhere else than help me come out on the other side.

I don't blame her. I wouldn't want my company either.

Yet, she's constantly running laps in my head, like right now, when I need to focus on the here and now.

I LEFT Noah to sulk alone in the snow, not caring that I ended practice early. There's someone more important I need to see and kindly yell at.

Making my way inside the main building, I search for Coach Jones, texting Maya to ask if she's seen her dad, when my body collides with a hard form. Hands steady me, and I look into the eyes of the person I'm looking for.

"Hey, Hannah, how's Noah out there?" he asks kindly, taking a step back to give me space.

Which is a good call, cause I might explode. "You knew, and you thought I could help him with that?" My voice rises a few octaves higher than intended, and Coach looks startled.

"Hannah... It's not as bad as it seems," he tries to reason with me, but I'm already past the point of no return. I can't believe he's trying to convince me it's not that bad.

"Coach, he has—"

"Is everything all right?" asks Anthony.

"Can we speak more privately? The three of us?" suggests Coach Jones, looking around, paranoid.

Most of the guests are asleep, and only the staff are lingering.

Anthony signals us to follow through a door that reads "Manager's Office." I take my seat across from Anthony, while Coach Jones stands by the case of snowboarding trophies, his face scrunched with worry.

"What's going on??" Anthony has no issue being stern with me, since he thinks of me as his own kid to begin with, but I can tell just by his eyes and the way they soften that he's having a hard time following through.

I point at Coach Jones, throwing my manners right out the window. "Ask him, because apparently, his best snowboarder has the twisties and failed to mention it."

Anthony almost chokes on air. "Is she serious?"

Coach Jones's eyes dart around the room, rubbing the back of his neck. "It's not like it hasn't happened before, he snapped out of it fairly quickly the first time."

"THE FIRST TIME?!" I shout, almost knocking my chair back to stand.

Anthony has to match my stance, keeping space between Coach and my wrath. It's not like I'm going to hit him, but I can verbally knock him down a few pegs.

"And how did he overcome this before?" Anthony questions, keeping me in his peripheral so I don't swing.

"Uhh...well, I don't know, exactly. The kid has a rough time handling failure, then he gets it in his head..."

"Now he's mentally stuck, thinking he's getting lost in the air," I interrupt, trying to keep my cool.

Both of them exchange a look, then Anthony says to Coach, "So you think Hannah can bring him back to reality?"

"Or enough where he snaps back on his own. That's if Hannah is still willing to help?"

Am I still willing to help? I've never met anyone personally with the twisties, but I hear the experience can cause a boatload of issues, resulting in retiring early from the sport.

The real question is, can I do it? Can I get self-centered Noah Hart to overcome his mental block and perform?

The weight of this whole ordeal rests heavily on my shoulders.

Both men look at me for my final answer, while I battle it internally.

If I say no, I'm not only letting Anthony and Jill down, but I'm also letting Maya down, and that's something I refuse to ever do in this lifetime.

Goddamn it.

I find Noah sitting alone in the dining hall, eating whatever's left over from lunch. His hair is a dark, curly mess, shoulders hunched over while he eats pizza, casually scrolling through his phone as I take a seat across from him.

His eyes flash, a surprised smirk appearing on his lips. "Red."

"Noah."

His eyes shine, like he enjoys hearing me say his name.

"And here I thought you'd given up on me?" he deadpans, putting his phone aside.

"Quite the opposite." Whatever mental issues he has, we don't have enough time to fool around.

"Oh? And what changed?"

Staring at Noah is like staring at the moon, bright in the darkest of night, inviting when you want something calm to whisk you away. Dangerous because of the pull he has without realizing you're leaning in.

I correct my position and fidget with my hands under the table. "It's clear we're not fans of one another. And I would rather be picking up horse shit than spend most of my mornings with you, but I love this place. It's everything to me, to others, and to see it fall under because I can't put our differences aside makes me no better."

He rests his elbows on the table, hands clasping underneath his chin. His mouth pouts forward, and I notice day-old stubble just above his upper lip. "Judging by your calm approach, I'm assuming Coach told you." Brown eyes search my face, making me squirm in my seat. I can't lie, Noah's attention is quite intimidating.

"Yes."

"I don't want your sympathy." His jaw flexes, eyes cold and distant.

"Even if I want to give it, you still don't deserve it." Especially from me. "But he told me some details of what happened."

"Then you know that your attempts are feeble. Coach is trying to force someone else on me, someone who doesn't know my past, hoping it'll knock the mental block down, but refuses to see that maybe I can't come back from this. Not this time."

My heart pounds, the sound pulsating in my eardrums. If I can't get Noah over his mental roadblock, then Snowy Peak will be buried along with his career. "Lucky for you, I won't give up that easily."

He rolls his eyes. "Great. Now I have a stalker."

"Right, not like a crowd follows you every day, what's one more?"

"Sometimes I want my privacy." With a somber expression, Noah looks off in the distance, avoiding eye contact. I might slightly underestimate him when it comes to enjoying all the attention, but it's no excuse for his behavior.

"Why did you try those moves, knowing you have the

twisties?" I ask instead. "Do you know how dangerous that was? And you let me push you?" I'm basically digging his grave for him.

His mouth slants, then he leans back in his seat, sighing. "Because I have a bad habit of feeding into the pain. At least it helps me to feel something."

Noah looks lost, and I wonder if it's been like that for a while.

But I can't feed into his melancholy. I stand. "If you want to continue to suffer and never snowboard again, then leave; otherwise, meet me exactly at seven a.m. on the halfpipe."

I'm about to leave when Noah's words flutter across the room. "And if I don't show?"

Hand on the door, I want nothing more than to rewind and never set my sights on Noah Hart, but letting Maya down eats me alive inside. "Then I'll know what kind of man you are."

BREATHING IN CRISP, winter air, the sun barely sits on the horizon this early in the morning. Light snowflakes cascade down to tickle my nose, dusting my pink puffer jacket. My breath can be seen in plumes ahead of me as I huff up the long hill, wondering if Noah actually jumped his own hurdle and wants to overcome this tricky battle.

To my amazement, he stands leaning against his snowboard, smirking in a way that makes me want to stare just a little bit longer, and I hate being aware of it. "You're late."

I stop. "I said seven."

"Did you?" He smiles big, exposing a perfect set of white teeth. "Hmm, I couldn't remember, so I came at six." Goggles hang from his neck, his tawny skin peeking through the white sweater beneath his black winter jacket, highlighting how perfect his complexion really is.

Not a single blemish in sight.

"Six?" What the hell was he doing all this time?

"Yeah." He shrugs, coming closer.

"I said seven."

"Like I said." He moves with grace, just like how he snowboards... Why am I focusing on the way he walks? Get it together, Hannah!

"What's next, Red?" He stands inches from me now, and I have to crane my neck at a weird angle to see all of him. Gosh, he's so tall.

He's so eager to start, I wonder where his defiant attitude from earlier went. At least he's trying...for now.

I coax him to stand next to me at the start of the course, looking over the cluster of log cabins below, where the mountain forms, finding peace in a quiet, chilly morning. "You feel that?"

I can sense his eyes lingering on my face. "No?"

"That's what peace feels like when it's you and your board becoming one."

"I haven't even left the start line," he chuckles, and I blush, loving the sound.

"You will. I want you to just glide down the pipe and remember why you love the sport in the first place."

Stepping back to give him space, he looks over his shoulder at me, confused. "That's it?"

"For now."

A playful wink comes my way before he hides behind his tinted goggles, coasting down fresh, even snow.

Every time he comes back, I force him to repeat, hoping it drills into his head that what he loves isn't lost forever. To reacquaint himself and not hold the burden of his past mistakes, even if it's coasting down the halfpipe, familiarizing himself with how it feels to glide, hopefully cracking the surface of his mental block.

He returns for the sixth time, not hesitating to start again when I say, "Again."

"Can I at least try the Alley-Oop?" He sounds hopeful, breathing heavy through his nose, lips parted, slightly chapped.

"Not yet." He mumbles under his breath and walks back to

the starting line...except Noah does the exact opposite I ask of him.

I'm running, skidding to a stop, watching from above as he gains speed. I brace myself and analyze his form, trying to catch a mistake before the trick is complete. But when he turns his shoulders uphill, fully immersed in the twist, I can't catch the moment that causes the mishap, resulting in his tumble straight down, snow spraying everywhere from the impact.

The twisties are definitely a mental obstacle, an issue I've never experienced personally, and wouldn't wish upon my worst enemy, not even egotistical Noah Hart.

I'm grabbing my board, strapping myself in quickly so I can reach him. He's groaning by the time I get to him, and I pray he didn't break a bone.

"Can we do something else?" is his first response as I huff a sigh of relief. Well, glad to know he's coherent enough to continue.

"No, you moron. I told you not to do a trick yet." I swear I'm talking out of my ass with him.

"You're a real Debbie Downer, huh?"

"Just being optimistic." And honest...cause, so far, he's a hot mess.

"I'm doing something else."

"No."

"Too bad."

"I'm trying to help you!"

He ignores my reply and moves faster than I can get the next words out of my mouth, running up.

"Noah!" I'm unfastening the stupid bindings, almost tripping over myself, and getting out of his way.

Looking up, he's already racing down the halfpipe, gaining speed faster than before, using it to his advantage, and glides up on the shoulder, the tail of his snowboard pointing straight in the air. He begins to spin, grabbing the toe end of his board when his spin is high, then lands over the halfpipe. Rushing forward, I find him lying flat on his back, swearing like a truck driver.

"Are you all right?" I hover over him, his arms spread in the snow.

"No, Red, I'm not."

Noah pushes himself to a sitting position and aggressively removes the binds from his feet.

"What move were you trying to do?"

He rips off his goggles. "Does it matter? As you said, I can't do it."

"I never said that...specifically."

"Didn't have to be specific." Noah chucks his snowboard, yelling in frustration. "Fuck this."

"Maybe if you listened to me—"

"I don't need your advice, Red. I just need—"

"A smack upside the head? Your problem, Noah, is that you do whatever you want, when you want, and you don't care who it affects!"

When he doesn't say anything, I continue, letting my frustrations and pent-up anger roll off my tongue. "Not for nothing, you would think that saving a family resort and its workers would make you feel somewhat good about yourself, but it only throws a goddamn wrench in your overinflated ego because you can't freely make out with every female guest that walks by. And for the last time, my name is not Red, it's H-A-N-N-A-H! HANNAH!"

I take a deep breath, the weight lifting from my shoulders finally easing some of the pressure off my chest. Damn, it feels good to tell him off.

Crossing my arms, I wait for his typical snarky comment. His eyes wander over my body, landing on my face, while I breathe heavily through my mouth, until our eyes connect, his pupils dilate slightly.

Why is he giving me that look? Heat rushes to my cheeks.

"When's the last time you had sex?" he asks nonchalantly.

"Oh, no, we're not having this conversation." I start walking before he can get another word in, a rush of heat spreading through my body. I can't believe he just asked me that!?

He catches my arm before I can escape. "The only way to help me is to help you."

"Excuse me? Are you clinically insane?!"

"Maybe, never been tested, so..." His big hand relaxes a bit, loosening his hold on my arm.

I ease away from his grasp, creating space so I can fucking breathe. "I don't think you need to be tested, because what you just said was proof enough for both of us."

"Red, I'm not asking the secret to life; I'm suggesting that if I help you, then in return, it helps me. I can't work with someone with that much anxiety rolling off their body. I nearly drowned when we first met."

Oh...so now it's my fault? "Are you going to add me to your very long list of conquests if I give you the chance?" Definitely not entertaining the idea, but...

He raises a dark eyebrow. "Think of it as...enemies with benefits."

"Oh, like that's any better."

"No strings attached, just to help meet your physical needs, which in return relaxes your uptight ass, then trickles over to my issue. My temporary coach is in bliss, and I'm less worried about being perfect."

I blink, trying to comprehend his reasoning. "So, I'm too uptight, and that's why you're failing?"

Noah shakes his head, letting me go. "No, Red. But your anxiety makes me anxious. Just think about it."

He picks up his snowboard and descends the hill, while I stand alone, hearing families and their kids exit their cabins below.

There is no way in hell I'll let Noah Hart touch me, especially intimately.

No.

HEAD HANGING LOW, water falls from the showerhead, soaking my hair. I use two hands to lean forward, palms flat against the shower wall. My muscles scream at me, pain shooting up my right side from my wasteful attempt at a stupid Double Cork, knowing the minute I gain air, everything goes blank. I can't grasp it this time, what's causing my anxiety to present as the twisties, but it's enough that I almost want to give up.

Red refuses to, even after finding out, continuing to stand by my side. Granted, it's to save Snowy Peak, but it's kind of nice to have someone go through it with you. At least I'm less alone.

So, why did my dumb ass drop such a stupid question to her? Because I want to fuck the frustration out of her? She is walking anxiety, prone to causing chaos wherever she goes, and it's coming off her in tidal waves.

Or maybe, as I stand under the showerhead, I admit I want to know what her skin feels like, and maybe I want to know if those lips really are as soft as they look. Maybe a few rounds of us tangled in sheets might do us both good. It's not like I'm looking for something stable, but rather just some fun to release some of her anxious tendencies and make me less frazzled while I try to kick this shit to the curb. It's a perfect opportunity, I hope she doesn't waste it.

But she should say no, she should run far away from me. Because no intelligent woman like her will say yes to a guy who has done nothing but tease and give her hell since my arrival.

I rub my chest, feeling some soreness near my left breast-bone. Even if she says no, I'll always wonder what her pussy feels like. Is it as tight as her ass when it comes to discipline? Can she get as soaked as I want her to by only using my mouth on her tits?

My hand is already traveling south, gripping my cock, stroking it lightly. Visions of her red hair falling delicately down her back as I imagine my hands running through each tendril, her mouth toying with the tip of my cock.

I'm pumping a little faster as a scene plays out before me of Red riding my face, her soft moans melting me whenever my tongue hits the right spot. My hands travel to her thighs, squeezing, my present self stroking faster along my dick, pressure building in my balls.

I flip her over, hear a little yelp from surprise when I smack her ass playfully, dragging her forward, just to tease her entrance with the head of my cock. I want to hear her call my name as I stretch her, while she scratches at my arms, trying to get leverage.

I fuck her senseless, our hot breaths mingling, sweat dripping down my back, her fingers dragging down, drawing blood.

I'm spilling into my hand seconds after whispering her name breathlessly. "Red."

Water washes my cum from my palm, swirling down the drain. I haven't masturbated in so long, struggling to even get myself aroused. Even with Cassy, only getting *her* off wasn't enough. But thoughts of Red have me going feral in seconds, barely holding on enough to make it last.

An antidote not prescribed, but something I'll gladly take over and over again.

CHAPTER 30

HANNAH

I SKIP breakfast and use the Maya method and hide out in my cabin, taking a long shower and throwing on a pair of comfortable sweats, then braiding my wet hair.

Noah probably won't care that I skipped our morning session, and honestly, he's not getting anywhere, so a break—mostly for me—is necessary.

I stare at myself in the mirror, observing my laugh lines and a minuscule wrinkle or two around my eyes, but no matter how hard I try to distract myself, I think of Noah's offer and what that might entail.

Noah is a man who walks around like he's some god reincarnated, so sure of himself that my answer is an automatic no.

I have never loathed someone as much as Noah, with his sarcastic drawl, his cocky personality, right down to those—and I'll deny it if anyone asks—gorgeous good looks. He thinks any girl will fall at his feet, worshiping the ground he walks on. And offering me an outlet for my sexual needs...the last time anyone has touched me so intimately was Liam...and the mere thought of his hands on my body forces a nervous shiver down my spine.

Liam knew my body, knew the lines and creases of every

imperfection across my skin, until he became ashamed of it, disgusted, even. My hands travel to my midsection, where my belly sits, mocking me for how hard it is to lose weight from that area. To let another man touch me, explore my tainted body, for someone as perfectly fit as Noah...we don't match in equal parts, and it scares the living shit out of me.

I drum my fingers on the counter, teetering on an alternative path, if I did say yes. It's been months since I've done anything sexual, let alone to myself, not finding the urge to because of my self-doubt, being repulsed by my own body.

Who wants to touch a girl with all these rolls and cellulite? Who would find an attraction enough to want to do anything sexual with me? I roll my neck, feeling the tension return to my shoulders.

If I did give him a yes, what's the harm in letting go and feeling for once without the expectations of a relationship? He did say to think of it as a transaction.

My god, why am I even entertaining the idea?

He's so...frustrating and rude and literally has a new girl attached to his hip every day.

I can only imagine if he's contracted any sexually trans-mitted diseases.

Liam was so safe and careful...before my diagnosis. He became a different person altogether in the end.

Tears prick at the backs of my eyes at memories of us, bodies intertwined, one clothed in doubt, the other free from inse-curities.

ONE YEAR AGO...

Liam caresses my cheek while he pushes his tongue into my mouth, our lips smacking together, the sound loud and wet. He pins me to the mattress, his hot skin tingling my fingertips as I trail them down his muscled back. He groans whenever my nails slightly dig into his heated flesh, while his hands find their way down to my pants. Liam tugs them roughly down, discarding my favorite black workout pants across the room. He must have removed my underwear at the same time because a cool breeze touches my core.

He flips us over so I'm straddling his lap, and his dick hits my shirt, but when I'm about to take it off, he stops me. "It's just going to be quick. No need to get fully undressed."

I hesitate, my fingers barely touching the hem of my shirt. "But you're completely naked?"

"Because I have to shower after, so it'll be easier," he explains. His blond hair flops in front of his eyes. I told him before he needed a haircut.

"So will I?" What's his issue?

"I'm trying not to argue here, Hannah."

All the frenzy I built up has dissipated within seconds, leaving a bad taste in my mouth. "It's me, isn't it?"

"What? Hannah, look how rock hard I am. It's definitely not you."

"Then why can't I take off my shirt?"

Liam's facial expression turns sour, and his voice takes on a defensive tone when he says, "Honestly, Hannah, this is so typical of you."

I get off his lap without being told, standing back near the wall by the window. "Typical of me?"

He walks toward the bathroom, barely looking over his shoulder when he says, "Making something out of absolutely nothing."

His words sting, a blow to the chest. I cower closer to the wall, hearing the door slam shut, the hinges rattling from the force.

I can't figure out what I did wrong. I can't understand how my questioning led to him leaving me, pantless and confused. My hands are shaking as I look around for my underwear.

Maybe I overreacted a little. Maybe I need to understand it from his perspective and how he's feeling.

Maybe...maybe it's my fault.

CHAPTER 32

HANNAH

MY FRONT DOOR echoes a few soft knocks, pulling me from a horrible memory, staring at myself through the mirror with wide eyes. Maybe Maya got my SOS and brought me food.

I wish the door had a peephole, because I open it to find Noah leaning casually against its frame, pouting. "Why are you hiding from me?"

Okay, he's full of himself. Second, I am DUMB for not asking who it is first. "I'm not?" Well, I am, but he doesn't know that... Does he?

"May I come in?" he asks politely, ignoring my weak deflect.

"Um..." He barrels in, not waiting for my answer, unbuttoning his black winter jacket and tossing it aside. He wears a forest-green sweater, dark jeans, and brown boots, hair a mess of unkept curls touching the back of his neck.

I shut the door. "Make this quick, I have things to do."

He spins around, eyes so dark they leave me a little unsettled. "You skipped practice because you had things to do? Oh, Red, don't play coy with me." His voice turns sultry, and goosebumps dance along my skin.

"Is it so hard to believe you're not the center of everyone's attention?"

Noah comes closer, and my back hits the door. "But you thought about it, our little deal, didn't you?"

I gulp. "Maybe."

"How easy it can be to let your frustrations go, your anxiety to calm down by simply saying yes and letting us play?" Both of his hands hit the door above my head, and he looks down, our lips barely an inch apart.

Letting us play.

Shit, he's heady, the smell of his cologne alone overpowers my self-control, even my mouth. "Maybe I want you to suffer. Maybe it's time you didn't get everything you want." I'm losing my mind.

"What I want, Red, is something only you can provide."

Noah leans in, grazing his nose along my neck, inhaling like he can't get enough. "Do you know what it's like?" He deliberately kisses slowly down my neck, humming in satisfaction, a moan slipping past my lips. I'm a traitor to my own desires. "How intoxicating you've become, right down to the smell of your skin?"

"Yes," I whisper breathlessly. Hannah, knock it off!

He hums. "Yeah?"

"More," I whimper. Well, there goes all my self-control, out the goddamn window.

Noah's nose continues to skim my skin along my neck. Oh no! Can he see any chin hairs I missed? Panic rises in my chest, but Noah takes it upon himself to take me in his arms and bring me over to the bed, a yelp escaping from my mouth when he plops me down on the mattress.

My body burns as he returns to kissing along my collarbones, my nipples peeking through my thin, white, cotton shirt.

Right over the fabric of my shirt, he lightly tugs on my nipple with his teeth, the sensation nearly crumbling me to pieces.

I'm at a loss for words as Noah tugs gently on the bottom of my shirt, eyes searching my face. "May I?"

May he? My god, Noah is the first man since Liam to see what's underneath...since my diagnosis. Will he like what he sees? Or will it disgust him to know this woman's body is tainted?

Asking for my permission, coming from him, who has been nothing but arrogant and crude...is a whole other side of him, catching me off guard.

And we haven't even kissed yet.

I nod, preparing for the worst, desperate enough not to stop him, because I'm already too far gone, and whatever common sense I had has clearly left my fucking brain.

His smile, slow and sensual, continues to draw my attention when his hand slips under my bra wire, cupping my right breast. My back arches on instinct, his fingers gently squeezing my hardened nipple.

I bite my lip, rolling my head back. "God, please." How can he make such a simple touch so intoxicating?

"Yeah? Who are you praying to, Red?" His other hand grabs my left nipple, giving it the same attention, tugging, teasing. "'Cause right now, it's just us, and if you're going to pray, it's going to be on your knees for me."

I arch my back even more, shouting yes in my head. Instead, I whimper, because whatever I'm about to say never makes it out of my mouth.

As if our touch is in sync, Noah's big hands cover my entire breasts, slowly using his palm to circle my nipples. My legs instinctively latch around his waist, shamefully grinding, trying to create friction. I'm gone, lost to my sexual desires; my body, which hasn't been touched in two years, is starved for the very contact Noah provides.

He chuckles, his mouth inches from mine. "You like that? You like being touched here? Say yes, Red. Otherwise, this stops now, and we can go right back to just hating each other."

He makes it so easy to give in, to forget my surroundings, and become consumed by the very essence of his presence.

If I say yes, I'm demolishing barriers I've kept up since Liam left, for it to crumble to the wrecking ball that is Noah Hart.

"Noah," I breathe, using my legs to pull him closer. His erection presses through his dark jeans, his length rubbing against my clit. I sigh once I find the right spot, rocking against him. "Noah," I repeat, mouth agape, his hands working against my nipples.

My bed is the only place to support my back as I grind against him, a sensation beginning to build, my body coating with sweat. Noah mimics my moves, using more force to entice a louder moan from my mouth.

"Noah, please," I beg, panting like a dog in heat.

"You're so fucking sweet when you beg," he purrs.

I need him to kiss me. Why won't he kiss me? Wait, why do I want him to? I shouldn't want this!

My sexual desires have other ideas. "I need more," I whimper, keeping my eyes closed so I don't have to face my awkward begging.

"Say yes, Red."

Fuck it. I want our bodies slick with sweat, intertwined for hours until we lose consciousness. "Yes."

Noah grips my chin. "Now, open your eyes, Red. I want you to look at me when you ask for something."

His command arrests me, how he keeps it gentle with his touch, yet his voice holds all the power. I squint harder, unsure of my desires, aware of the force those brown eyes can do to a girl in just seconds of contact.

"Red, baby," he coos, halting his movements, slipping his hand free from under my shirt to stop my pelvic thrusts against him. "Open, please."

My left breast misses his touch. I peek at him, and he hovers over me, waiting, his hand keeping my chin raised. "If I ask, please don't laugh. Promise?"

His smile is soft, reassuring as he nods, waiting, keeping his body hovering over me. "I promise."

"I... I—"

Loud knocks rattle my front door, freezing my speech, the breath escaping from my lungs. Reality comes rushing in, forcing us to face what transpired, reminding us with just one look, how much we truly loathe one another.

And I fucking said yes.

CHAPTER 33
HANNAH

NOAH REMOVES himself from our heated embrace, adjusting his dick through his dark jeans, then makes sure his sweater isn't twisted in a weird position.

"Hannah, you missed breakfast. Are you okay? Ill? Avoiding a certain someone?" Maya calls through the door.

Noah smirks, placing a single finger to his lips to keep quiet. He tiptoes across the room and opens the nearest window.

"What are you doing?" I hiss under my breath.

His playful wink tells me all I need to know when he removes the screen and hops out, but one of his boots' shoelaces catches on the corner of the windowsill, and he grunts as he faceplants in the snow.

I have to cross my legs to keep from peeing myself and muffle my laughter. Trying to contain my hysterics, Noah waves me over for help. Through calming breaths, laughter still caught in my throat, I tried to release his shoelace, finding it stuck.

"Are you okay?" I quietly ask, some of my laughter coming up.

He throws a thumbs up, struggling at the same time to reach

for his laces. "Yes! Hurry!" Snow coats his eyelashes and brows, face red from the impact.

My doorknob starts to turn, halting us in place. Panic mirrors our expressions, and I turn as she comes inside, shaking off snow from her shoulders.

"Girl, where the heck were you this morning? And why is your window open?" she inquires, coming closer.

"I woke up late, then got hit with an intense hot flash, so I needed some air." There, a simple enough answer for no further questioning. I adjust my position so it blocks Noah's boot from view, sitting down so my ass almost hangs out the window.

"Right, and it's not because you had a screaming match with Noah on the halfpipe yesterday?" Leave it to Maya to hear the latest gossip within twenty-four hours.

"When am I not yelling at him?"

"Nice job trying to deflect. Now, tell me the truth."

Maya is a true friend when it comes to secrets; never once has she told any of my darkest, but I'm not sure this one with Noah is such a good idea. Not yet, anyway.

Shit, I can't believe I said yes to him.

She waits, tapping her foot. "Well?"

"Menstruation shit, nothing new. Period side effects, but nothing major." I really don't want to keep it from her, adding another lie to the list, and I'm afraid it might get bigger.

"Huh." She scans my room again. "Right." Maya's eyes land on Noah's black jacket, half draped over the couch, then to me, and her dark eyebrows rise almost to her hairline. "Whose jacket is that?"

I swallow hard, hands clammy. I have to be quick with my response; otherwise, Maya won't stop until she finds out who owns it. "Mine, it just came in."

She picks it up, examining it, right down to sticking her

hands in the pockets, thankfully coming up empty. "It's huge, Hannah."

"Yeah, I realized that after I opened it. They must've messed up on their end. I'll return it when I get home." I bite the inside of my cheek, hoping she takes the bait. Fuck, she might pick up Noah's cologne from it.

She does another examination of the jacket but changes the subject, tossing it back on the couch. "My parents are setting up a meeting to go over the possible food vendors that are participating. Would you like to come?"

Relief floods my body. "Sure, let me just change."

"All right, I'm grabbing some muffins. Do you want anything?" Her smile returns.

"Yeah, a blueberry one." I cross my arms, freezing my ass off from the open window, Noah's boot hanging on for dear life.

"Okay, see you in a few." She leaves, the door softly clicking shut.

I inhale a deep breath, and my heart begins to slow its erratic beating, when Noah's boot starts to move.

"Um, help?"

CHAPTER 34

NOAH

MY WHOLE back is soaking wet from sitting in the snow for too long. Hannah is trying to get my boot laces unstuck with scissors, and my teeth start chattering, watching her. Her long, red hair, plaited in a braid, falls past her shoulders as she tries to cut the lace away. It's a fucking sight to see.

She bites her bottom lip, slowly cutting, trying to tear it in two. "I'm almost there."

Yeah, I need more time to bite that bottom lip. More time to undress all those layers, right down to her soft skin, wanting to roam my hands all over her curves. My dick is rock hard as my mind concocts an image so detailed of her on top of me, tits bouncing, kneading that thick ass, I have to refrain from making a noise. She's right in front of me, and—

"I did it!" My lace comes apart in her hands, and she waves it at me. My leg starts to fall from the windowsill, my body sinking a few more inches.

Hannah leans out her window, hands stretched toward me. "Here, let me help you." I grasp her small fingers as she pulls me with all her strength to a sitting position, giving me the leverage I need to hoist myself up to stand.

I'm shivering now, and Red lets go of my hands to grab my coat, tossing it at my head.

"Thanks." I put it on, but it barely keeps my body warm since my clothes are wet, probably starting to freeze. "I'll see you soon?"

She shakes her head, about to reattach the screen, when I force her to stop, her hands shaking under my touch. "Red?"

"What?" She seems agitated, her lips in a hard line.

I come closer, and our noses almost touch. "Do I need to remind you what our agreement is?" Removing one of my hands, I brush a loose tendril of red hair behind her ear. "Because I don't mind holding you up to remind you." Taking my thumb, I trace her bottom lip, knowing I haven't kissed her yet.

I want more time, and I'll get it. I just want to take my time with her.

She shivers, releasing a shaky breath. "Like what?"

I smirk, tracing her top lip now, her hot breath expelling along my skin. Up close, I can see more of her freckles, each one unique in size and shape. "I want to get you out of those clothes, Red. Strip you all the way down and pin you beneath me, bury myself inside that sweet cunt."

Her inhale is sharp, a soft gasp as her eyes widen. Her cheeks flame a stunning crimson, and I stick my thumb inside her mouth. "Suck."

The risk of getting caught is so high, it makes my dick rock solid, it's almost unbearable in my pants, begging to spring free.

If she does as I say, it's all over. I'm forcing my way back in and devouring her right then and there. To hell with her plans with Maya. I'll have her up against every piece of furniture, either plastered to the wall or bent over.

Red closes her eyes, and my breath hitches at the back of my throat, anticipating those soft lips to close around my thumb. She starts to back away. "I have to go."

I'm instantly blue balled. It's my own damn fault.

Blue eyes are now wide open, stepping away. I retreat as well, watching her secure the screen and lock the window, drawing both curtains closed, shutting me out.

Except her yes has already let me in.

WE MEET her parents in a nearby conference room in downtown Burlington, the group consisting of Maya, me, their accountant, and a couple of local vendors from the area. A spreadsheet is laid out of other possible vendors who might attend. Snowy Peak's first-ever snowboarding event will commence on December 28th. So far, they've sold roughly eighty tickets, not including guests already in attendance.

Henry texts Anthony a report of the boys going live on their social media to help promote and garner tickets faster. They go live in a couple of hours, and to be prepared, the site may have some difficulties staying up. Nobody can resist their charms, even Noah.

Go figure.

Some buzz has reached neighboring towns, courtesy of Elise and Ella, without the help of ads yet. I already told Anthony and Jill I'll add new content to their site tonight and run two major ads for an extra boost, hoping it'll start a domino effect for ticket sales.

Dennis gives me a look, probably not a fan of the idea, as we're using some of the budget to run such lengthy ads, but I know in the long run it's going to pay off. As long as I get Noah off his ass, find a miracle to cure him from his twisties, which, apparently, involves me relaxing, he'll be able to focus.

I internally roll my eyes at his logical thinking.

Flashes of his hands along my breasts, plump lips kissing my collarbones, his thumb in my mouth, asking me to suck, make me adjust in my seat, getting a weird look from Maya.

"You good?" she whispers.

I nod with a forced smile and continue to take notes.

Knock it off, brain.

Jill opens a PowerPoint and goes through each slide of confirmed vendors. Stanley's Famous Hot Dogs, Fried Dough Mania, and Little Delights will attend with their food trucks. Anthony suggests we move the hot chocolate stand outside, along with a vendor who handles Coke products.

We reach the end of the slideshow with a picture of Snowy Peak's giant Christmas tree in the center of the resort. "This weekend, we are lighting our new Christmas tree. It's open to the public, and an ad is already running for it. Hannah, I would love for you to take some photos for the ceremony?"

I smile. "Of course!"

We're about to wrap up when an idea comes to mind. I raise my hand. "I think for the kids, we should have a make-your-own mini snowboard station. Some can get restless, and I think having side activities available will be a great benefit."

Dennis eyes me through his thick lenses. "I think that would be pushing the budget."

My cheeks stain red.

"I think that's a great idea, Hannah," responds Jill, ignoring his remark.

"I'm just pointing out it's a bold risk to toss more funds out for something so irrelevant. If it doesn't succeed, at least you'll have some extra funds to fall back on." I can't tell if his comment is directed toward me or Anthony and Jill.

"It's not irrelevant if it applies to *all* guests. It's a family resort, in case you forgot." Anthony crosses his arms, a dark eyebrow raising to challenge his rebuttal.

Tension rises, and Jill has to redirect the conversation. "We're not here to argue, we're here to try everything, we've got to save this place."

Maya and I are excused for the rest of the meeting; most likely, they're discussing a more private matter.

"I hate him," Maya mutters.

"Your parents' uptight accountant?" I ask.

She snorts. "Dennis thinks that cutting corners is risky. Yet, if we can't make this work, there's no point in arguing over a budget that will cease to exist in the new season."

Swinging my arm out, Maya halts in her tracks. "What?"

"Maya Juliette Gomez, we will save your family's resort. Okay?"

"I'm just preparing for the downfall, that's all." She unlocks her white Jeep Wrangler and puts the heat on full blast.

I buckle my seatbelt, watching from the passenger side as she fiddles with her aux cord. I can't let her succumb to negative thoughts. We have to hold out hope. "We'll save it."

She gives me a quick look. "I hope so, Hannah, I really do."

CHAPTER 36

NOAH

JERKING off is not on my to-do list, but not getting my fix from Red, leaving me horny beyond belief, my only option is to relieve myself in the shower again, thinking dirty thoughts of her mouth... again.

Hot and heavy, I pump my cock, imagining her full lips sucking my tip, her saliva dripping down my shaft. My movements become sloppy the more I picture Red on her knees, my hands entwined through those thick, red locks. Her nails dragging down my thighs as she takes all of me.

I reach my destination, and my body tenses up as I spill into my hand, the hot water from the shower washing it all down the drain.

My breathing is ragged, like I ran a fucking marathon, but damn, what a weight off my shoulders, at least for now.

Finishing my shower, I get ready to meet the guys for dinner, dressing in black slacks and a cream sweater, with brown boots. I style my hair away from my face; it's still wet, making it more curly. Spraying one of my most expensive colognes, I slip into my black peacoat and meet the fuckers at the main building.

The air, cool and crisp, is a pleasant relief for my too-hot skin, cooling my face and providing a cleanse of all things Red, at least, for now.

Families have gathered to watch staff members decorate the enormous Christmas tree, stringing lights and gold garlands along its thick branches. Snow has taken a break from falling, and people are taking photos of the twilight sky, hues of pinks and oranges splashed like paint across the horizon. Red peeks at the edge where the sun sets, lighting the whole sky on fire. It reminds me of a feisty woman with plush lips.

She infiltrates my very thoughts, making my dick twitch in response. I flex my hand inside my pocket, trying to keep myself from skipping out on dinner plans, looking for Red instead.

I need to control myself better. We only agreed to hook up casually, nothing more.

Lamp posts glow a soft yellow, illuminating my way toward the main building. Maneuvering through pockets of guests, I say thank you to someone holding the door, breezing my way inside to find my teammates huddled by the roaring fireplace.

"There he is," comments Taylor, gripping my shoulder and shaking me. "Where were you?"

I push him off. "Getting ready, ya pinhead."

"What? Were you shaving your ball hair?"

"Fuck off."

Coach Jones comes through the front doors, heading our way, when he says, "Plans still on?" He's in dress pants and a brown peacoat, hair slicked back in gel. "My kids are in bed early, so I can hit the town with everyone."

"DD, hell yeah!" Mark fist pumps the air.

"Whoa, hey, that's not my job tonight." He comes to stand next to me. "We can rent a cab."

"Gonna need a bigger vehicle," mentions Cody, barely

looking up from his phone. His fingers blur as he types vigor-ously to his on-again, off-again girlfriend.

"We invited a few extra people, by the way," adds Mark, thumbing behind him to a couple of girls and one guy.

A familiar brunette winks at me, lips stained a ruby red.

Cassy.

She saunters over, hips sashaying like she's on a runway in Paris. Her beauty is undeniable; all eyes are on her, no matter where she is. But I can't find it in me to want to go to her.

All my thoughts are jumbled because of one fiery woman who just so happens to walk right through the front doors.

MAYA CATCHES me by the front entrance, looping her arm through mine. "Where have you been?"

"Finishing up some portraits for your mom," I say, waving my camera at her.

She leans her head on my shoulder. "Thank you, Hannah. I don't know what I would do without you."

"Hmm...you might still be the same, maybe a little crazier."

She pinches my arm. "Brat."

People are already inside the dining hall, but Maya stops us from entering, forcing me to spin around. "What?!"

"Noah is grilling you from across the room. Did you piss him off again?" She gives a quick look over her shoulder. "I can't tell if he's pissed or has a dildo stuck up his ass. No hate if he's kinky with it."

I stare up at the ceiling, shaking my head. "Maya, why does it always revert to an object being lodged up someone's butt?"

She shrugs. "It's more common than you think."

"Riveting news, Maya."

But I can't help but look past her head, catching Noah

staring straight at me. He wears a cream sweater under a black peacoat, dark dress pants, his hair curlier, wilder. I can't help but wonder how the texture would feel between my fingers.

Oh my god, Hannah, you fucking said yes, remember?

My palms are clammy. I said yes to Noah Hart because I think with my vagina and not my goddamn head.

There's no way this can happen. Noah will see underneath my clothes and vomit all over the floor; he might even call animal control because I'm simply a wolf growing hair in places that a woman shouldn't.

My hands lay a protective shield over my mid-section, the weight I'm having such a hard time getting off. Noah is going to see all my imperfections and wonder what the fuck he was thinking.

Maya snaps her fingers in front of my face. "Hannah? Did you hear me? I asked if you're ready for dinner?"

He blinks, shaking his head, and returns to his teammates, chatting.

I'm about to leave when the same girl from a couple of days ago snakes her arms around Noah's waist, forcing him to hug her. Her long brunette hair is loose over her shoulders, with a toned physique and a cute nose people would kill for. She is the epitome of perfection, with someone as devastatingly handsome as Noah.

My heart pumps hard, my ears pulsate, and a tightness in my chest I haven't experienced in a while hits me, almost knocking the wind out of me.

I'm shaky now, and quite agitated. All I can picture is his thumb in my mouth, telling me to suck, and now he's here, cozied up with the pretty brunette woman. No, no, I can't think this way... I can't let jealousy taint something that never began.

It's just sex...that we haven't done yet. We haven't even kissed.

No strings attached. Heck, we haven't discussed rules.
So, why am I acting this way?
Why?

CHAPTER 38

HANNAH

BARELY EATING dinner the night before is one thing, but skipping breakfast is a whole new kind of torture. And it's all my own doing. Because why train on a full stomach and risk barfing around Noah, since, ya know, we've been here since seven in the goddamn morning. Not a single peep about yesterday's extra activities, I might add.

I'll call it intermittent fasting, but not even my bottle of water can suppress the sounds my stomach is making.

At least Noah is too preoccupied with my constant direction to pay attention.

But I'm also hyperaware of every move he makes, right down to the way he adjusts his winter hat, even his goggles hang seductively from his neck. Sometimes I catch a vein, thick and pulsating against his tawny skin, whenever he fingers his collar to readjust.

Last night, I remained wide awake, going over every possible scenario, wondering how to bring it up, but every time Noah has a few minutes in between my commands, the words fail on tight lips.

Then again, he hasn't uttered a word either, so does it have to be up to me to start the conversation?

No, but someone has to do it, right?

Not quite sure how I'm holding myself together at this point.

And then there's the matter of his stunning brunette friend. Is he also screwing her? Is he using protection with her? Shit, does he see me after he has his fun with her?

My eternal spiral continues as Noah tries to practice edge changes. I hear f-bombs before he topples, somewhat sliding down the halfpipe on his ass.

Thankfully, news hasn't broken over his catastrophic demise, and I wonder if that has something to do with his freakishly quiet PA, Henry.

It doesn't help that Noah still can't overcome his mental block.

He climbs the side of the halfpipe, head down, board somewhat dragging along with him, winter hat skewed. He claims my anxiety is distracting him, the pressure to be perfect. I don't get how it relates to his previous record or how he snapped out of it in the first place, but if it's an excuse to get into my pants, he's already halfway there.

But judging by his attitude and constant swearing, then yeah, maybe I can ease up the tension a bit.

He tries again, barely getting the tail above the lip, and falls backward, screaming fuck across the resort. Noah's voice echoes across snowcapped mountains when I coast down to where he lies sprawled out.

He shouts, almost close to the sound of a lion's roar, digging his gloved hand into the snow, throwing a chunk over our heads.

I smirk. "Broadway already had their auditions for The Lion King."

Noah looks at me through his goggles, breathing heavy.

"Your one-liners are lame." But I swear the corner of his lips perked up slightly at my joke.

Unless the lack of food is causing my brain to malfunction, making me see shit.

Noah pulls out two granola bars from his pant leg pocket, tossing one at my feet.

We eat in silence, chewing on peanut butter granola.

"I heard your stomach, thought you might need something." He finishes it in two bites, removing the binds from his boots. Watching him chew is oddly sensual, especially because his jawline is cut to perfection. He swallows, his Adam's apple working to push the food down. Why is it so hot? Shut up, Hannah. "Should really eat something light because not eating at all is dangerous."

"Since when do you care about my health?" I say in between bites, almost choking like an idiot. Nobody ever has before, not even Liam. His kindness is out of the blue, and I'm not sure how genuine he is.

"Since you're supposed to be my saving grace in fixing me? I can't have you half dead, barely focusing because your lapse in proper dietary needs goes unchecked."

I blink, swallowing the last of the bar down my very dry throat. "I'm perfectly capable of taking care of myself."

Underneath the surface of our conversation lies the more serious one, the one where I said yes to something deranged. Maybe I was silently malnourished, barely focusing when I agreed.

His sultry eyes pin me in place, making my heart accelerate at an abnormal speed. I wonder if he can hear it and see the anxious look in my eyes. How my hands sweat profusely inside my thick gloves, to the point that sweat soaks my clothes.

Noah moves an inch before I'm backing away, looking for an excuse to dip early.

"I forgot that Maya needs me soon to go over event details, so..." I'm already retreating, and he mirrors my steps by walking forward.

"Freeze, Red." His voice, a low, sexual tenor, halts my movements.

Gripping my snowboard to my body, trying to create some barrier between us, is honestly pathetic on my part because no amount of obstacles is going to stop Noah Hart from getting what he wants.

"Coach Jones wants an update on my progress by the end of this week...if I remember correctly—"

She's back, the pretty brunette that was on his arm last night, stealing his attention. She sashays over, hips swaying with more force than necessary. Her outfit consists of a sleek black puffer jacket with matching snow pants and boots, while her makeup is done like she's heading out early to a nightclub.

She's everything I'm not. Everything Noah should have.

They make sense. We don't.

So why give me the choice? Why not ask for someone else to help you get over your mental block, who isn't dripping with anxiety everywhere she walks?

She playfully rubs his arm, flipping her perfectly styled hair over her right shoulder.

Using the brief interruption to escape, because I've person-ally had enough of watching her sexualize him, I nonchalantly dip out, but take one last look behind me. Noah is completely engrossed in their conversation, and I run as fast as I can away, trailing my snowboard behind me.

COMFY SWEATS and a good book are all I need right now. Maya is aware I'm hiding out in my room, explaining I need some time to recharge after today's training with Noah. She doesn't bother to question further; instead, she offers to drop off food, but I suggest catching up with her later for dinner and grabbing some trail mix I find in the minibar.

Deep in my favorite romance novel, soft knocks pull my attention away. I frown, because sometimes Maya doesn't listen and makes herself at home. Well, I wouldn't mind some extra snacks, and I'm getting to the good part where the main male lead confesses his love to her.

Slipping in a bookmark to hold my spot, I scuffle over the hardwood floor in my slippers, opening the door, only for me to immediately regret it.

I'm suggesting a peephole the minute I get rid of him.

Noah stands outside my cabin, hands in his pockets, still wearing his thick, black puffer jacket, with a matching winter hat. He never changed out of his training gear.

A sour expression taints his face. A nice reminder of the person he truly is. Moody, arrogant, rude...

"Where's your brunette friend?"

"Cassy? Probably back at her cabin, I don't really care."

I try to forget our little sexual encounter, but it burns like a thick wick, bright and inviting. His stare alone sets my skin ablaze.

Gosh, if I can just run my fingers through his ha—

"May I come in?' he asks, watching me curiously.

I shake my head. "Depends, what do you want?"

He smirks. "To talk."

"Noah Hart wants to talk? About what?" I'm stalling, and he fucking knows it because his smile only widens.

"My, do we have a lot of questions? You know, the longer you keep me out here, the more fans will notice and want to be nosy."

I step back and extend my arm to welcome him inside, plastering on a fake smile.

Definitely a bad idea.

Noah moves with grace for someone so tall and takes a seat at the edge of my bed. I stand before him, knowing exactly why he came here.

"Practice is over," I stress, shifting my stance.

"I'm aware," he responds, watching me watch him.

The imaginary candle wick continues to burn.

"Then...?" I'll continue to play stupid if it gets him to leave.

Noah slowly starts to remove his winter coat, and my lungs constrict as air leaves me. "What are you doing?"

"I told you, I can't have you wound up, and since we were rudely interrupted the other day..." he trails off, tossing his knitted hat on a nearby chair. "I remember quite clearly you consented to our agreement."

My feet remain glued to the floor, at a loss for words. He can't be serious? "Noah, what happened the other day was a simple lapse in judgment."

"Was it?" he hums, standing now.

I gulp. "Yes."

He smirks as he runs a hand through his dark, curly hair. "You're lying."

"I'm not. Are you that cocky to believe you can make any girl drop to her knees before you? My god, you really know how to slip a mask on and cover your shitty personality, and I'm the dumb ass who fell for it."

"Hannah," he says, his voice thick and raspy. Noah's dark eyes burn right through my core. I've become the mouse, caught in his trap.

He never calls me Hannah.

The tension between us grows heavy, my chest feeling exposed through the thin material of my pajamas, revealing my need before him.

He licks his lips, eyes darkening more and sensually.

I can stop this. All of it. Right here and now.

But I'd be lying to myself, because the first taste of Noah Hart, of what we can do, what he can do to me...letting us play, had me hooked.

"How obvious do I have to make it when it comes to my visceral need to touch you?"

Noah thumbs his bottom lip, my heart pounds like a sledgehammer, working overtime. He wants this just as much as I want to feel what those lips are like against my own. I want to know where those big hands can roam, or what it's like to straddle his lap while his fingers are tightly entwined in my hair.

I'm already across the room before I can think rationally, and jump into his arms, our lips colliding.

My imaginary candle has gone up in flames, engulfing everything in its path, igniting my veins from the inside until a white-hot burn scorches my very being.

Noah cradles my head and cups my ass, sitting right back on

the edge of my bed as I devour the kiss, straddling his lap. Our tongues collide, teeth scraping against teeth, the sound of our heavy breaths and small whimpers of need infusing the air.

Kissing him is euphoric, a high I'll constantly chase once it's over.

I grind shamelessly against him, his sharp intake of breath from my movements only heightening my need, my very core slicking with wetness.

God, he's right. I'm too wound up, and this kiss alone has already started to release some of the tension along my shoulders as Noah flips me over onto my back, never breaking our kiss.

The more our tongues collide, the more his hands travel along my body, once again tugging at the hem of my shirt.

Noah breaks our kiss, looking into my eyes. "May I take this off?"

It never ceases to amaze me his manners when it comes to my comfort level. How can someone come off so arrogant and rude, only to act soft and respectful behind closed doors?

I run my fingers through his hair, so soft and so easy to pull.

I tug lightly, and he chuckles. His eyes look lighter today, more of a honey color. Noah looks...happy.

"Yes," I breathe, lifting my body up so he can remove the shirt, tossing it behind him. Thankful I wore comfortable pants to hide the stretch marks on my midsection.

I lay back down, and his pupils are blown from my exposed chest.

Noah traces a delicate finger down the center of my cleavage, my body trembling from his touch alone. "Absolutely perfect." His swollen lips descend to my right nipple, my chest rising and falling at a rapid pace, when the first kiss lets a loud moan escape my mouth.

Noah licks and sucks until it's swollen and red, leaving

behind a hickey near my nipple. He begins again with the other, giving my left the same attention, my moans escalating with each tug and nibble.

"I don't think you realize how fucking perfect these are." His tongue flicks across my peak before covering it with his entire mouth, sucking.

My fingers grip his hair, my nails digging into his scalp as his mouth on my breast has me begging, desperate for him to be inside me.

He groans, sucking hard.

A loud pop comes from his mouth when he releases my nipple, and my back arches as he kisses past my stomach, right on my navel.

Shit, he's close to an area I can't let him see, not yet. Before he teases the elastic band on my waist, I pull him up, wanting another kiss. Our bodies mold together, his hand traveling back down to my waist, teasing along the band.

Noah slows down our kiss until space is created between us, leaning his forehead against mine. "Can I touch you?"

I swallow, nodding, and say, "Can we leave my pants on?"

He smiles, kissing the tip of my nose. The action is simple... delicate. So unlike the Noah I experienced outside these four walls.

He doesn't question me, just nods, accepting my level of comfort.

He trails little pecks of his swollen lips down my neck, his long fingers teasing my waistband once more, my skin prickling with goosebumps from his gentle touch. Every second he prolongs it, the more I get antsy, waiting for his warm fingers to—

Noah moves two of his fingers down past my waistband, massaging my inner thigh for a brief moment, then the tips of his fingers graze my clit.

My toes curl, panting, anticipating his touch. "Noah," I groan, throwing an arm over my face to hide it.

"Oh no you don't," he tsks, removing my arm and tucking it behind my head. "I want to see you come undone, knowing it was me who got you to the end."

His possessive demeanor is enough to roll my eyes in satisfaction. "Please, touch me." My wetness has already begun to soak my underwear.

Noah moves up so we're back at eye level, his mouth agape as he finally slips two fingers in, massaging my clit.

I gasp, a strangled whimper escaping with each stroke, circling around and around.

"So wet, Red," he purrs.

I roll my hips, matching his pace as he continues, then he plunges one finger inside my entrance, wetness soaking it.

Thank God I fucking shaved.

The sensation has my hips thrusting in the air, just as Noah sucks on my nipple once more. The combination of his fingers, along with his hot, slick mouth around my breast again, has incoherent words bursting from my mouth as I ride out the pleasure.

He unlatches himself from my nipple, and even with my eyes closed, I can feel his hypnotic stare. "You like being touched, Red? You like it when someone sees how undone you become? I can do this all day, touching you, never getting tired of how you break apart beneath me."

He adds another finger inside me, my pleasure building with each thrust, while his thumb circles my clit.

"Noah," I moan, eyes opening to find him staring deeply above me; he's breathing just as heavily as I am. I reach for the front of his pants, desperate to touch him.

Noah catches my fingers and guides them perfectly against the waist of his snow pants. "Is this what you want?

I nod earnestly, flexing my fingers over his hardened cock, tucked safely inside those stupid snow pants.

He surprises me by adjusting himself at an angle on the side of the bed so my head lies on the pillow, his fingers still deep inside me, then takes his free hand and undoes the buttons, grabbing his cock and pulling it out.

"Turn your head, Hannah," he orders.

I oblige, finding the tip inches from my mouth, pre-cum oozing. My mouth waters at the sight.

His height makes it easier to keep his position.

"Show me how much you can take."

I make no hesitation and use my free hands to massage his length, and Noah groans, still keeping momentum with his fingers.

I lick from the base to the head, then suck greedily at the tip. Noah grunts, adding another finger inside me.

I almost shatter then, trying to hold out my focus between his pleas and my own.

Another string of pleasure coils tightly, wetness now drenching my underwear and Noah's hand.

Inch by inch, I slowly insert him into my mouth, tasting his soft skin, hearing a hushed sound, almost like the word fuck falling from his lips.

Bobbing my head up and down, I take him almost fully in, enjoying the way he tries to steady himself from fucking my mouth. Trying to enjoy his pleasure while receiving mine is a hard enough task on its own, but somehow makes me wetter.

He moans the further I take him in, almost gagging but holding myself together.

"Such a good girl," he praises.

I moan in agreement, relishing the praise coming from his mouth.

Noah hooks three fingers against my inner walls, while I'm

trying to focus on him, but lose motion, my erratic movements causing Noah to come early, his semen spilling into my mouth. I swallow quickly, his fingers still inside me.

He takes a shaky breath, moving my hair away from my sweaty face, and shimmies himself down to eye level, his long fingers moving out of my core to massage my clit.

"Focus, Red, just focus on your needs." He gently takes my head and leans it against his chest, using two fingers now to circle my clit.

I'm almost there, my climax coming into view.

My moans are loud the closer he gets to me. I tug at his shirt, grasping at anything, anchoring myself for what is about to happen.

It's been a year since I've been touched by a man, and I've let Noah be the first in a while, astounded by how well he already knows my body, pushing me right over the goddamn edge.

A ragged moan rips from my throat, and Noah clamps a free hand over my mouth, talking in a soothing voice in my ear. I'm too far gone to understand a single word.

He removes his fingers and graciously hands me back my shirt. I'm too limp to put it on, so he takes it upon himself to help me.

I fall back on the pillow, eyelids heavy, legs and arms moving like Jell-O.

Noah adjusts his pants and starts to get ready to leave, looking over at my spent body, smiling, pleased with his work. "I'll see you later, Red."

Eyelids half closed, I watch a blurry Noah grab something off the couch, then cover me with its warmth.

I'm fading before I can say goodbye, hearing the soft click of the door.

I sleepily think, if this is how foreplay is, I can't imagine the intensity of having sex with Noah. It might cause a catastrophic explosion.

CHAPTER 40
NOAH

RED CAN MAKE me cum in minutes, and now, her hot mouth is all I think about as I trek through mounds of snow from behind the cabins. As I reach my cabin, kicking off my boots at the front door, I throw most of my clothes off while heading towards the bathroom. I almost trip face-first into the shower with how hard I'm pulling to remove my goddamn sweater.

But it's worth it. All worth it. If I can have more time with her, which I will, then I'll hide in snowbanks forever just to taste those soft lips, to run my fingers through her thick hair.

To hear her whimpers whenever I get her close, or touch a spot she desperately craves.

My dick is already twitching again while I hang my head under the water, sighing in relief from its warmth.

I go over every moment between us as I massage my muscles, relieving tender spots. Red has no idea what beast she's unleashed in her room, no idea what I can really do with her once I take all her clothes off.

She's hesitant; regardless of how she came at me with that kiss, she's holding back.

I can't wait to unwind all her frustrations and watch her let go, like a wind-up toy finally set free.

Dissipating her anxiety, in return, helps me focus better... for now.

Her quick, witty comments and sharp tongue are perks added to our agreement. It's nice to verbally spar with someone who isn't afraid and won't back down.

My phone won't stop chiming by the time I make it to my bed, nearly naked. I'm already regretting opening the message thread with the guys.

> Taylor: Drinks tonight, there is a local bar, and they have $1 margaritas.
>
> Cody: We all have practice in the morning, and Mark has his wife coming early.
>
> Taylor: So? I wanna get sloshed.

I start to type out my response when Mark swoops in.

> Mark: Did your "one-night stand" turn you down?

Taylor sends a GIF of the middle finger.

> Mark: That's what I thought.

I feel bad for Taylor that no one wants to join in on his festivities, so I agree to attend. Probably going to regret this later, but I'm going to enjoy the time we have together before we all head back to our separate homes.

> Me: What's the attire?

> Taylor: Noah, my man, is back! Dress like
> you're going to the VIP lounge at Sip & Slide in
> downtown Manhattan.

I give him a thumbs up and start rummaging through my suitcase, which I've failed to unpack since arrival. My favorite black slacks are folded, surprisingly, neatly at the bottom, and a light blue sweater.

My phone chimes another six times.

> Mark: If I go, you're buying me a drink, and we
> leave no later than eleven.
>
> Taylor: Since you didn't specify which drink
> you want, I'm going to choose. Cody? You
> coming?
>
> Mark: Fuck you.
>
> Cody: I guess.

What a bunch of sourpusses.

> Me: Cheer up, fuckers.

> Mark: Bite me, Hart. I have a pregnant wife
> coming in the morning, and I don't want to
> tend to her with a hangover.

I sent a GIF with surrendering hands.

> Me: Fair point

> Cody: What time are we leaving?"
>
> Taylor: 8, and bring your A game. It's time we
> show the people of Burlington how we party.

Lights blind us as we enter the only club Burlington has to offer. Needle & Pine is nothing short of strobe lights and cheap drinks, but they know how to bump their music loud until the room rattles. Bodies collide on the dance floor, hips swaying, grinding against their partners as heavy thumps from the bass make my body vibrate. My shoes already stick to the floor, and they're going to be a goddamn bitch to clean after.

We find a small booth to fit all five of us, then we down our drinks. Taylor orders another round, waving a few hundred bills around. The waitress comes back with shot glasses of green liquor.

"Drink up!" Taylor shouts, throwing back his shot like it's nothing but water.

It hits my tongue, and sour green apple coats my throat, burning right down to my stomach. Pushing my empty glass aside, I take notice of some pretty women here, but search among the crowd for that familiar, fiery hair, coming up disappointed because I know she's not here.

It's not intentional, yet I can't help myself. Even now, I check my phone, knowing damn well we don't have each other's numbers.

But I wish, and I have no goddamn idea why.

"All right! Phones away!" shouts Taylor over the music.

I tuck it back in my pocket, tapping my fingers on the wooden table. "Yes, Mom."

Cody is ruthless and texts right in front of Taylor's face. "You too, man." He snags Cody's phone, locks it, and slips it into his front pocket. "No texting tonight. We party and let loose. Remind ourselves to have fun and get the town rooting for Snowy Peak!"

Mark shakes his head. "Did you take your own shots before we left?"

He kisses Mark's cheek and jumps out of the booth. "Fuck yeah, I did!"

Mark wipes his face in disgust. "Why are you such a sloppy kisser!?"

Taylor is already heading toward the crowded dance floor, and people start cheering when he slithers his way through.

"That fucker has my phone," mutters Cody.

"I think you can go one night without talking to Kara," says Mark. He calls over a waitress and orders water for the whole table.

"I'm done talking to her," he states.

I'm about to ask why when his eyes follow someone behind me. Peeking over my shoulder, Henry comes closer, clutching a water bottle for dear life. "A club? Really?"

I roll my eyes, groaning. "My babysitter has arrived."

He kicks my legs, forcing me to slide further into the booth, taking my seat. "Your fault for inviting me on this trip."

"And you're here right now because...?" God forbid the bastard takes a night off or picks up a hobby. Yes, I hired him for his expertise in keeping my shit together, but I can't remember the last time he's taken time to relax for himself.

"You're here now. Let's just get through this night so I can go home and sleep." Our waitress returns with glasses of iced water. Mark takes them off the tray for her and hands us each a cold glass. "Otherwise, my wife is going to murder me if I'm late meeting her at the airport."

"Adelaide is coming?" asks Henry, smiling. "Please tell me she's bringing—"

"Her famous chocolate chip cookies? Yeah, she made sure it was a part of her carry-on."

"Fuck yeah!"

One minute we're chilling in our own booth, the next, Taylor comes barreling through the crowd, out of breath, leaning against Henry for support. "We gotta go. Now."

"Why? Whose boyfriend did you sleep with now?" Mark comments, sipping his water.

Suddenly, Maya shows up, waving at Cody.

He smiles and waves back. No way...he can't be...Red's best friend?

Henry stiffens beside me, staring between them. Cody forces Mark to move and joins her by the dance floor, greeting her with a hug.

"Huh, never would've guessed," I say.

"What is she doing here?" Henry crosses his arms. "Isn't she too young to be here?"

I smack his back, making him jump. "She's probably the same age as Red."

Speaking of Red, I wish she came—

"We need to leave. We should've left two seconds ago!" Taylor is white as a ghost, shaking the shit out of Henry to move.

"Are you all right? Why are we trying to flee like criminals?" I never get my answer, because I never hear past the roaring in my ears. No, all I see is familiar dark hair, a woman, and a man... a man I once called my best friend at the edge of the dance floor, hands intertwined.

How, out of all goddamn fucking places...

Because they're on vacation and Olivia never tagged the place. It's my shitty luck she's here with him now.

I'm pushing Henry, knocking Taylor on his ass, when his hands grip my pant leg. "Let go!"

Mark has his arms around my waist, pulling me back, shouting in my ear. "You're gonna cause a huge scene and ruin everything for Maya and her family if you go over there right now."

I can't do that...not to Maya...especially not to Red. Her face comes to mind, taming my wild beast, simmering my anger to almost nothing.

They don't see me, but I catch every move, every touch, between them. Holding onto Red's face is the only thing keeping me in control of my emotions. "Why the fuck are they here?"

"They probably don't know about the event," mentions Henry, helping Taylor to his feet. "I mean, if they did, they wouldn't be stupid enough to come here of all places for a vacation, let alone this fucking club."

But they're here now, unaware of how close I am to landing a good hit to Sean's face. But my anchor, for some strange reason, is a woman so feisty, she has no idea she's keeping me grounded, and she's not even here.

Fuck, I can't wait to see Red tomorrow.

MORNING CAME FASTER THAN EXPECTED. I wake up, finding myself warm and sprawled out on my bed, a wool blanket covering most of my body. My stomach rumbles, demanding to be fed, and I come to my senses about what happened last night.

For starters, I never got dinner, skipping it altogether. My phone is nowhere in sight, and the smell of some type of cologne lingers on my sheets. I sniff, finding notes of cedar and cinnamon.

Noah.

Oh, it hits me harder than expected. His fingers inside me, the way his lips moved against mine, and heat bloomed in my chest, expanding out, my toes wiggling in appreciation. That dark, unruly hair my fingers sank through effortlessly, tugging at the roots. The noises he made whenever I sucked deeper on his cock, the size was quite enjoyable to look at. How he calls me a good girl whenever I do something he's pleased with.

I shoot up from my bed, finding myself getting aroused. "Gosh, Hannah, focus."

He might have been right about needing a release, but how

long will it last before he breaks through his mental block and we go right back to hating each other?

I can't worry about that now. No, right now, he has to get better to perform at the event; otherwise, our efforts to save the resort will all have been for nothing.

Shit, I never peed. Forcing myself to the bathroom isn't easy. I'm still groggy from my climax, but happy to admit that the release helped unwind some of the knots, not that I'll ever admit it to him—no need to inflate his ego even more than it already is.

Relieving myself, I rub my eyes with the back of my hands to remove any lingering eye boogers, blink a few times, then wipe, flush, and check myself in the mirror. A reddish spot catches my attention, and I move my shirt along my collarbone to find a medium-sized hickey. My fingers trace its shape, not sure how or when he had time to make one.

But... I like it... I like knowing he's leaving his mark. It makes it real and not some weird fantasy I conjured inside my head. A reminder that last night did happen and I'm not totally delusional.

I move around my cabin, tidying and freshening up, telling myself a shower after snowboarding is better than taking a second. Next is to locate my stupid phone, digging my hands into the cushions of the couch, hoping it slipped through the cracks. With no such luck, I mosey my way over to the bed, checking behind pillows, in between the table and mattress, when something buzzes inside the drawer.

Pulling it open, I see my phone sitting neatly tucked against miscellaneous items, a yellow sticky note stuck to the front of the screen. Crumpling up the paper, I tap the screen, finding an unknown number has texted me.

Unknown: Morning, Red.

> Me: How did you get my number?

Unknown: Your bestie.

Maya.

> Me: She doesn't give it out to anyone. How did you coax it out of her?

I quickly add him as a contact, receiving a quick response.

Noah: Someone named Gift Card Dude ring any bells?

My mouth drops, laughter bubbling up my throat.

> Me: I do know of this individual.

Noah: She no longer has that date with him.

How the hell did he pull that off? Maya must be skipping around, relieved to have dodged him yet again—the poor bastard.

My stomach yells, reminding me to hurry the hell up.

I type out a quick response and hit send, grab my gear, and head over to the halfpipe, wondering how Noah and I will act face-to-face after yesterday's encounter.

> Me: Bring me one of those granola bars.

CHAPTER 42
HANNAH

OVERCAST SKIES GREET ME, the smell of possible snow giving a boost of serotonin. Guests have yet to awaken; the silence leaves me with the sound of my boots crunching in the snow. Crows squawk somewhere in the distance, echoing off the Burlington mountain range.

I catch Noah coasting down the halfpipe, and a smile touches my lips. He's following my advice, and it's progressing. Now, to get him to master his tricks and stick the landing.

Another battle for another day.

I hear another set of footsteps behind me, and I jump, almost whacking the shit out of his PA with my snowboard.

He looks down at me, blue eyes cold and distant. His blond hair is hidden under a winter hat, his outfit free of wrinkles. I wonder if he wakes before five in the morning and follows a rigorous routine. I wonder what goes on inside his head. He's stiff and emotionless. Henry seems to be waiting for me to say something.

I clear my throat when he speaks. "How long are you practicing with Noah today?"

I shrug. "Depends on how long I can stand him." Or focus, or end up in a private setting, begging him to touch me again.

Henry doesn't find my joke funny. "I need him in the lounge right after. He's been ignoring my texts, but I can see from here he's actually making use of his time."

A question comes to mind. "Were you with him when he got his first hit with the twisties?"

Henry blinks, caught off guard by my question. "Yeah, yeah, I was."

"Do..." Am I crossing a boundary by prying it from his PA? Not like Noah will tell me himself. I don't expect deep conversations from the man or anything, really, besides consensual sex and an unrelenting attitude. But any insight can potentially help. "Do you know how he overcame it?"

He crosses his arms, becoming fidgety with his legs. "He would kill me if I ever talked about it again. Even his own teammates are sworn to secrecy."

"Oh." Fantastic.

"Noah...can be difficult, but it's not intentional. It's who he is, how his brain works. A stubborn mule, but damn can he snowboard."

I know very little about Henry, but even he seems in awe of Noah's talent and hard work. I just wish I knew what saved him last time.

"Thanks, and hey, I'll make sure he sees you after."

"Thanks, Hannah." We part ways, and I follow the trail up the half pipe, inhaling the winter air in my lungs.

Noah and I meet, our moves slow, until only inches separate us. I hug my board, watching him, not caring how obvious I make it. I thought things were going to come off awkwardly, but instead, my heart pounds hard against my chest, anticipating when we'll be alone again.

He smiles, removing his goggles to hang around his neck.

He's breathing heavy, and I notice more stubble grows along his chin and upper lip. His tall stature is one of the qualities I enjoy about him. He overtakes a room just by standing idle, attention instantly drawn to him.

Noah cocks his head to the side. "Red."

A nickname I once despised has begun to grow on me, though it might have something to do with our agreement. "Noah."

"I thought maybe we could fix your Alley-Oop today," he suggests.

"And how does that help you?" I question.

He closes the gap and tugs on my braid. "Maybe helping someone else other than myself might retrain my brain."

Henry's words come to mind. *Noah can be difficult, but it's not intentional. It's who he is, how his brain works.* "Sure, why not?"

He cups my face. "Really?"

I playfully push him back, making sure nobody catches us getting too cozy. Regardless of the fact that it's early in the morning, someone might spot us. "Yes, but then it's your turn. We can't waste too much time. Coach Jones needs an update by the end of the week, remember?" And I need a freaking miracle, he's able to perform at least one move.

Noah grins. "Was that before or after I felt how wet you were?"

"Noah!" I choke, checking around if anyone heard. "Before!" My face heats, knowing damn well the color of my cheeks matches my hair.

His laugh is deep and rich, the sound heavenly to hear. "Let's go, Red, we're burning daylight."

I prefer this version of Noah, carefree, less rigid, and I wonder if it's what he needs to ease his worries and overcome his inner insecurities.

He waves me over to the edge of the starting point, watching me strap my boots into the mounted bindings, pushing my goggles down over my eyes.

"You need a little more speed and to start your turn earlier. Try to keep the nose of your board steady, cause once it goes over the lip of the halfpipe, you gotta lead with your shoulders. It should all be in one swift movement to grab your board and land."

I watch him explain, in awe, finding he's more patient and passionate when it comes to teaching someone else the sport he loves, wanting to help someone perfect the move and get a high from achieving it.

"All right, more speed, turn earlier," I repeat.

"Nose steady and grab your board," he adds and pokes my actual nose with his gloved finger. His smile is contagious, making it easy to return one of my own.

He steps back, giving me space to start my run. Taking a deep breath, I let my board guide me down, making sure my speed is increased by the time I get myself angled for the Alley-Oop. The base of my board is now flat against the pipe. The nose makes it slightly over the lip when my turn begins, gaining more air than before, gripping my board as I complete the one-eighty turn, landing with ease.

Noah cheers from the top, and I raise my hands in celebration. Making my way back to the top, he gives me a double high five. "You're an incredibly quick learner. What else can you do?"

For the next thirty minutes, I perform a front-side 180, then I transition into a front-side 360. A little wobbly at the end, but it's been more than four years since I did the trick.

Noah already knows what I need to fix, giving pointers in an encouraging tone, but he's excited to meet someone who shares his love and energy for his favorite sport and is not afraid to improve their craft.

I try to push Noah before we end, but he insists a break is needed, and we'll go back to his work tomorrow.

I'm not going to ruin the mood by nagging, so I let it go, walking side by side down the hill. Guests are now awake, flooding the resort with their kids or significant others to start their day on the slopes.

Noah stops short, forcing me to follow. "What's up?"

"I have to get something back at my cabin. Do you want to come with me?"

"Uh...sure?"

We make our way over to cabin twenty-four, and he unlocks the door, telling me to lean my snowboard against the wall by the fireplace.

A suitcase is wide open on the floor, pants overflowing in every direction. Door shut, he rummages around, looking for something. A bottle of pills from a pharmacy sits on the bedside table in the other room, and pairs of shoes are lined up by what looks to be color. His disorganization skills remind me of my place back home, and I smile, finding our similarities quite funny. I make my way further in, entering the bedroom, catching something shiny on a bureau. Gold and silver watches line the top of a wooden bureau, expensive and flashy.

"Can I help you find whatever it is you're looking for?" I offer, observing his belongings, lightly touching a silver watch. Small diamonds are encrusted around the clock face. When I don't get an answer, I stop hearing him move, but I know, judging by his silence and the weight of the floor, he's right behind me.

Hands snake around my waist, covered by my winter jacket. His nose grazes along my neck, right into my hair. He sniffs, sighing in content. "I already found what I was looking for."

I shudder with pure pleasure. "You could've just asked." My heart has already picked up speed while I naturally lean into his touch.

"And risk you hiding again? Absolutely not."

"I already said yes."

He chuckles. "Somehow, I don't believe you."

"I thought yesterday proved my willingness."

"True, but a man can never be too sure."

I back up a bit, moving my ass along the front of his pants. "Is this good enough to convince you?"

Noah squeezes my hips, groaning in my ear. "It's all I've been thinking about during our training. It's so hard to focus on what that sharp tongue says when I can put it to better use."

Things are different now that we're in the daylight. He can see everything more clearly, and panic rises in the back of my throat, teetering on keeping just my shirt on in case it's too much for him. Because judging by the feel of his dick against my backside, he's ready to move on to the next step.

It's what we agreed on anyway.

Noah probably senses my hesitation and turns me to face him. "Second thoughts?" Brown eyes search my face, pupils blown out from desire. I won't lie, my needs have arrived, already soaking my underwear.

"I'm afraid of what you'll see underneath." My cheeks heat. Because for all I know, Noah will take one look at my body, one look at the stretch marks and rolls, and go running for the hills.

Noah cups my chin, making sure my attention stays put. "I don't care about whatever imperfections you think you may have. All I care about is making you come."

My breath hitches, and his words are final as he grabs a hold of my face. His thumb moves across my bottom lip, a groan rumbling in his chest. "I'm gonna bite this lip while I'm buried deep inside you, Red."

He doesn't give me time to respond, takes my mouth, claiming my space and the very air I breathe. Noah's tongue collides with mine, the kiss deepening, my body burning up.

The straps on our snow pants fall, taking turns between kisses to remove layers of clothing except for our underwear. I hug my midsection, shame rushing through my body.

Noah gently removes my arms, exposing every inch in broad daylight. All my stretch marks, blemishes, and the weight that sits too comfortably above my private area are on full display for him to pick apart and ridicule.

Instead, he takes my chin, making sure our eyes collide. "Your body is a fucking temple, Red. I'm ready to worship it."

NOAH LAYS me down gently on the bed, our kisses soft and slow, almost like we're savoring the moment, but I'm on edge, waiting for the other shoe to drop and watch him run for the hills, or projectile vomit in the bathroom. Either way, the outcome sucks.

He cups my face, controlling our movements, tongues teasing over swollen lips.

Noah can sense I'm holding back and breaks our kiss, smoothing away any hairs from my face. "Do you want me to stop?"

I take in a deep breath, finding comfort in his concern, knowing this is a lot for me. Something Liam would never have done, or asked. "No, I trust you." Because at the end of the day, underneath the armor to shield his own insecurities, Noah is willing to see all of me, the good, the bad, even the ugly.

He kisses the tip of my nose, then both my cheeks, smiling. "Good. I want you to trust me."

His dark eyes somehow glow, a shower of emotions raining on me, making my breath hitch. Noah starts to kiss parts of my skin that are usually covered in layers, spending extra time on my hips, nipping my skin. I keep my eyes closed the whole time, knowing he's looking at all my imperfections, the stretch marks of my battles, hoping I removed every hair on my body, praying he doesn't catch a strand.

Instead, I feel his rough fingers graze along my skin, lightly touching my midsection, humming, "So soft."

Tears prick behind my closed eyes, threatening to escape. A gentle kiss shocks me as Noah pecks the area that has ruined my self-esteem since my diagnosis. His hands then travel back to my waist, gripping my love handles, groaning as he continues to kiss and lick my skin. "God, Red, can you be any more perfect?"

I swallow back the emotion that is building in my throat. "I'm far from it."

Noah tsks playfully, then tugs at my hair. "Open your eyes and see what a starved man looks like."

I hesitate, peeking slowly, when I notice Noah's pupils are blown out, hovering over me, his stare sensual, a predator ready to strike at its prey, starving. "You look hungry," I tease.

Noah squeezes my hips, then bites my lower lip, pulling until a whimper escapes. "I've been hungry ever since I laid eyes on you." His fingers roam to the waistband of my underwear. "Lift your ass, Red. I'm ready to feast."

I oblige, my chest rising and falling with rapid breaths, the cool air hitting my most sensitive area. He discards my underwear over his shoulder, props my knees up, and spreads my legs further apart. I inhale a sharp breath, finding his eyes half closed, in a daze. My nipples peaked, hair wild, fanning over pillows. Noah watches as I let my hands wander, finding confidence from his stare alone. I begin to massage around my nipples, moaning. I've never done this before, let a man see me touch myself. But with Noah, it comes so easily.

Noah's chest starts to mimic my own, our heavy breathing

matching in tempo as I pinch my nipples between my thumbs and pointer fingers.

"Fuck, Red." He steps off the bed and removes his underwear, his erection hard, while he strokes himself. "I'm taking my time with you."

I nod vigorously, continuing to massage myself, the cool air making me slick with need. Noah falls to his knees, wrapping both arms around my thighs. He leans in, sniffing some of the pubic hair I left behind on my shaving escapade. "I love this. Please keep this."

My heart soars out of my chest from his compliment, finding myself completely in awe of his words.

I yelp as he blows cool air on my pussy, then slowly runs a finger through my lips. I arch off the bed, moaning, panting. "Noah."

"I know, Red," he coos, then drags his tongue through the center until he finds my clit and begins to lick and suck like it's a goddamn lollipop.

Keeping my thighs firmly in place, Noah devours me, driving his tongue in and out of my entrance. I try to rock against him, but he holds me back, using only his tongue and lips to coax the most guttural sounds from my mouth.

My hands have fallen away from my chest as I clench the sheets, my pleasure rising, the coils beginning to wind tight.

When I'm sure I'm about to climax, Noah backs away, licking his lips, eyes black and feral. "Not yet." He flicks his finger at my clit, stinging, making me squirm. He goes at it again, his hot mouth feasting like a king. I'm climbing that mountain, my body shaking the closer I get, but he stops just before I reach the peak.

He starts up again, making me groan in frustration, and I stop his movements, coaxing him to me with my finger.

He smirks, crawling on top of me. "Yes, Red?"

The sound of his nickname for me on those swollen lips makes my toes curl, desperate to hear it whispered in my ear. Funny how something that pissed me off so much became my new favorite thing.

When he reaches me at eye level, I curl my arms around his neck, my pale skin against his bronze a colorful combination, our flushed bodies pressing us together, my nipples rubbing along his chest.

My fingers trail up the back of his head, toying with his soft curls, pulling gently. I smile with bliss, the way it feels in between my fingers, pulling a little harder when his kisses turn to sucking, marking my skin.

I was never one for hickies, but since Noah has given me one, that's all I want stained on my body. I kiss his shoulders, chest, neck, right back up to his lips, a satisfied sigh escaping his mouth when our lips move, tongues flicking each other.

Noah's hands cup my ass, squeezing, then he slaps lightly, my mind going insane from the tiny sting.

We break apart. "I have a condom, Red. I can use it if you're more comfortable with it?"

Where did the nasty, condescending Noah I met before go? All I have in front of me is this sweet version of him, who has a wicked tongue. "Yes."

He reaches over to his nightstand and pulls open the drawer, taking the first wrapped condom he sees, looks down at the label, and smiles. "It's fire and ice."

"Never tried that before," I laugh.

Ripping the wrapper with his teeth and spitting the remains out of his mouth, he leans back and rolls it over his erection, then spreads my legs wider. Noah teases my entrance as whimpers escape from my mouth. He smirks, clearly pleased with himself that he's prolonging what I desperately want.

"Noah," I scold, digging my nails in his arms.

He pushes in another inch, my body reacting to his size. I'm having a hard time controlling myself, almost tempted to take over and sit directly on him just to get what I want. Instead, I bite his shoulder, making it known that what he's doing to me is absolute torture.

Another inch, and the coolness of the condom makes it that much more pleasurable. "Do you want more? What if I just fuck you like this? Barely getting all of me, teasing until you break?"

I grip his hair, moving his head until our eyes are at the same level. "Fuck me like you mean it, Noah Hart."

At the same time, he drives himself forward, filling me up. My back arches on the bed as he works inside me, breathing heavy with each thrust. Our breathing syncs, picking up pace.

He slows to a torturous rhythm, then takes his teeth and bites my bottom lip, my eyes rolling back in my head. He releases my mouth, absolutely pleased with himself, and my hips start to match the tempo, trying to feel more.

"Red, you feel so goddamn good, " he mumbles in my hair, "tight and sweet."

"Oh!" He starts to hit the spot, pushing me high in the sky.

Noah moves my right leg up, gaining a better grip, and pushes even further in, his size filling me up. I grip the back of his head, then my nails drag down his back, knowing this time I might draw blood.

He then flips me over on my hands and knees and fucks me from behind. Faster, he thrusts and slaps my ass, a stronger sting shocking my senses, the sounds coming from my mouth are incoherent, my face pushing into the pillow.

I know for a fact a hand print is left, and that makes me more wet at the mere thought of another mark left by Noah on my skin. Claiming territory.

I'm beyond coming back, my climax just around the corner, my walls beginning to tighten.

"I feel you, Red, so close for me?" Noah doesn't waste any time; he drives into me with such force that the bed starts to move with us.

I've never had a sexual experience like this before. He's an animal in the sheets, and I want nothing else but this from here on out.

"Noah," I moan, my climax almost tipping over the edge.

"Come, Red, come for me."

His command is my undoing, my moans growing louder; I'm sure the nearby village can hear them.

Noah finds his release seconds after, groaning, rocking back and forth in a sloppy manner. "Fuck."

We break apart, collapsing side by side in bed. My chest rises and falls, sweat coating my skin, body limp.

Shit, he knows how to fuck.

And I might have just developed an addiction to it.

CHAPTER 44

HANNAH

STARING AT THE CEILING, our breathing is all I hear, our arms touching, our skin sweaty. What a mind-blowing experience, feeling a million times lighter simply because of how Noah helps me let go.

He suddenly jumps from the bed and enters the bathroom, leaving the door ajar as he relieves himself, peeking out from the door with the comment, "Make sure you go, okay?"

I smile and follow suit, doing the same. It's nice to have someone else to remind you that peeing after sex is incredibly important.

Liam would leave to do his business, just to end up back on the couch watching a golf tournament.

Noah pats the bed beside him when I'm finished, handing me a bottle of water. "I'm always thirsty after."

I sip it. "Really? It's not like we're exerting ourselves or anything."

He kicks my legs jokingly and chugs the rest of the water bottle, then cracks open a second one, swallowing half. "Sometimes I think I'm part fish."

I grab a fistful of blanket and throw it over my body. Now

that I'm more aware of his wandering eyes, I'm not one hundred percent ready to lay exposed in front of him unless we're fully embraced. At least his body covers mine.

He notices but doesn't comment; instead, he starts up a conversation about his childhood. "As a kid, my mom couldn't get me out of the pool. I shriveled up like a raisin by the time she dragged me out by my hair."

"I find that interesting, because you ended up becoming a snowboarder." I lean on my hand, turning to face him. "For someone who loves the water, why not swimming?"

"My dad loved the sport, taught both my brother and me at a young age, and I ended up being good at it." He looks off into the distance, most likely recalling a memory.

"What's your brother's name?" I'm intrigued because it's more than I'll ever get out of Noah on a normal day.

"Cameron, he's about sixteen." Noah looks over at me. "You?"

I shake my head. "Only child, my mother had a hard time." I guess PCOS is hereditary, and she's lucky to have had a pregnancy at all. Unfortunately, she passed it on to her only daughter.

But Noah doesn't need to know that.

"Do you like it? Being an only child?"

"It never bothered me, and I was lucky to have met Maya; she became the sister I was meant to have."

Noah throws his arms back behind his head, rubbing the heel of his foot on his leg. "And you became a snowboarder as well, why?"

"Honestly, my school system gave us a choice, and I randomly chose it. That's also where I met Maya. It kept me grounded after my dad passed away."

"I'm sorry, Red."

"It's okay, it's been years. But for snowboarding, it was a chance for control when everything else in my life fell apart."

"How did photography come into play?"

I smile. "My father gave me my first camera, took me to some of the most beautiful places to practice, and I found a passion for it the older I got. I grew my clientele through high school and college."

The parallels of our upbringing are similar, especially when it came to our dads, teaching us something new without realizing how it would shape us in the future.

The thought comforts me that people can share similar journeys, bringing them together by chance.

But I can't believe it's Noah.

"What do your parents do for work?" I'm not sure when I'll get another chance to ask him such personal questions, and maybe it can help trigger some memory as to why he's suffering again with the twisties.

"Mom is a chef, Dad is dead."

My heart constricts, my mouth goes dry. He says it so casually, I wonder how long it's been.

Noah reads my face and answers my unspoken question. "He passed away four years ago."

"Noah, I'm so so—."

"Don't. He may have taught me everything about snowboarding, but the dead bastard cheated on my mom several times. Died in a car accident on his way to the other woman's house. Quite poetic if you ask me."

I open my mouth only to close it. Noah looks over at me and shrugs. "It's truly okay, Red. We were distant before his death because of his bullshit. I'm not mourning a loser like him."

Our dads are both deceased, Noah's a cheating ass, mine from ... "My dad died of cancer when I was sixteen." It comes out like word-vomit, and my hands shake a little. It's been a while since I spoke about him, about what took him from me.

"I'm sorry, Red." He reaches for my hand and squeezes, so simple and unlike him to show sincerity for my loss.

I realise then, I never want this version of him to fade away.

He scoots toward me and pats his chest. "I'm cold, move closer. You're hogging all the blankets."

Scooting enough to curl along his side, Noah drapes some of the blanket over himself, my head resting on his pectorals. "Better? You big baby."

His laugh shakes my head. "That was probably your weakest insult yet."

"Don't get me started."

"Oh? Red, I'm waiting."

I'm about to start when the door handle starts to shake, Henry's voice loud and irritated on the other side. "Noah, you better be fucking in there."

Maya's voice comes next, giving me a rush of panic. "Move over. I can unlock the door."

Henry huffs while Noah and I scramble to get our clothes.

"Why didn't you say you could unlock the door?" he mutters.

I know Maya is giving him a dirty look when she says, "For someone with all that forehead, you're still forgetful."

I need to stifle my laughs, rushing to the bathroom and closing it quietly. I can hear Noah throw his belongings all over the place when the front door bursts open.

Henry's voice gets louder. "You were supposed to be back at the lodge at ten. Why are you just sitting here?"

"And where's Hannah?" Maya's feet are lighter when she moves, coming closer to the bathroom door. "Hannah, are you in here?"

Fuck, I'm throwing all my gear back on in haste, almost falling into the goddamn tub.

"How do you know it's her?" asks Henry.

"Her snowboard is against the wall."

FUCK. Why isn't Noah saying anything?!

With my snow pants back on, I finally respond. "I need a minute."

"Oh...uh...okay." She backs away from the door, her voice fading a bit, confronting Noah. "Why..." her voice cuts off.

I quickly fix my hair, doing the braid over so it's cleaner and doesn't scream I just got fucked.

One last look, and I open the door, making my way to the living room area.

Noah sits perfectly at ease on the couch, texting on his phone, relaxing in a black shirt and gray sweats. Hair combed back, you wouldn't even know he was breathing heavily over my body, fucking my brains out moments ago.

Maya spots me first. "Hey, we didn't know where you went?"

Henry gives her a weird look. "Who's 'we'?"

I've never seen Maya so taken aback. "Is there a monkey in your brain banging on a set of symbols?"

Noah looks up from his phone and winks at me. "Guys, play nice."

"You were told to meet me after practice," scolds Henry.

"By who?" Noah leans forward, intrigued with this new information.

Unfortunately, Henry points a measly finger at me.

Yeah, I most certainly fucked up.

I wave sheepishly at Noah. "Oops."

He starts to laugh, so much so, he's in tears. I'm not quite sure how to react, nor are Henry and Maya.

They look at me for an answer. I shrug, not sure how to understand it myself.

When Noah gets himself together, he wipes away his tears. "Sorry, I don't know why that got me."

"Are you on drugs?" Henry looks at me. "Did you give him some?"

Maya comes to my defense...in her own way. "Please, Hannah barely drinks."

Noah has calmed down at this point and crosses his leg, that's when I notice the used condom hanging from his pant leg.

I almost collapse from embarrassment.

How the hell do I alert Noah without the others seeing? My phone is back in my cabin, and so far, Henry and Maya are too busy swapping horror stories.

"Get yourself dressed in a suit, we have interviews in an hour. You're incredibly lucky they had to push back the time." Henry doesn't look my way again, too busy grilling Noah.

How does nobody see it dangling off his pants?!

I start to sweat.

Maya huffs in annoyance. "I can't believe he's your PA. What a goody fucking pants."

Using my eyes, I try to get Noah to look down, making them wide so he catches sight of my panicked state.

The guy is fucking oblivious, trying to come off nonchalant with their intrusion.

I'm moving before I can think, and stand in front of Noah, blocking his view, grabbing the others' attention. "I'm sorry, it's my fault we ran a little late with practice. Noah's cabin is closer to the slopes than mine, and I really needed to pee."

I know, rooted deep in my bones, that Maya doesn't believe a goddamn word I've said; rather, she entertains herself by asking the most obscure questions. "Is his toilet made of gold?"

"Yeah, and it's got a seat warmer too."

Henry is on the phone now, shouting at someone on the other end over time stamps and incoherent details. I try one last time to get Noah to look at me, and he finally realizes I've been using my eyes to make him see the used condom dangling from his pant leg.

Mirroring my own horrific shock, he tries to tuck his leg behind the other on the floor, hiding it from sight.

I know he feels it ooze out of the condom by the disgusted sound he makes.

"Hart, you got twenty minutes to change, don't be late." Henry leaves, but Maya lingers by the door.

"Just give me a few minutes. I'll meet you for lunch."

She nods, looking at both of us before heading toward the door, she shouts. "Hey, tight ass, wait up!"

Noah jumps up from the chair and grabs the used condom. "Gotta dispose of this."

"Noah, how in the world did that happen?!" Giggles escape, and I try to stifle them, but it's too late, I'm in hysterics, bent over, legs crossed, trying not to pee myself.

He's already in the bathroom, disposing of it, muttering under his breath.

Now I'm on the floor, fetal position, laughing so hard I'm crying.

He catches my laughing fit and starts to join, his shoulders shaking when he joins me on the floor. "I swear, I tossed it out!"

I shake my head and can barely get a word out from how hard I'm laughing, falling on my back. Noah lies next to me, trying to catch his breath, and we roll into each other, hands finding hips, lips suddenly kissing, bodies grinding hungrily.

"Round two?" he whispers, both hands are up my sweater, massaging my skin.

He has one of his fancy watches on. I grab his wrist to check the time. Lunch is approaching fast. "I can do a lot in fifteen minutes."

MORNINGS ARE NEVER EASY, but lately, it's been doable, and I won't admit out loud that Noah has something to do with it.

We laugh at the top of the halfpipe over some out-of-pocket joke he made. Our typical banter of insulting one another has diminished, now leading to light topics and flirtatious quips.

Sometimes I catch his stare lingering on my ass, other times we can't help but brush against one another, addicted to each other's touch.

Noah starts his run, and I count on bated breath, waiting until he hits the ground from the Alley-Oop, but he can't even finish the turn, the nose of his snowboard hitting the lip of the halfpipe, tumbling down the side.

There's still a mental block, somewhere deep in his subconscious, distorting his reality.

Noah lies flat along the half pipe, staring up at the morning sun. I go to him, skidding to a stop, kicking up snow from my board, and peering down at his limp form. Noah breathes heavily, goggles blocking his eyes, and I can't tell if he's looking at me or not.

Removing my bindings and then Noah's, I try to get him up, but he's dead weight. "Come on, pretty boy, let's run it again."

He doesn't budge the harder I pull on his arm. "Noah, come on."

I yelp when he tugs back, falling on top of his chest. He wraps his arms around me, nuzzling his nose against my hair, inhaling deeply. "I wanna fuck you so badly right now."

My heart pounds, his hands resting on my hips. I take off his goggles and find his pupils are wide as saucers. "You need to practice first, and I'm relaxed, so you can't use my anxious behavior as an excuse."

He grunts. "Red, I am an eager man right now." He thrusts his hips forward, and I feel his erection through his snow pants. "Let me touch your perfect skin."

Most of the time, his compliments don't affect me; I try my hardest to let them go in one ear and out the other. But lately, one will slip right past my barrier and curl along my spine, forcing me to take a step back and panic to rebuild the walls I built.

This is one of those times.

Why let someone in when they don't need to be there?

It's a transaction, nothing more.

Untangling myself from his touch, I get to my feet, clapping my hands together. "Move, let's go!"

Noah follows without protest, but I can sense disappointment as we climb to the top.

Because he needs to participate in the event. Without Noah, his star quality and amazing performance, we lose the hype and possible revenue. It all weighs on my shoulders, and if I can't get him to complete one solid trick...

Noah snaps me out of my self-doubt monologue and kisses me, hot and with tongue. I cave, the sensation hitting all the way to my core. Our kissing turns sloppy, teeth and tongues colliding, wet sounds of our lips smacking, hands tangled in hair. Noah pushes me against a solid pile of snow, claiming all my senses and thoughts. My gloved hands reach for his face, wanting to take control. Our breaths become labored, bodies rising in temperature, toes curling in boots, he's sex on fire, and I'm caught in the flames.

Screw what others might see, I need him now. I break us apart, gasping for air. "We take a break, then go back, okay?"

He nods, not wasting any time, and demands we snowboard down the halfpipe. We make it in record time, crashing through his front door as he hoists me up around his waist.

Noah ignores the bed entirely, bringing me to the bathroom instead. I'm soaked and horny when he lets go to turn on the shower.

I look at him, puzzled. "Shower before sex?"

He removes the straps from my shoulders. "No, Red. I want to fuck you in the shower."

He takes the liberty of discarding my hat, bending to help me out of my boots. Noah takes off his pants and shirt, his muscles defined by hard work at the gym and snowboarding, a body so sculpted I wonder if it will shatter like stone.

My fingertips trace along his defined muscles, humming in appreciation of his disciplined routine that keeps him fit. He stands completely naked, not afraid to show all of himself under the fluorescent lights. Then again, if I were someone of perfect caliber, I might do the same.

Noah's eyes follow the pattern I trace, teasing my touch along his neck, watching him swallow, his Adam's apple bobbing up and down. His veins are thick and protruding, deliciously capturing my attention, as I find him utterly perfect.

I trace his lips, mouth slightly open, and stick my finger inside his mouth. He gently sucks, pulling me by the waist closer to him, then releases my finger with a loud *pop*, brushing my cheek gently with the palm of his hand. "Meet me when you're ready." Eyes of the deepest brown hold me still, just for a moment, forcing anything negative away, keeping my mind at peace.

He steps back and enters the shower, leaving the sliding door half open.

Water runs, steam clouds the mirror, and I wipe it to catch my reflection, red cheeks marked where the chilled wind touched. Freckles coat my nose, fading across my face. I stare intently, triple-checking my chin hair, making sure it stays at bay.

Slowly, I remove my clothes, layer by layer, watching as more of my skin is exposed—freckles dotting my shoulders, fading down my forearms. My breasts are round and heavy; I check to be sure my nipple hairs are gone. My pants come last, my thighs thick, cellulite glaring under the light. I hug my midsection. Maybe if I suffocate it, it'll fall off my body. Noah said this body is a temple, but all I see is the wreckage after a tornado.

Liam's projection of negativity tries to penetrate my walls, but Noah's acceptance keeps it safe.

I step into the shower, finding him facing it, dark hair wet and slicked back, water cascading down his body, catching the beautiful sight of his round ass. His presence does something to me, an instant reaction, and I'm drawn like a moth to his out-of-control flame.

He senses my stare and turns, smiling. "You made it."

No point in hiding now, he's seen everything, and if he wanted to run for the hills, then it would've already happened. "I did."

Noah adjusts our positions, making me stand in front of the showerhead. He stands behind me and removes the showerhead, running the water along my skin. "I was getting worried you were going to chicken out."

He moves it along my scalp, the warm water running down my back. It feels good having someone else take care of you.

"I like to experience new things."

"Yeah?" his lips kiss my shoulders, moving the water further down my stomach. A click sound, then the pressure changes to jet, more force, circling my belly button. "Lift your leg on the lower shelf."

I do as I'm told, using the bottom shelf to widen my stance, exposing my core. Soft lips kiss, then teeth nip at my skin, making me lean my head back against his chest. The high I feel is something I'll never have the right words to explain. With Noah, everything is euphoric; his hands alone can wreck me, cause floods, even crumble the very ground I walk on.

My breathing quickens as Noah moves the showerhead even lower, just above where my clit is.

"Noah," I whimper, legs spread, and every sensation hits me at once; his lips on my skin, water dripping down to my center, calloused hands gripping my waist. He sets me ablaze.

"I like it when you say my name, you make it sound sinful." He moves the water over my clit, erupting a loud moan from my throat. God, it's divine how he circles the water around and around, my hips rocking along with it.

He laughs, a deep, tenor sound in my ear. Sucking on my neck, he continues to circle my clit with the water, my strings coiling tight. My hands move up into his hair, putting my full weight against his body for support, his hard erection against my lower back.

Pleasure builds fast from the hot pressure of the water, shattering when I come, letting go, climaxing so hard I think I see stars.

Noah takes my chin, forcing me to look up, and muffles my

moans with his lips, kissing me like his life depends on it. We drink each other in, needy fingers gripping and tugging skin.

He puts the showerhead away, and I waste no time wrapping my arms around his neck, kissing him. Our tongues move, sounds of pleasure heightening my sensitive skin, already wet. Noah is a dream, a wild dream I know I could wake up from at any point, and it'll be all over.

I crave him constantly, and not only his touch but the sound of his voice, how he walks, and forces the entire room to shift its attention to him. But in a crowded room, he finds me, and our bickering suddenly becomes inside jokes and deep conversations.

He became a friend...with extra benefits.

I break our kiss, moving to face the shower door, bracing my hands on the glass. "Take me here, Noah. Please."

He groans, the sound of a wrapper tearing from teeth, a minute of adjusting the latex condom on, and he's already inside me, sighing with satisfaction.

My breasts are pressed against the glass, my hands above my head for support. The more he fucks me, the louder I get, thankful running water creates a buffer.

We fit perfectly together, our bodies molding into each other, while Noah circles my clit with his finger at the same time.

"Red," he moans, taking a fistful of my hair and pulling me back so I'm seeing him upside down. His lips find mine, kissing me until my head spins. My legs shake as I try to stay upright, getting lost in one another.

"Noah," I whimper against his lips, and my insides coil, bracing for the fall. I'm almost there, almost at the top. He drives into me.

It approaches fast, crashing down into rough waves when I come, knowing he's following right after. He presses into me, my breasts sticking to the glass door, calling me by my nickname like it's the sweetest sin.

I've never come so fast before, not even with Liam.

Noah lingers inside me, kissing my shoulders, his nose dragging up my neck as water continues to spray down on us. "You always smell so good after sex. Why is that?" He nibbles on my earlobe, then slowly pulls out, leaving me empty.

I whimper from lack of contact, easing myself off the glass doors, hearing my skin peel away. "Do I?"

Noah nods and guides me under the showerhead. "Let me wash you."

Taking my favorite shampoo, Noah lathers it in his big hands and motions for me to turn around. He rubs my scalp, massaging behind my ears, down to the base of my neck. It's heaven how he uses his fingers to rub the shampoo in, taking his time, being so gentle. My eyes are rolling, and I'm moaning by the time he rinses it out.

I lean back into his chest, watching him squirt body wash gel into a cloth, squishing it together to create suds. He glides it around my skin, washing my arms and chest, right over the peaks of my nipples, adjusting me forward to get my back.

"I don't think you realize how good this feels," I moan, dropping my head.

Noah reaches my ass and washes it in circular motions. "You're right, I don't."

I blink and move, forcing him to stop. "Really?"

"Yeah, it's not a big deal." He says it's like a meteor might crash any second, and he's totally fine. "I enjoy washing you."

I grab the cloth, making him turn around. "Let me."

"Red, you don't have to." He's trying to grab it back, but I keep it secured in both hands behind me.

"I said, turn around, Noah," I command.

He looks, lips in a hard line, definitely holding back from

protesting. But he surprises me by giving me his back, head bent forward.

My hands shake for some reason, maybe it's me realizing in this moment how intimate our showering together is, especially washing one another, but I don't care. I want to wash him, to cleanse away any negative thoughts. To ease his muscles and tension along his back.

He flexes under my touch when I begin to wash from shoulder to shoulder. He's truly a work of art, Michelangelo's David, if I had to describe the perfection of Noah's body.

His skin is smooth, not a single scar or blemish taints his tawny canvas. The urge to bite it and leave my mark has me biting my lip to keep myself in check.

Noah sighs when I touch his ass, mimicking his moves with the cloth. "You're right, this feels amazing."

I'm smiling so big I must look ridiculous. Noah Hart is letting me wash his body, he's letting me intimately touch him, and I'm thoroughly enjoying every second of it.

Slipping my arms around his waist, I rub the cloth over his chest lightly. "Can you turn back around to face me?"

He turns, sadness touches his eyes, and it makes my heart ache. "Noah?"

But I never get the chance to finish, because Noah makes it his mission to kiss me senseless, leaving the cloth completely forgotten on the shower floor.

WE FUCK several times before Red passed out, drooling on my chest. She's wiped, and our legs are intertwined under my thick comforter. Sunlight has faded behind snow-capped mountains, and the only light by my bedside table illuminates the room in a soft glow.

Red snores softly, hair falling down her back while I stroke it, her warmth keeping the chill at bay. She's small in my arms, and it goes against our rules...wait...we never established any, but I have zero intention of giving a shit. Not right now. Not when I need her comfort.

I selfishly want to enjoy this because I know it can never be...

She'll never feel the same. And I will never let myself get to that point. But for now, her company is enough.

Cause once it's all over, I'll leave and never look back. Never look at her again. Never see those bright blue eyes stare directly into my fucking soul. Or her mouth when it wants to talk back or kiss me with as much urgency as I give in return.

No, I can't let it consume me. I can't let her fully in. Lying here is already a mistake, but it's so easy to give in with her... for her.

So why can't I move? Why can't I remove myself from her limp, warm body, her soft legs, and light snores?

Why do I continue to mull over every detail of her features, from the way she walks to the way she talks? Her very essence takes over all my cognitive thinking; it's maddening and intoxicating.

I don't think I can leave.

My chest starts to hurt at the thought, and that scares the living shit out of me.

She's insecure, and I knew instantly when she tried to hide parts of her body from me. She has no idea how goddamn beautiful she is. I want to sucker punch the fucker who ruined her self-esteem, who made her see any imperfections because there are none.

I kiss her forehead, staring down at her freckles that dot her nose like the constellations in the sky.

Red stirs in my arms and snuggles her face against my side, her fingers gently stroking my skin. She lifts her head slightly to peek up at me, her eyes squinting when she smiles, and it takes all of my power not to crumble, to give in and let her become... mine.

But she's not mine. Can't be...won't be.

I'm a piece of shit who can't get his act together, who's known for having a new girl every hour. It's a miracle she agreed, a miracle I don't deserve.

Selfishly I stay, holding her because for once, my world becomes quieter when she's in my arms.

A silence I've been searching for such a long time, and somehow its been here all along.

CHAPTER 47

HANNAH

THE SOUND of a snowboard skidding across freshly leveled snow never gets old; however, for Noah, it's a constant reminder that he can't grasp his turns and landings. At one point, about forty minutes into our practice, his Alley-Oop looked promising, except his strength wavered, causing his unbalance and skidding down the halfpipe.

But he persisted, getting right back up and making it to the top hill every time, only to meet another failed attempt at his tricks.

It's dangerous to let someone with the twisties perform, but he's showing promise, and not only is he more relaxed with his thoughts, but he also proved me wrong and stomped most of my own anxieties.

Eventually, I call for a break, watching his face fall when he sits in the snow, patting the seat next to him.

I join him, enjoying the morning air that fills my lungs. Noah keeps his head low, goggles swaying from his fingertips. If only I could get inside his head and rearrange the gears to move him away from self-deprecating thoughts.

Because it's not his dead dad that's making him lose control, it's something else entirely.

Instead, we sit in silence for the remainder of practice, hoping the peace at the top can settle the unease I know is creeping near. It comes off his body in waves, dread filling the small space we share in such a wide-open area.

It's suffocating, even for me.

I wonder if it's like that all the time for him.

"Noah," I say, watching him from my peripherals.

"I think my career is over." He chucks the goggles on the ground and removes his winter hat, twisting it between his hands. His voice sounds so small, making my heart ache.

"Noah, it's not over. This happened before, right?"

I barely get the words out when his eyes turn dark. "Who told you?"

"Coach Jones. I confronted him when I realized what was happening at our first practice. But you overcame it before, didn't you? Henry wouldn't delve into the details eith—"

"'Cause it's nobody's business but mine, Red."

"But if we can use how you overcame it before—"

"NO." It's the first time he's raised his voice at me. "You think because we're working together, you have a right to know my personal business? It doesn't work like that. So, stay out of it."

But it's not the first time for me when it comes to a man yelling at me. It makes me sick to my stomach, shrinking my size down to a tiny ant, his boot keeping me stuck to the bottom of his heel.

Where is the man I washed in the shower? Who let me sleep in his arms after he touched and claimed all my intimate parts?

Noah catches the hurt in my eyes and my silence, reaching

for me, but I back away. Because when trauma meets trauma, everyone gets hurt. "Red, I'm—"

"Hart!" yells Mark from the bottom, waving his arms.

"What?" Noah shouts back.

"Coach Jones is looking for you both!"

"Shit," he hisses under his breath.

Up until now, I totally forgot Coach Jones wanted an update on Noah's progress by the end of the week, and we have nothing to show for it.

I'm failing Maya and her family, getting too distracted by Noah's touch rather than making sure he overcomes his mental block.

It's too much, everything. And now I have to meet with Coach Jones to discuss another failure.

Coach Jones takes a comfortable position behind the desk, rocking back and forth in his chair. He clicks a blue pen with his thumb, waiting for one of us to speak. Noah looks only at his coach.

I, however, want to fucking hurl my breakfast up.

"Update?" Coach Jones says, continuing to click that stupid pen. I want to throw it at his head.

Noah shrugs. "I keep eating shit, if that's what you want to hear."

The room falls silent, and Coach Jones looks about ready to explode. His face turns a deep shade of red, veins protruding along his neck. "You can't be serious." He turns to me. "Is he serious?"

"I—"

Leave it to Noah to start an argument with his own coach. "Who else have you told about my past?"

"No one. But I think you should shed some insight for Hannah, at least that'll give her a chance to reverse the mess."

"Or we can just admit it's over. No point beating a dead horse."

"Listen to me—"

"Save the lecture. It's going to make my ears bleed anyway."

His words are sharp, and before Coach can respond, Henry comes in, eyes darting back and forth between the three of us.

Well, this can't be good.

"Now is not the time, Parker," Coach advises, continuing to grill the shit out of Noah.

"I believe it's the perfect time." Grabbing a chair and wedging it between Noah and me, he continues, "Cause someone alerted the press, and Anthony and Jill are trying to get the staff to control the mob outside."

"Fuck," hisses Noah.

"Who in the flying fuck alerted the press!" Watching Coach Jones lose his shit is one thing, but witnessing him take a stack of books and launch them off the table, screaming, "Fuck!" is another.

"The rest of the team is aware and is hiding out in their cabins." Henry starts making phone calls, trying to keep it under control.

"I don't understand," I finally speak, my voice sounding off.

Noah finally looks at me, his eyes holding no emotion, slipping on a mask.

I hate it. I hate this version of him. It's like when we first met. His arrogance and coldness push me over the edge.

Coach Jones storms out, most likely assessing the situation outside.

Henry eventually answers my question. "The media is

already aware of the Olympic team doing the event; however, they never swarm this fast unless a story breaks about one of the players." He side eyes Noah. "You guys practice before the guests are allowed on the slopes, right?"

"Yes. From seven to nine." Like we agreed.

"Apparently, it came from an inside source, according to the article on page six in the L.A times. Once they get hold of information, it spreads like wildfire." Henry gets another phone call, barking orders to some poor soul on the other end.

My stomach turns. If people know of Noah not being able to perform,it might turn others away from coming altogether.

My breakfast rises in the back of my throat.

"Red?" Noah claims my attention, eyes wide with panic. "You're as white as snow. Are you okay?"

Afraid to move, my fingers dig into the upholstery, trying to breathe through my nose. My hearing is shot as a loud ringing in my right ear penetrates my skull, pounding at my temples. Dizzy, I feel dizzy and out of control.

Noah pushes Henry out of the room, but all I catch is the sound of my erratic heartbeat pumping, no chance of slowing down.

Noah gets on his knees and shifts my chair to face him. But I need to get away. I can't stay here, not like this. Not when he's this version of himself, too much back and forth with him.

No, I have to go now.

Bolting from the room, I catch sight of the mob outside the foyer, cameras flashing, blinding in all directions. Someone shouts for Noah; Anthony and Jill are trying to get the staff to shuffle the paparazzi outside.

I can't see, but someone shouts for Noah, then more follow after, when strong hands touch my shoulders.

"Who's the girlfriend, Hart?"

"Give us a kiss!"

"Hart, is it true you're retiring?"

"Red—"

"Hannah!"

Maya! Thank god.

Another set of hands grab me, taking me away from the chaos. We duck into the dining hall, skirting past the staff and into the head chef's office.

Maya pants, hands on knees, trying to catch her breath. "I'm so out of shape."

Sliding down to the floor, I hug my knees, panting as well. "Time to head back to Zumba."

She pretends to gag. "Fuck that, I'd rather walk a mile at my old high school track than be surrounded by all those sweaty bodies."

"It's because that chick removed her tank and slapped you in the face by mistake."

"I wanted to die, okay. How do you just blatantly take off your stupid tight-fitting tank top and just swing it around like you're riding a goddamn bull! THIS ISN'T A RODEO. It's fucking Zumba in the North End."

Her outburst makes us pause, then laugh, holding our stomachs. Maya joins me on the floor and rests her head on my shoulder. "I think Noah putting his hands on you really put the paparazzi in a frenzy. I wouldn't be surprised if your face is plastered everywhere now."

I groan, banging my head back against the wall. "Did you hear what they called me?"

"I mean, it's better than calling you his booty call."

I give her the side eye. "Doesn't help."

"Why did he come out in the first place? He looked disheveled. What happened there?"

"Told Coach Jones he's done. It's like he didn't want to try anymore." Does that also mean our arrangement is over, too?

Would it be so bad if it were? After he yelled at me at the top of the halfpipe, maybe it's for the best. Maybe our transaction has expired, and it's not doing any of us favors. It fueled a fire brighter than the sun, and I think it's starting to sizzle out.

But to tell Maya all this right now, I don't have the mental strength to deal with her questioning.

"Do you think he's done?" Maya asks.

"Does it matter what I think?" Because at the end of the day, Noah is going to do what he wants, when he wants, and will never apologize for his ways.

The door opens, and the head chef looks at us huddled on the floor.

He hesitates stepping in, wondering if it's safe to enter his own office. "I...just...uh, need my master copy of the menu." He stretches his long legs almost into a split, grabs the menu off his desk, and shuts the door without another word.

It sends Maya and me into a fit, not expecting the head chef to make an appearance in his own office.

"Gosh, what a mess," I say, taking a deep breath to suppress any more laughter.

"Well, someone leaked Noah's business. My parents are most likely calling the cops right now. I think they'll add a new policy to the resort after this, with no paparazzi allowed."

"Can they do that?"

"Yes." She plays with the gold ring on her middle finger. "It sounds like you do care about what happens to Noah." Leave it to Maya to find a deeper meaning than intended.

"I'm lucky I got his ass out of bed."

"True. But he can't resist you."

He can't, but not in the way she thinks, and oddly, it hits me hard in the chest, a somewhat dull ache starting, making it difficult to catch my breath.

JILL AND ANTHONY announce a cocktail party before the tree lighting ceremony. Maya and I get ready together. Her parents hired a special catering service and gave their staff the night off. Maya explains how he had a stroke over the expense for the catering. I guess Jill told him to shut up in a few colorful words, and they beelined straight to the best food in Burlington.

Invitations are sent via email to guests and staff, and attire is dressy. I'm thankful to Maya for keeping me in the loop since Noah takes up most of my time and now my bed.

My mind tends to stray whenever I think of him, or his hands, the way he rocks into me, calling me Red in his husky tone.

Then he yells at me, ignores me in the office, and the paparazzi blinds me with their flashing cameras.

I'm still mad at him, but it doesn't mean I still don't want him.

I shake my head and return to reality, deciding on a floor-length, emerald dress with spaghetti straps and nude heels.

Maya straightens my hair when I remember Noah saved her

from Gift Card Dude. "So, how did Noah get you out of your date?"

She parts my hair in sections, running the straightener through. "Honestly, he told him the truth. I'm too nice to say no, and I didn't want to hurt his feelings. And might've given him a gift certificate to the restaurant we met at."

"To ease the blow?" I muse.

"Yes. Now, I have a question for you." She starts on another piece of my wavy hair, moving the straight pieces aside. "Why were you really in Noah's cabin? And don't say to pee because you looked hella flushed for someone who just peed, unless you dropped a shit."

"Oh my god, Maya!"

"Well?" she laughs, trying to keep still with the hot straightener close to my face. Any closer and my eyelashes will singe off. "Did you poop?"

"Gosh, no!" I can't be shocked by her question, but sometimes I wonder if she has a few screws loose.

"Okay, okay. So what was the reason then?"

I normally tell Maya everything, trust her with the basic stuff right down to the top secret gossip, and now... I hesitate, wondering why I can't tell her. Why am I compelled to keep something as intimate and private as mine and Noah's "transaction" to myself?

Her judgment is nonexistent when it comes to our friendship. If anything, she would be relieved that I went back out there and got my socks rocked. But Noah isn't a potential anything, he's just...convenient...and understanding, and isn't all arrogant and egotistical, as he had first come off. And deep in my caged heart, a tiny sliver likes the idea of us becoming something more.

But as much as Noah cares and is gentle with me, I'm only a placeholder, not a prize to be won.

And maybe I'm ashamed of judging too quickly and can't face the truth of my own actions.

It's just sex.

So, why does it feel like more?

She finishes my hair, running her fingers through the soft strands. "I know we tell each other everything, and it's okay if you want to keep it to yourself. Just know I'm always here for you." She squeezes my shoulders.

I reach to grab her hand. "Thanks, Maya."

"And if you want to tell me now how I totally think Noah is banging your brains out, that's good, too." She finishes the last section and unplugs the cord.

I sit there, jaw hanging open, stuttering like a fool.

"Oh no, don't worry. I support your decision to keep it to yourself." She brings out her makeup bag and starts to riffle through its contents.

"Maya..." I'm so dumb to think she wouldn't figure it out. "Listen, I wanted to tell you.. I just wasn't sure..."

She winks at me, popping the cap off a face primer and applying it to my face. "Hannah, I'm messing with you. Yeah, I figured something was going on between you two, but when you're ready to tell me, I'll be here to listen."

"I know we tell each other everything, and for some reason... I wanted to keep this a secret...to convince myself it's not just some game that passes the time." I begin to pick at the little balls of cotton on my sweatpants.

She fans my primer down and starts with some light foundation. "Noah's time?"

I swallow a hard lump in my throat. "Is that wrong?"

Dabbing my face with a makeup sponge, Maya bites her lip, her telltale sign when she's thinking hard. She moves on to setting my under eyelids, then eye shadow, not saying a word.

When we get to the eyeliner, I stop her. "Maya."

She steps back, eyeliner in hand. "You're my best friend, and I want what's best for you...Noah is...might not be the best? I don't know. By all means, knock your socks off, but I worry. Especially since what happened with Liam, which you still refuse to tell me how it ended. So, I don't want you getting hurt."

Two secrets I've kept from Maya. One from shame, one from... I don't even know anymore. "He'll be gone once the event is over. Nothing more can come of this anyway." It's definitely one-sided. Noah will never feel the same, even if I entertain the idea... But that stupid candle flickers to life once more.

If I don't snuff it out soon, it's all over.

Maya finishes the look with setting spray and hands me a mirror, and I find a happier version of myself staring back at me. Lighter, even. Is it due to being back at Snowy Peak, yes, but if you asked me on a deeper level, I'd say Noah's presence has everything to do with it.

Maya completes her look with a rouge lip stain, then we both dress and throw on our sleek, black dress coats. I can't wait to freeze my ass off in this.

The dinner portion is first, followed by the tree-lighting ceremony and dessert. Maya says her parents refused to give away any of the details and wanted us to enjoy the night, not have to worry about anything.

Fine by me; however, Maya isn't happy being out of the loop. She likes to be in on the plans, always helping, and it's hard for her to sit back and let others take control.

It's actually quite comical to watch her point out all the details of her parents' plan.

We leave the cabins, my camera bag on my shoulder, walking on a newly shoveled path, where lights have been added to guide our way down to the main building. A light snowfall kisses my cheeks; the taste of newly fallen snow always tastes heavenly on the tongue. I stick it out, and Maya catches me, joining in. We catch sight of other guests starting to gather along the path, dressed in elegant clothing, even the kids wear cute dressy coats and tights.

At the top of the stairs, a balloon arch of white and silver greets us at the entrance, and standing under the arch is the rest of the Olympic team. I scan the group, not finding Noah among them. My heart hammers as I reach the top of the steps, greeting the boys and the twins. Ella and Elise are in stunning matching long-sleeved red dresses, glitter teasing the waist and gems fanning down into the silhouette. Their hair is styled somewhat similarly, with big, loose curls in a half-updo; they even added tinsel. With ruby-red lips, they both smile at Maya and me before heading inside, arm in arm. The men are dressed in suits of varying shades. Mark sports a velvet green, fiddling with the cuff links. Taylor chose a deep maroon, while Cody has a sleek man bun, in an all-white suit.

All of them look ready to walk the runway.

Maya smiles playfully, snaking her arms through Mark and Cody's. "Let's go, boys. Taylor, sweetheart? Watch the rear."

Taylor shakes his head and offers me his arm. "Thanks, but you don't have to."

"Nonsense. Every woman deserves to be escorted."

I blush, not used to chivalry. Taking his arm, he escorts me inside the main foyer, where more silver and white are splashed about the room. The reception desk is draped with a crisp white cloth, silver snowflakes dangling on the edge. White roses in silver vases are displayed around the room. The tree's once-colorful lights are changed to white, and silver garlands now weave through the fake branches, complementing the red ball ornaments that hang at the ends. A red carpet is rolled out, directing the flow of guests to designated spots to gather.

Chatter fills the air as guests pile in, dressed in beautiful clothing.

Soft, instrumental music plays as we make our way over to the coat room, where a staff member takes our coats and gives us a claim check.

Taylor notices my dress and whistles. "Noah is gonna drool when he sees you in that."

My face flames a crimson red. Taylor either knows the truth or suspects. Either way, I'm not willing to correct him. "I don't think so."

"Why not?" he seems offended.

"'Cause he's not here?"

"Yet."

He offers to get me a drink, disappearing into the crowd. I linger in the room, catching sight of Maya flirting with Cody.

Maya's parents are by the entrance to the dining hall, Jill's black satin dress complements her beautiful dark hair, a mirror image to Maya's, while Anthony matches in a sleek dress coat and pants.

Taylor hands me a flute of champagne, clinking his glass to mine. "Cheers, Hannah. For helping us get our Noah back."

Our Noah.

Little does Taylor know that he was never mine.

And Noah's twisties debacle is ongoing.

I take a little sip, not a fan of alcohol, but trying to be polite for his kind gesture. Taylor wanders away after a comforting pat on the shoulder. Maya is nowhere in sight, while the twins are talking amongst themselves, and I stay in a corner, observing the crowd mingling with one another.

Until my eyes find a familiar back and light blond hair. He walks with confidence among the crowd, dressed in a black tux.

It's when he turns around that I drop my champagne flute and lose my ability to speak.

CHAMPAGNE SOAKS THE FLOOR, and the flute smashes into pieces. People around me look and stare, and a waiter comes over to clean my mess.

I stand frozen, the heat of the fireplace warming my backside, as Liam, my shitty ex-boyfriend, enters the main building. Never in all my twenty-four years did I think he would return, knowing how close I am to this place—or Maya being my best friend.

Brain cells are lacking.

Liam hasn't noticed me yet, but it only takes seconds for me to clock the girl that follows him in: a tall, wavy brunette with smoky eyes and a flawless complexion. She calls him some weird nickname and kisses his cheek.

She is everything I'm not—the epitome of beauty.

Her dress is navy blue satin, legs for days, not a single hair out of place.

Together, they belong in a magazine for a perfume ad, while I belong in a zoo near the elephant exhibit.

He's the same: cool-toned blond hair, sky-blue eyes, a killer jaw, and—most importantly—his "winning" personality.

A total tool bag.

My heart hammers in my chest; I'm not sure what it means yet, but most likely fear of his past words, his harsh tones, and disgusted looks whenever I changed in front of him. But he can't hurt me anymore, not here, not ever again. Though his actions and mental abuse left a permanent scar, tainting my view on relationships and men in general.

Of course, my reflex is to run, hoping to avoid him, when he catches sight of my movement, and we stare at one another like we've each seen a ghost. His new girlfriend follows his line of sight and pans over to me, trying to understand what's happening.

Liam shakes his head, releasing me, bringing me back to reality, and ushers the beautiful brunette to the reception desk.

I manage to blend in with the other guests, trying to inch my way to the back corner. At least I'll be safe here until they leave for their cabin.

But what are the odds Liam comes straight over to me, model brunette in tow?

The Gomezes must make an escape route for situations like this.

They haven't seen me again. I'm currently up against the bay window, surrounded by teens taking selfies. I take a seat, keeping my eyes on them.

It's almost like he's scouting me out, waiting for me to emerge and then pounce. He's admiring the fireplace with his newest victim. They're extra touchy, hands constantly needing to grasp some body part, giving me the major ick, it's not like kids are around or anything.

Men and their need to make the world know how desirable they are.

He needs to leave. Why the fuck won't he leave?!

"Hannah?"

It's over.

If I play like I can't hear him, maybe he'll go away, mistaking me for a lookalike, but sure enough, the son of a bitch comes right into my peripheral, hands interlocked with a Victoria's Secret model.

Dare I look up?

Too late, I cave and meet the stare of the worst ex-boyfriend in existence.

The closer he is, the more memories resurface, and I try to plaster on a fake smile, like he didn't mentally hurt me and eviscerate my self-esteem.

"I forgot you came here," he says.

Liar. He knows damn well I practically call Snowy Peak my second home. He's seen photos, my collection of sweatshirts, and even the stickers on my insulated water bottles.

"Yeah, well, it is Maya's family resort." Pretty sure he doesn't remember my best friend either.

The brunette model looks uncomfortable. I take this chance to introduce myself, keeping the topic off me. "I'm sorry, where are my manners? I'm Hannah."

She gives me a half smile. "Gwen." We don't shake hands, might be because she's too busy touching fuck face over here.

"Well, it's good to see you." Liar. "Did you come by yourself?" Nosy jackass.

"She came with me." I'd know that voice anywhere. The husky tone when he's claiming what's his, mostly in the bedroom. Noah strides over, at ease with himself, fully aware of fans in the room, and not giving a single shit as he snakes his arm around my waist, tucking me into his side.

"Oh my god, you're Noah Hart?" Gwen looks like she's ready to pass out.

Liam, however, is not impressed. "Rumor has it you're not performing at the event. Something to do with...mental issues?"

Noah must have caught the snarky tone, because he pulls me in a little tighter. "That's why they call them rumors."

"Huh, the source was a personal friend." Liam's eyes wander to Noah's hand on my waist, then look back at me.

"Not a personal friend if they're willing to sell them out to the tabloids for cash."

I try to remove Noah's grip, but it's no use against someone who's built like pure steel.

One of Gwen's hands snakes up Liam's chest, exposing a ring...a very familiar ring.

Suddenly, the room slows, and time is halted as I stare at the diamond sparkling on her long, tan finger.

It's only been a year.

One whole year.

The ring promised to me enjoys its new home.

Waves of anxious emotions rise, my heart pumping, and Noah's touch becomes too much. I elbow him when they're not looking, getting a grunt behind me, and he releases me from his hold.

Liam turns around, eyes flickering between us.

I hate him. So fucking much.

He smirks, clearly pleased with the fact that the ring he caught me looking at before our breakup rests nicely on Gwen's finger.

But does she know what a narcissistic pig he is? Or how he belittled my diagnosis?

"Well, it's been nice chatting, but I gotta go see if Maya needs me," I announce. I just need to escape.

Liam cocks his head to the side. "Maya? Oh, yes, that's right. I forgot her parents own a ski resort."

What a conniving fuck.

"Yes, this one, to be exact," I mutter.

Liam brushes it off like it's old news and turns to Gwen,

stroking her cheek. "They're offering sleigh rides now, let's go take one before dinner."

Hand in hand, Gwen gives me a sheepish wave, while Liam barely bats an eye and leads her away.

I'm left with lingering insecurity from our past relationship and Noah's intense gaze.

"RED," says Noah, his tone quiet. I wonder if he can sense how my emotions have fucked with my nervous system.

"Don't," I warn, trying to calm myself down.

"We need to talk," he says, touching my arm lightly, completely ignoring my request not to say anything else.

Just breathe, Hannah, in and out.

"About what?" I hiss as rage fills every part of my body. I'm surprised steam isn't coming out of my ears. So much for calming myself down. "Because the last time I checked, you told me to stay out of your business."

"I know what I said was fucked up, and I'm—"

"Leave me alone, Noah," I snap, trying to remove myself from his touch.

He ignores my demand, instead focusing on the one question that chips at my armor. "Who was that asshole, Red?"

His inquisition almost makes me want to slap him. "Wow, how fucking ironic."

"Are you going to answer the question? Or do I have to beat the shit out of him for it?"

"What makes you think he's the problem?" Now look who's the observant one.

"Anyone with eyes can see how you locked up when he approached. What the fuck did he do?"

"You wouldn't cause a scene."

"Watch me." Those brown eyes swirl a darker shade, his promise laced with malice.

"Don't you dare. Do not ruin this for the Gomezes." His touch never falters, but somehow we're closer than before. "Why does it matter to you anyway?"

Noah's eyes linger everywhere, almost like he's taking mental pictures. His fingers start to slip, releasing me finally. "Nobody deserves to get hurt."

The twins' voices come to mind, of Noah's troubled past relationship.

How bad was the fall he experienced?

I shake my head, remembering the vow I made to myself. Swearing off men is the whole reason I avoid shit like this. I won't let him rope me back in, already regretting the yes I gave him before.

I mean, sort of. I also sort of don't regret his touch.

No, I don't want to hear his excuses or watch those goddamn gorgeous eyes plead for me to listen. He doesn't get to cast me aside and shut off, then ask about my personal bullshit. "I'm returning your favor from earlier. So, stay out of my business."

I leave him alone and crestfallen in the corner as I search for Maya. My breathing escalates while I weave through the guests, and my chest tightens with every excuse me to slide by strangers, people's faces blurring as my panic starts to rise. Every noise, down to the kids running and screaming in their suits and dresses, hurts my ears, making it harder to focus.

Where is she?!

I spot Henry, Noah's stiff personal assistant, checking the watch on his wrist. He catches me staring and saunters over, clearly taking my wild eyes as an open invitation to bother me.

"Where's your short friend?" he asks, adjusting his collar.

I backpedal, letting our conversation become a distraction from my mounting panic. "Maya?

He checks his surroundings, searching for her. "Yeah, she muttered something about incompetence, then stormed off, taking my drink with her."

"What did you do?"

He looks offended. "Me? The woman complains that I'm an eyesore, and yet it's my fault?"

Sounds like Maya. "Have you tried to apologize for something you didn't do?"

Henry rolls his neck. "You don't believe me either."

"I didn't say that, but I can't help but wonder what stupid sentence came from your mouth. Maya doesn't yell at just anyone."

"Wasn't yelling, per se, more like chastising me like a dog who shit on her carpet..." he pauses, catching my insult. "I bet Noah really enjoys your company."

"He can go kick rocks, for all I care."

A sea of guests starts to close in, gathering by the entrance of the dining hall as a bell chimes, signaling all of us to silence.

Anthony stands on a nearby chair, clapping his hands to gather any wandering conversations to a halt. "Thank you so much for joining us tonight for a feast and a night that will surely be memorable for years to come. Please, make your way inside, and check the seating chart. We are excited to get this night rolling!"

Henry gestures to me to go ahead. "Ladies first."

"At least you have manners. How did you end up working with Noah, anyway?" I ask, leading the way inside.

Anthony and Jill have transformed the dining hall into a luxurious space. They switched out the long, ornate tables for round ones with red tablecloths, candles flickering in the center. Crystal snowflakes hang above us, casting rainbow hues on the floor.

Henry follows me over to the easel, where our name and table numbers are displayed.

He plucks our cards, waving the table number in my face. "Looks like we're together."

Dread fills my body, because if he's seated with me, that means...

By the foggy windows, I spot Maya looking just as annoyed as I when she catches us coming her way. And there's Noah, bracing his elbows on the back of his seat, staring right into my soul. A face so stunning it can knock the wind out of anyone.

Heart? Why does it have to be him?

Henry is oblivious to the tension when we take our seats, finding an empty spot with my place card right next to Noah. He pulls out my chair, while my heart hammers against my rib cage as I try to remind myself of our argument we had moments ago, and that his chivalrous gesture doesn't give him a free pass.

Regardless, it makes my stomach flip one too many times.

I mumble a simple thanks, feeling his legs brush against mine when he takes his seat.

Henry takes his seat on the opposite side of Maya, her mouth in a hard line, arms crossed like she can't be bothered.

I elbow her gently to get her attention and whisper, "Hey, everything okay?"

"I'm contemplating tying my hair to the ceiling fan in my cabin and going for a ride," she deadpans. And she's not quiet about her comment, either, because Henry is already rolling his eyes. "I don't get why you're the one who's mad."

"Want me to rewind the tape for you, Parker?" she snipes.

He takes a long look at her, his lips in a hard line. "I'm not the one who took my comment out of context."

Before she can respond, Liam arrives with Gwen on his arm, and my hands clench under the table as I grind my teeth. Because it didn't register until now that two empty seats remained.

Maya's eyes bulge, then she turns to me and mouths, What the fuck.

A rough hand covers mine and squeezes. I look over to find it's Noah's, and my breath hitches in the back of my throat.

Gwen takes her seat, while Liam casually leans into his, a smirk on his face. "Well, this is interesting."

"And you are?" asks Henry.

"A walking disease," mutters Noah. His hand gives me one more squeeze and pulls away.

Maya looks to me, then Liam, and finally Noah. I catch her texting on her lap, my phone buzzing inside my clutch.

Dare I look? Knowing she's asking what she's missed. I mouth the word later and try to take a sip of the water that's already provided at the table. Slightly chilled, enough to clear my dry throat. I keep my eyes down, admiring the intricate snowflakes on the white china plates, hoping Noah's remark is left behind.

But it's hard when the one person you never thought would come back to plague your world again is grinning at you across the table.

I look up, Liam leans forward and snags his water, swirling the glass around like it's a wine testing session. "Hannah, nice to know your company remains the same. Tell me, does Noah here beg like a dog? Does he sleep on the floor when you kick him down?" Liam's laugh is a sound I was hoping to never hear again. It's like nails on a chalkboard, a constant loop, making me want to curl in on myself.

He's doing it on purpose, making comments to have everyone else at the table think I was the abusive one.

I hate it. I hate him. I hate how he's here, sitting across from me with his new fiancée, flashing that ring, how she has no idea what mental abuse he graciously bestowed upon me. Where I second-guess every action, how I move my body, what I wear, hiding behind layers of self-doubt because he's the one ashamed.

Ashamed of what I had to go through.

A year of therapy, and yet all the crap he put me through slips through the cracks in my defences.

No, I can't sit idle anymore. I can't cast my eyes down and watch him make comments or laugh and try to belittle me in front of everyone.

I look him dead in the eyes, a sly smile creeping up on my face, catching a snake in his trap. "Why? Because your current treats you like a pussy?"

It's a low blow, I'll admit, and knowing Gwen is stuck in the crossfire isn't fair, but there's a good chance he's twisted the story around in his favor to ensnare her.

She sits in silence, avoiding all eye contact. Her silence is enough to know he's most likely mentally abusing her, too.

Maya spits her drink out; Henry has a hard time controlling his laughter.

Noah, however, slings an arm behind my chair, smiling with pride. He tugs at my hair and winks. "Why, Red, you're feisty when you're hungry?"

I hear Maya choke even more, having to smack her back to get her to stop, knowing damn well his nickname for me caused the fit.

I keep eye contact with Liam, raising an eyebrow to the challenge. He's already setting his lips in a hard line, eyes dangerous and threatening.

Finding comfort in Noah's presence, I scoot closer, playing a game way out of my league right now. I won't forget our fight from earlier, but that doesn't mean I can't use him to bend the rules and force Liam to show his hand.

"Red? Is that a pet name? Why, you know what they call female dogs?" He takes a sip, and eyes sharper than knives cut through my armor, now tarnished and broken at my feet.

Waiters arrive with fresh salads and depart. Nobody touches their food. Noah is fuming beside me, his chair creaking from clenching the seat too hard. He's about to rip him to shreds when Henry holds him back, shaking his head.

He's baiting Noah by getting to me, so he has a story to run to the press with. He's trying to ruin Noah's career even more.

"Liam, didn't I see you in an ad for those new Viagra pills?" Maya stabs her salad and takes a huge bite, chewing obnoxiously, waiting for his reply.

I don't know what surprises me more, Maya being able to shut a man up with one sentence or Henry losing his composure and busting out the most hearty laugh from someone so reserved.

Gwen tugs on Liam's arm, whispering something in his ear. His face contorts in an ugly expression, lip curling in disgust. "No, we're staying here."

She's like a wounded puppy, making me regret my previous remark.

Maya pushes her empty salad bowl aside, dabbing her lip with a white napkin. "If you stay, I'll continue to roast you until there's nothing left but your ashes, Liam."

"Yes, it would be such an unfortunate thing for your parents to receive a bad review of their resort, considering they might not make it to the end of the season," he comments, amused with himself.

"Funny, I don't remember hearing about that publicly?" Maya is trying to fish for his source, keeping her face neutral.

"You'd be surprised at what money can do to get you what you need."

Maya mutters a trail of curses under her breath. I didn't realize I tried to lunge at him when Noah moved, wrapping his arms around my waist, keeping me at bay. His breath tickles my ear. "Do not give him the satisfaction."

"You may be a guest, but you're under no authority to threaten any of us. I suggest you keep your comments to yourself," Henry warns.

"And who the hell are you?"

"Someone who can send you to the hospital if you continue." His voice, a few octaves lower than normal, drives the point home that he will most likely beat the crap out of him.

Maya whistles, eyes wide.

Liam adjusts his collar, looking like he's about to break into a sweat. He finally accepts defeat and chews on his salad, Gwen following suit like an obedient fiancé.

Dinner is silent for the rest of the evening, while around us, tables are full of enthusiasm, people chattering and clinking glasses. The main course arrives, a beautiful display of steak slices over a mountain of mashed potatoes, with green beans as a side. The smell is simply mouthwatering, yet my appetite was gone the minute Liam sat down at the table.

I pick at the green beans, Noah watching every move I make like a hawk, nudging me to eat more. But how can I when the one person who is supposed to stay out of my life for good keeps coming back? It's been a year, and now he wants to show up with a new girl at the one place I call home? Claiming he didn't remember and then pulling the ultimate UNO reverse card and finding out the truth behind the event?

He came here with a mission to maintain his abuse and remind me that no matter how far I run or go in my life, he's right behind me, destroying it at every turn.

Noah leans in, speaking in a hush tone only I can hear. "Red, you have to eat. Please." His hand brushes along my thigh, using his thumb to stroke through the thin material. Goosebumps rise, a chill runs down my spine, and I have to keep my breath controlled because his touch alone does something to me.

Stabbing a couple of pieces of sauteed green beans with a shiny, gold fork, I nibble, getting a satisfied grunt of approval from Noah in my ear.

The sound alone makes something in my brain go haywire, like pouring water on an electric fence.

Dessert options are creme bruleé or a slice of chocolate ganache cake. Both desserts look absolutely delectable. I opt out, my stomach twisting in tighter knots. I need to get outside for some air, to escape, and get as far away from Liam as possible.

Making a rash decision, I text Maya, letting her know I need a quick exit and to distract the table. She gives me a thumbs up, sits up in her seat, and then faints to the floor, taking half the tablecloth with her. Dishes hit the ground, shattering into pieces, and several waiters rush over.

Henry is instantly at her side, and Noah is standing, checking to make sure she's all right. Liam mumbles something about dramatics, giving me the easiest escape of my life, dashing from the room.

I owe her big time.

I bypass the woman assisting with the coat room, hearing her complain over the sound of me shifting through the thick, winter jackets, muttering about people and their ostentatious designers and fur hoods.

Squeezed in between two dark trench coats, I find my stuff and make haste, almost tripping when I run into Jill.

She steadies me with her hands. "Hannah, are you all right?"

"Uh...yeah, yeah, I'm fine," I breathe, slipping my coat on.

"Are you sure? You look—"

One of the waiters comes flying through the double doors, shouting Jill's name.

"Whoa, what's going on?" she halts him.

"Maya...your daughter," he bends over, hands on his knees, trying to catch his breath, "... fainted."

Jill raises an eyebrow at me, knowing damn well her daughter is faking it.

"I'll explain later," I say, heading toward the door.

She steps forward, only to retreat, nodding once, and ushers the waiter back inside the dining hall.

A blast of frigid air hits me when I open the front doors wide, running out to my sanctuary.

Snow is light but falls quickly, and already my hair is coated. I run to the other side of the building, leaning against the wall. Part of the roof sticks out, giving just enough cover for me to dust off the snow before I'm buried in it.

Out here, the quiet comforts me, a peace that I've been chasing for a while. Coming here, I never thought I would be wedged between my past and hazy present. What started out as a trip to take some photos for the Gomezes turned into a steaming pile of garbage, confusing feelings, and unnecessary drama.

My breath puffs like a cloud of smoke, lips starting to chap. I inhale deeply just to exhale all my emotions, the action keeping me sane, and hopefully, stable for the rest of the night.

I'm about to head in when I hear footsteps pound down the front stairs, a voice all too familiar echoing in the quiet night. "Red! Where are you?!"

FROZEN MID-STEP, I peek around the edge of the building, catching sight of a disheveled Noah, frantically checking his surroundings. He wears only his dress clothes, hands in his hair, tugging at the strands in frustration. Henry comes shortly after, halting his pacing.

"Noah," he says calmly.

"I have to make sure she's okay." Noah is about to head toward the cabins, but is blocked by Henry.

"You need to be more careful," he warns.

"Careful? I don't give a shit about being careful anymore. Did you not see the look on her face when he made those comments? Don't ever hold me back again."

Henry has to grab Noah by the collar and force him to listen. "I get it. Why did you think I told him to shut the fuck up? Your career is on the goddamn line, and it's my job not only as your personal assistant but your friend to remind you this shit can spread like wildfire if you're not careful."

"Good. I hope the whole fucking world burns to the ground." He shoves Henry off him.

"Holy shit." Henry doesn't try to fight back. He stares at Noah in disbelief.

I'm finding myself inching closer, clearly exposing myself to eavesdropping, but it's the way Henry is looking at Noah that has me on edge.

"What? Oh, don't fucking look at me like that," he snaps.

Henry is smiling now from ear to ear, all perfectly straight teeth showing, shaking his head. "For how long?"

"None of your damn business."

Doors open, and voices drift over to where I stand, people pouring out from the main building while Noah and Henry get lost in the crowd. What does Henry mean, how long? I'll never get the chance to find out because Maya runs my way, my camera bag slung over her shoulder, catching sight of my stalker stance, and keeps us out of sight.

"Pulling that tablecloth down and watching Liam's face react to the wine splashing on him was well worth it," she laughs, proud of herself, handing me my bag.

"I wish it had been the hot meal instead, but thank you for distracting everyone." I squeeze her hand, grateful to have a best friend like her.

"Anytime! Are you okay with taking pictures of the lighting ceremony?" she asks, swaying back and forth on her feet.

I can't let what happened back there take away from what I'm about to do. Everyone is counting on me, and this is an important moment to document for the people I love. "Absolutely."

We make our way over, shuffling through the already crowded front to get the best view. Anthony and Jill are in the center, a microphone in hand, smiling at their guests. I take out my camera and throw the strap over my head, adjusting a few settings and taking a few shots, getting them both at the microphone.

Jill taps the mic to make sure it works, then hands it to her husband. "A few words, for our amazing guests. Thank you for returning, and thank you to the new ones as well. Snowy Peak has been a family business for over twenty years, and I'm truly grateful for the time we've had with this place. From making family memories to our first official Olympic snowboarder event."

I whisper in Maya's ear. "Why does it sound like he's already saying goodbye?"

She bites her lip. "I don't know. The event hasn't happened yet."

Jill now has the mic. "We wanted this season to be extra special, knowing how much our guests mean to us, for returning and telling your friends and family, Snowy Peak would be nothing without any of you." Jill has tears in her eyes, smiling at Anthony.

Maya grips my arm. "Do they not think the event is going to work?"

Anthony is handed a big, red button, a grin so wide I wonder if his face hurts. "So, tonight, we celebrate our very first tree lighting ceremony!" He smashes down the button with his gloved fingers, and the crowd holds their breath as the tree from the bottom up lights the whole space.

Its soft, white glow illuminates guests' shadows on the snow, and blue ornaments twinkle, reflecting in a shimmery light. Silver garland is strung through its branches, where an iridescent star sits on the very top. Guests cheer and clap; others take pictures with their phones. Children giggle and run around, some stare at it with wonder, and I capture it all through my lens.

More begin to gather, and I'm already looking for Noah in the crowd, a knee-jerk reaction to how strong his magnetic pull is. But who I spot him with almost rips me to shreds from the inside out.

Standing, beautiful as ever in a sleek, black winter coat, hair that reminds me of melted chocolate, is Cassy. She takes center stage, angled toward him, speaking in a hushed voice, then flips her hair back away from her shoulder, casually running her fingers through Noah's hair. He pays little attention to her because he has his eyes directly on me.

My throat goes dry as anxiety comes in waves, rippling over the stone wall I've made. He's not stopping her from touching him, nor is he engaging. He doesn't move; he only continues to hold me in place with those captivating brown eyes. Trying, unsuccessfully, to put my stupid camera back in my bag, I finally get it in, zipping it tight. I'm edging away, Maya lets go automatically, probably seeing what I see.

Why is this affecting me?

Why am I even letting it get to this point?

We made a deal, no strings attached. Granted, I told him no other women because I refuse to contract any sexually trans-mitted diseases, and vice versa, but am I that much of a fool to trust him?

Or is it something else, something deeper I refuse to admit, because even now, as I blend into the crowd, the last thing I see is Cassy pulling Noah into a hug, forcing me to run away, back to my cabin.

My stupid heels make it unbearable to run, especially through the snow. More starts to fall, heavier now, covering the shoveled path. It smells fresh, and nostalgia sits on my chest, making it ache as I climb up the stairs to my cabin. I drop my camera bag to the floor, huffing from exerting myself, then take off these stupid heels and chuck them aside. Next is my jacket, shaking off any excess snow, watching it melt into the carpet.

I'm just about to undo my dress when my cabin door swings wide open, scaring me half to death.

Standing under the threshold is Noah, snow on his long, thick eyelashes, breathing hard.

"Red." A stupid nickname he can't seem to give up, but the nickname I never want to go away.

"I don't want to talk right now, Noah, please just go." Why can't he see I'm literally drowning in my own tidal wave?

Noah gets on his knees, the door wide open, snow blowing in at his back.

I start to panic. "Noah, what are you doing?"

"Would it make you feel better if I crawl to you, Red? To show you that you're the one who holds all the power here?" Snow starts to coat some of the floor, but Noah remains kneeling, waiting for my command.

"This is ridiculous!" I throw my hands up. I'm over this and over men in general.

"If you're going to yell, yell at me. Throw all your hatred right here." He points to his chest. "Yell, Red."

The lid to my pressure cooker heart starts to rattle, the raging emotions boiling over, spilling out into the cabin, swallowing us whole. "Do you know what I want? I want to be free of these goddamn shackles I put myself in just to please others. He hurt me, and he mentally abused me, because he couldn't handle a girlfriend who wasn't perfect in his eyes anymore. I was blamed for something out of my control, something I have to constantly deal with on a daily basis, so I don't succumb any further to the pain. I just want someone to look at me for once, see everything, and accept who I am. WHY IS THAT SO FUCKING HARD?!"

I'm breathing heavily, and Noah continues to kneel on the floor. Snow is now covering parts of the furniture, even his hair. Gosh, that hair.

Somehow, he knows I have more left to say. "Are you done?"
I shake my head.

"Yell at me, Red." He's not giving me permission, he's ordering me. He knows how he recently treated me wasn't okay, and I have every right to knock him down from his pedestal.

"And *you*. You made a deal with me. Why? Why couldn't you just let me train you and call it a day? Huh? I have sworn off men since...since Liam, and then you come in and ruin everything! And when I actually try to help, you shut me out, and you think you can just turn around and try to apologize? After the shit you pulled with Coach? No, Noah, that's not how that works, not with me. Letting you in..." But I can't say it, I won't. Because how I feel about him bulldozing through my life won't matter after tonight.

My knees hit the floor before I realize I'm crying. Noah starts to crawl to me, kicking the door with his foot to keep out the cold. Snow coats his dark curls, and when he reaches me, he cups my face in the palm of his hands.

"Do you want to know why I call you Red?" he says gently.

My lips quiver, shrugging in response since my words have failed me.

"It's because it was the first thing I noticed about you. How the color is nothing I've ever seen before, and when the light catches it? You caught me." He stops a tear, swiping it away.

I smile through my tears. "So it wasn't just my award-winning personality?"

He takes his thumb and skates it across my bottom lip. "Then it was this mouth. How could I find a way to touch it, if only for a few seconds? I'd pray to any god that would listen, just for that one chance."

His words are so raw and honest, it's crossing the line we drew in the snow, and I can't let myself fall backward when I've come so far on my own.

But I'd be lying to myself if I claimed his words didn't warm my heart, even if he said them just to make me feel better.

Our foreheads connect, and I keep my eyes closed, inhaling a shaky breath and counting backward from ten so my heart can catch up.

Then I remember seeing Cassy running her hands through his hair, stealing his attention. Jealousy is an ugly thing, toying with my mind.

I've sworn off men for good, and this is part of the reason. Somehow, Noah weaseled his way in.

Noah strokes my cheeks, then kisses my head. "How are you feeling now?"

"Cassy," is all I say, watching his face change emotion.

His eyes narrow. "Whatever you saw, it's not what you think."

"I know we never agreed on any other partners, but if you're getting tired—"

He shushes me with his finger. "We made an agreement. I'll never go back on it."

Relief hits me like a bus, all at once.

"Now, are you okay?" Noah asks again.

Taking another deep breath, I open my eyes to find him staring at me. The way he looks at me is so overwhelming at times, it's enough to stop my heart. "I'm okay. I really just want to get out of this dress."

"Good."

"Good?"

He hooks the strap with his pointer finger and tugs it down my shoulder. "This dress almost sent me into cardiac arrest."

"I want it off." I stand, letting him remain on the floor, and walk over to my bedside table to remove my earrings. I check over my shoulder to find him stationary, in the same position. "Will you help me?"

Noah is suddenly behind me, fingers gently easing the zipper down. I don't move, holding my breath, waiting to see what he'll do next.

I want him to touch me, begging internally but too damn embarrassed to ask. Embarrassed because I yelled, because I brought up Cassy, because I'm tired of being judged. Why does he want to be around a girl like me who has crazy mood swings?

Maybe I am crazy. Maybe Liam is right.

No...no, Hannah, don't go back there.

Soft lips brush my shoulder, fingers trailing the straps of my dress to hang off my arms. Noah's nose glides along my skin, right up to my neck. I'm barely holding myself together, trying not to collapse from the anticipation.

I lean my head back against his chest, breathing as if I've just run a marathon, as he pushes my dress down, dropping it to my feet.

He hums in appreciation, his fingers tickling my skin, descending toward the clasp of my bra. "May I?"

One thing about Noah: he always asks permission, even when we've already established consent. He always asks.

I nod, hearing it snap off, dropping to the floor. Chest fully exposed, my nipples harden from the air and his proximity. He makes his way to my underwear, playing with the waistband, snapping it back a few times against my skin. I'm whimpering now, grinding my ass against his dress pants.

Wetness is already pooling between my legs, and I grip his thighs with my nails when he takes my underwear with two hands and rips it off my body.

Shreds of fabric are tossed across the room as I say goodbye to my favorite pair.

I hear him undress behind me, clothes dropping to the floor, my body on fire.

"You're so beautiful from behind," he muses.

I blush hard because no man has ever complimented me like him. I glance over my shoulder. "I think you might be blind. Or severely starved and seeing shit."

"You want to get on the bed for me?"

"Why?"

"Because I'm going to show you exactly what I've been fucking craving."

CHAPTER 52
HANNAH

NOAH BENDS ME OVER, softly caressing my ass cheeks, teasing just near my entrance, which is utterly soaked, dripping down my thigh.

I whimper, completely at his mercy, loving how he takes control, loving how he's so open to my body. He worships it like a prized possession, kissing my flesh so goosebumps rise along my skin.

I'm so ready, yet he takes his time like always, admiring the view.

He bites one of my cheeks, and a sensual moan leaves my lips, begging for more. He licks where his teeth are embedded in my skin, then sucks, leaving his mark. He's so close to my asshole I'm shaking, wondering if he'll take it that far.

"God, Red, you're just what I need." He inches inside, the condom creating a safe barrier. I have half a mind to remove it just so I can truly feel him.

I fist the sheets, Noah entering at such a slow, torturous pace, it releases a crazed sound from my throat.

He moans approval, starting at a slower pace, reaching for

my hair, weaving fingers through thick strands of it, using it for his own leverage.

His ruthless rhythm starts to pick up, and his balls smack against my backside, the sound causing incoherent words to leave my lips.

"Fuck, Red, I want you all the goddamn time. Like this, completely willing." Noah grunts with each thrust, then uses both hands to reach for my chest, moving me so I'm half leaning over, working twice as hard to keep pace. My nipples peak between his fingers, squeezing them while he plows into me.

He moves so his lips brush the shell of my ear, and his heavy intake of breath nearly sends me over the edge. We're in sync, since the beginning, our bodies seem to understand the high they need to reach at the same time.

Our movements become erratic the closer we climb, our climax just over the horizon, but I want it to last longer. I'm not ready to lose his touch.

Truthfully, I don't ever want to. And it's a realization I can never admit to him out loud because it'll always be a transaction.

He pulls out just enough, giving me time to turn around and push him on his back. I climb him like a feral cat, then he grabs my face and kisses me until my head spins. Blindly reaching for his cock, I shimmy myself higher and sink perfectly down, moaning with him.

I splay my hands across his chest, and he grabs my hips, squeezing my love handles while biting his lip, moving with me. I arch my back, leaning my head back to face the ceiling, letting our bodies explore each other.

I ride faster, bouncing, my breasts doing the same, and Noah cups one, squeezing, moaning. My nails dig into his chest, red lines forming from my assault.

"Noah." His name slips past my lips, breath escalating the higher I climb.

I'm seconds from coming undone when Noah moves, sitting up, and I feel more of him enter me.

"Ahh!" His mouth latches onto my nipple, sucking on it so hard I lose all control, a shattering moan falling from my lips. My walls clench around him, and Noah follows seconds after, burying his face in my chest, groaning, and it's the first time I hear my name, my real name.

"Hannah," he whimpers, resting his head on my chest.

Sweat slicks our skin while we hold each other, coming down from our high. My nails somehow clawed his back during our orgasm, because I glanced down to see red marks claiming his skin. Marks I'll give again and again to get lost in one another, blinded by pure pleasure.

Then it hits me, he always calls me Red. I can't tell if he said it by accident or...

Noah looks up, long, dark lashes revealing tired eyes. He smiles blissfully, cupping my cheek, then kisses me softly and helps me move off him, the absence of him leaving a lingering ache in my chest. A feeling I swore I would never return to again.

We clean up, taking turns using the bathroom, then return to the bed naked. I join him under the sheets, expecting distance between us, when Noah tugs me against his chest, sighing in contentment. Like, I'm his favorite person in the world to share space with.

And I want to believe it.

I really do.

CHAPTER 53

HANNAH

NOAH PLAYS WITH MY HAIR. I'm half asleep, legs draped over his, my head resting on his chest. I hear his heartbeat thump, matching the tempo of mine, the sound soothing. Our bodies are naked, blankets having fallen to the floor during our sexcapade. He hums an unfamiliar tune, running his fingers through my hair, making me sigh contentedly. Tawny skin, smooth under my touch, the smell of Noah reminds me of home, making my chest ache with nostalgia. He makes it bearable, though, and I continue to immerse myself in his touch, squeezing against his waist in joy. Something I haven't felt since Liam left. Or at all when we were together.

Our fight earlier, looking back on it now, shows me a side of Noah where he's not afraid to right the wrongs he's caused. His apology for his outburst on the half pipe to the shitty paparazzi swarming the resort, Noah's playboy demeanor starts to slip, the mask breaking off in chunks.

Hours must've passed, my body is kind of stiff from resting in the same position for so long, and I stretch, catching sight of Noah admiring my body.

"Maybe you should take a picture, it'll last longer," I tease, ruffling his dark, curly hair.

He smirks, then sees my camera bag on the coffee table, helping himself to it and playing with the lens.

Noah zooms in on my body, and it's the first time I don't hide behind the covers, showing who I truly am.

He takes shots from every angle, even hovering over my body on his knees, capturing me from the waist up. "Your skin flushes after sex, and it's my favorite shade of red."

"Yeah?" I can't help but smile widely, enjoying his compliments. "I thought it was my hair?"

"That too. And this," he squeezes lightly on my hips, taking a picture of my flesh in his hand.

He cups my cheek, forcing me to look down the barrel of the camera and snaps a picture, then looks at the shot, smiling.

I can already feel myself getting wet.

Noah takes his time, making sure his hand is touching some part of my body in the shot. Lines have blurred, and I'm sinking deeper into his snow bank, with no intention of getting myself out.

To admit it out loud that I want something more...

I wonder if he knows something has shifted between us. Or it's all in my head.

I take the camera out of his hands, ready to take his picture, when he stops me.

"Not me, Red. Only you. Promise me if you ever doubt yourself, you'll look at them, okay?" Noah comes closer, lips brushing my cheek, then my chin, hovering over me. "Promise me?"

I try to close the distance, but he waits for my answer, pulling back as he holds my gaze, knowing I'll say yes regardless.

Knowing all I want is to continue to hide out in this room, rolling in these very sheets until we're completely spent.

"Yes," I agree.

He pecks me lightly, then devours me, our bodies connected, making it easier to slip back in, engulfed in flames of desire so intense the whole room might combust, maybe even set the whole resort up in flames.

And for the first time, I enjoy the way it burns my skin. The way it keeps me alive, rather than half dead, walking among the living.

Because maybe it's the most I'll ever get from him.

From us.

SEVEN IN THE morning comes quicker these days, forcing Noah and me to break apart, withstanding the icy air to work on his mental block.

He tries different tricks, hoping it'll break the cycle of his thoughts. I want to question more about his past, desperate to know what runs through his head, but after the last time, I'm afraid to try again.

And that's where the line in the snow continues to stay, even if it blurs with time. We're not, nor will ever be, at that point of trust.

I haven't even told him about my PCOS, so he has a right to protect his peace, too.

But I lie and say it doesn't mess with me.

Noah's attempts to twist, spin, or flip are all caught mid-air, distorting his reality and landing him hard on his ass in the snow. At one point, his board gets stuck on the lip of the half-pipe, and he hangs over. We have to ask maintenance to come help us remove him from his bindings.

Luckily, we get him out, and we lie flat on our backs in the center of the course, laughing.

"Maybe you should take my place," he suggests.

"I haven't snowboarded competitively since high school, and to do it in front of a crowd with other Olympians makes me want to hurl. So, no thanks." I take some snow and chuck it at his face.

He wipes away the excess and flicks it back. "I'm gonna be washed up, hosting game shows."

"You're only twenty-six."

He catches my comment. "Oh? I don't remember telling you my age."

"You know, the Internet is quite handy these days, especially when you look up a popular figure."

"Twenty-one questions?" His eyebrows quirk up, a goofy grin to match his playful tone.

I've been given a second chance to understand the workings of his mind. "Sure."

He reaches over and tugs at my braid. "How old are you?"

"Twenty-four." But he smiles like he already knows. "Oh, so you did your own digging?"

He winks. "Maybe."

"Fine. Color?"

"Red."

I roll my eyes. "Be serious."

"I am. It's one of my favorites."

"If you're not going to play fair..."

"All right, all right." He holds up his hands, laughing the whole time.

I raise an eyebrow. "Well?"

"I wasn't kidding, it is by far my favorite color."

My eyes narrow, and I gesture for him to go next. Knowing damn well he's fucking with me.

"You? I bet I can guess." He rolls on his side, using his elbow for leverage.

"Yeah? Go for it."

"Yellow." He's so confident in his answer, I can't help but laugh.

"Was I right?" He's poking my cheeks, making me laugh harder

When I finally catch my breath, resulting in a cramped stomach from all the laughing, I respond. "Not even close."

He pouts. "Tell me."

"Brown."

The look on his face is priceless. "Brown?!"

"It's warm. It makes me feel cozy and safe."

"My god, woman, you are different."

I roll closer, lips a hair's breadth away, shared air mixing together. "Yeah, recently, it has become a color I enjoy." Not that it's the color of his eyes or anything. How goddamn pathetic am I?

It's just sex, Hannah.

Just. Sex.

I roll away, reminding myself we have to get back to business, no matter how much I enjoy his company and this fun side of him.

We have a resort to save.

"Let's go, we've fooled around long enough," I chastise.

He grabs my waist and rolls me closer. "We didn't answer twenty-one questions yet. It's my turn."

I roll my eyes. "Fine, hurry up."

He boops my nose with his finger. "Favorite place to travel?"

"In or outside the US?"

"Out."

"Never been."

His eyes widen, his mouth drops in shock. "Red, are you serious? What have you been doing? Hiding in a cave?"

"Not everyone can afford the luxury to travel, Hart." But I know where my first stop will be if I have the chance.

"And if you had to choose? Cause I bet it's some place with a sunny coast and vibrant people, where it's summer, and you're in a floral dress, taking my breath away with your sun-kissed skin." It's like he can read my mind, his mouth coming closer to my own, his hot breath fanning my face.

"Italy," I whisper back. If I don't get up now, I'm going to do something wildly inappropriate on the halfpipe. My body is sweating through all three layers of my snow gear.

I swallow, suddenly very aware of how close his body is to mine and what a little bit of friction can do if you move just right the way. "We must get back to practicing." Rolling away, I get up, only for Noah to get on his feet, pulling me into his arms by the waist.

I panic, scanning the area for early risers. "Noah, what are you doing?"

"Maybe I just want to hold you for a little bit. Maybe it'll help my fucked up brain." He nuzzles his nose in my hair, inhaling deeply like he's committing it to memory once all of this is over.

The tickle of his touch makes me squeal when he lifts me up in the air.

"Fucking the help, Hart?"

Liam's voice hits me like a freight train, knocking the wind out of my lungs.

I'm put down. Noah is already getting in his face. "This is a private lesson. Leave."

"Doesn't look so private, does it? What would the guests think? Or the press? That their favorite Olympian gave up saving a shit resort for some worn-out pussy?" His words are like a viper's whip, harsh, stinging the skin, leaving its mark, red and raised, blood seeping from the wound.

Noah swings without thought, hitting Liam right in the nose. I can hear yelling from below, sounding like Henry, trying to race up the path in time to stop whatever is about to go down.

Liam gets up and throws his own punches, grazing Noah's cheek, but Noah's quicker and tackles him to the ground.

"Noah, stop! Please!" Because if this gets out, it's all over, and I am damned if I'm the cause. "Noah! I said Stop!"

Blood stains the snow. I'm not sure if Noah's now added to the mix because they're both rolling around, the sound of fists pounding makes me want to scream.

"NOAH, STOP!" Henry is sliding through the snow, followed by all the men from the team, coming in to break up the fight.

I'm backing away, clutching my chest, trying to breathe while I watch Taylor and Mark pull them apart, Cody keeping them separated.

"What the fuck," snaps Henry.

Anthony is already halfway up the pipe when he says, "At a family resort? What the fuck were you two thinking?" I'd never heard Maya's dad swear, never seen him this puffy-faced and angry in all my years I've known him. This is a whole new level of rage. I don't want to be in the crossfire.

Liam shrugs out of Cody's hold and spits in the snow, wiping the blood from his nose with the back of his hand. "Ask pretty boy here. I'm just a paying guest."

Noah keeps quiet, a bruise beginning to form on his right cheek.

"Well?" Anthony watches Noah, taking his silence as compliance.

"You may be a guest, but this is a private practice. You're not allowed to be here," states Henry, looking ready to knock the lights out of him next.

"There's no sign stating otherwise? I thought this was a safe, family resort." His upper lip curls, staring straight at me.

I want to reach for Noah out of instinct, an anchor to the ever-changing tides, swirling in a storm coming at high speed, before I'm swept under again. A current so perilous, I wonder if I will ever come back from it this time around.

Except, I can't.

I can't go to him. I can't reach for that safety net, where it's not mine to receive to begin with. I'll float in the abyss, my fingers barely grazing the material to save me. Noah and I are simply nothing but a deal, no obligation toward one another.

He's defending me because it's the right thing to do, not because he wants to.

I hold Liam's stare, trying to appear unaffected.

Anthony forces them to stay away from each other, calling maintenance to clean up the mess. Henry orders Cody, Mark, and Taylor to clean up Noah.

Noah lingers, wiping away the blood from his upper lip as his eyes take me in; some of it has dripped down his chin, even his neck is stained. His hand flexes and tries to take a step toward me, but his teammates are coaxing him to clean up.

He pushes them off. "I got it." His voice is rough, like he's physically in pain.

"Noah," warns Mark.

Taylor takes one look at me and says, "For Hannah, Noah, please."

Noah's eyes soften, and he wipes his mouth one more time before I watch him make his way down the cluster of cabins with the guys.

Why does it hurt so much now?

But I know. I painfully know why. I have no guts to speak it into existence. Not now and most certainly not ever.

Anthony escorts Liam away, nursing his stupid face with the palm of his hand.

I haven't realized I'm crying, hands holding my chest, gasping for air. Henry comes to me, holding me in a tight embrace, hushing my agony with each comforting caress to my back.

Astonished by his empathy, I let myself fold over, Henry keeping me afloat, when he's not the person I want to keep me whole.

But I will take what help I can get for the time being.

Once I'm done, snorting back my disgusting boogers, Henry takes inventory of my well-being. "Hannah, I won't ask you what happened, because I already know. I hope you understand that Noah's reputation is important for his career, but not if it hurts you. Not if other outside sources affect you."

I blink a few times. "It's okay. I should know by now the level of his status—"

"It's not okay. You're putting your personal life in harm's way for someone who can't get over his demons. All I can say is I'm sorry, and if you want to step back, I won't blame you." His words are sincere, and it's nice to hear that someone else cares.

"Let me think about it." I won't. I can't give up on Noah and Snowy Peak. Not now, not ever.

He nods, accepting my answer. "I was also looking for you specifically. We found the person who spread the rumor. Actually, Maya did."

"Oh, really?"

"Yeah, her tactics are...questionable, but she did it." Henry half smiles, probably recalling his conversation with my best friend.

I brush myself off, collecting my snowboard. My tears have now dried, my eyes are definitely puffy, but it's a therapeutic experience I never thought I would share with Noah's publicist.

Better him than some stranger.

"She has her in a room," comments Henry, casually strolling down the hillside.

"She what?!" I exclaim, now I'm running down the hill, Henry at my heels.

"She's not handcuffed to a table, if that is what you're thinking!" he shouts behind me.

"Doesn't matter!" Maya is a *Law and Order* junky; if this is her chance to live out her fantasy, she'll do it.

And most likely get the cops called on her in the end.

Now I have to save my best friend from jail time.

Awesome.

HENRY, thankfully, is an honest man, and Maya didn't handcuff the culprit who is spreading the rumors. However, she duct taped her mouth and somehow got a hold of some rope to tie her hands to the chair.

"I leave you alone for five minutes, and you already have her bound?!" Henry is removing the restraints, muttering words under his breath.

Cassy sits in a storage room full of sacks of potatoes and jars of different labeled jelly spreads. Garlic hangs from a couple of hooks, along with other various kitchen items.

"She didn't believe my threats, so I proved her wrong." Maya crosses her arms, glowering at a mute Cassy, who in return squints her eyes, mumbling through the tape, most likely cursing at Maya.

Ella and Elise stand guard outside, both are also responsible for holding Cassy hostage.

Henry takes a piece of the duct tape and says, "This is going to hurt." He removes it in one go and Cassy shouts, about to dive after Maya when I block her path, forcing her back in her seat.

Red splotches form around her mouth. "Why the hell am I here?" she yells.

"Deflecting your own stupidity isn't cute," retorts Maya, taking a step forward to show dominance.

Henry inches with her, like he wants to protect her. "You're only making it worse."

"I don't care! She's ruining the resort!"

"Oh, I'm sorry, am I supposed to care what happens here? It's just another washed-up place that'll go under like the rest." She flips her perfectly curled hair aside, raising a sculpted eyebrow. She's taunting Maya, hoping she takes the bait.

What I don't expect is Henry pulling Maya back, already clocking when she's about to rage and tackle Cassy.

She flinches, eyes darting around the room, trying to find an escape route.

I take over, mustering whatever confidence I have left, and calmly approach her. "Did you spread the rumor about Noah?"

"Not a rumor if it's true." Her snake-like attitude rubs me the wrong way. Even up close, she's blemish-free, not a wrinkle in sight. "But why would I tell you? You're only temporary to him. He'll come right back to me."

Maya and Henry are too busy arguing about safety and not to overstep to care that she outed my and Noah's intimate encounters.

But I will be damned if she tries to ruin us and Snowy Peak.

"So, you spread private information about Noah's condition to the press because he dumped you?" She can't be serious.

Her silence is all the answer I need to confirm the truth.

I snap my fingers to get Henry and Maya's attention. "It's her. Report her to Coach Jones and Anthony. I need to find Noah."

She tries to grab my arm, but I'm too fast, creating space between us. "I don't understand why you're so goddamn special.

Did you win the prize for the biggest pig? Is that why?" she sneers.

Maya is being held back by Henry, arms swinging, ready to fight for my honor. I stare at her sour expression, the hatred in her words, the pure, hostile look in her eyes. Cassy is probably someone who's been burned more than once, her bitterness masking any common sense. She will stop at nothing to seek revenge on anyone who's wronged her in the past, including ones who never inflicted it in the first place.

I happened to catch her at a bad time. "It's okay, Maya. I'm fine."

Henry calms down her swings, and she slumps against his body. "Just one hit, please."

I give Cassy another look over, feeling sorry for her. "No, she's not worth it. Let her go."

Maya shrugs out of Henry's hold and knocks twice on the door. Ella and Elise poke their heads in, getting the okay from Maya, and escort Cassy out of the room.

A light touch of someone's hand pulls me back into focus. "Hannah, are you okay?" Maya will go up to bat for me every time, and I can't get mad at her for going to my defense.

But am I okay? Will I ever be? Yeah, maybe, when the dust settles after Snowy Peak is in good standing again.

But I know what she's really asking, and I don't have an answer for her. Not anymore.

I pat her hand in reassurance and look over to Henry. "Is Noah in his cabin?"

He nods, eyes flicking back and forth between Maya and I. "Triple knock, he'll know it's someone important."

We briefly exchange goodbyes, and Maya mumbles about alerting her parents of what transpired, while Henry scolds her for almost causing a fight. Those two bicker so much they remind me of an old married couple.

Noah's cabin is in the third cluster, number twenty-four. Snow crunches underneath my boots, shoe marks imprinting most of the path. The stairs are slippery, so I take my time, using the railing for support. All is quiet upon my arrival, even the curtains are drawn shut.

I'm happy we figured out who started such rumors, even though it's true, but I'm worried about how he'll take it. If he cares at all, because it's Cassy.

Hugging myself close, I triple knock, counting down the minutes in my head, when the door cracks a few inches open, and Noah hangs an arm along the threshold, shirtless, a body sculpted to perfection. The very same body I've been exploring for days. Gray sweats hug his hips, that faint hair line down his stomach teasing me to touch.

Hair wet, dripping down his shoulders, he allows me inside. His face is bruised, a deep, purplish hue across his cheek, a small cut on his lower lip.

"Did you get an ice pack?" I ask.

He swings the door wide open and points at the first aid kit on his bed. "I wanted to shower first."

"Right." The air is charged with something I can't identify, simmering under the surface, waiting to shake our foundation.

I start to rummage through its contents, while Noah takes a seat at the end of the bed. An ice pack is hidden at the bottom, one of those gel ones you get from the hospital. I crack it, placing it against his cheek. He sighs, eyes closed, breathing at a steady pace.

He looks so young and tired. Dark circles are faint, but I see them, sitting underneath his eyes.

"Are you in pain?" I ask.

His eyes fly open. "No."

"Good." I'm trying to make light conversation before I drop the bomb.

"Are you?" he asks in return, keeping his eyes on me, a slight brush of his knuckles along my arm makes me shiver.

I shrug, moving the ice pack a little closer to his mouth. "I guess."

His hand covers mine, his brown eyes soften. "Red, I didn't mean—"

"Cassy was the one who spread the information to the press," I interrupt.

He freezes just for a second, eyes blinking, but he seems to recover quickly and says, "Not surprised. How did you find out?"

I move the ice pack up, closer to his eye. He hisses from the pressure. "Maya, she made Ella and Elise stand guard."

Up close, I notice flecks of gold in his brown eyes, a small scar above his left eyebrow. Lips pink, his bottom one is a little swollen. "You need to be more careful, Noah."

He clenches his fist, hearing some of his bones crack. "He insulted you. I couldn't let him get away with that."

Somehow, I manage to stand in between his legs, ice pack numbing my hand. "Liam isn't worth it. Hurting him isn't worth it."

"It was worth it. I'd do it again. I'll shed more blood if that means he can't come close to you ever again."

I sigh. "I can take care of myself."

"I'm fully aware you can kick someone's ass if you want to."

"Then why bother?" Why defend me like...like we're something more? We can never be something more.

"I don't tolerate fucks like him, running his mouth to belittle women. He's an insecure piece of shit."

"And my ex." Might as well remind him of those open cans of worms.

Noah touches my hand that holds the ice pack and removes it from his face. "How long were you with him?"

"Does it matter? It's over."

"How long?" He looks...hurt. No, no, I'm imagining it.

"A year. " Where is this conversation going? What is he gaining from this information?

He gets up, forcing me into an embrace, the ice pack dropping out of my hand. It's unexpected, something we've never done—a simple hug, where he rests his chin on my head, rubbing my back. I feel so small in his arms, fragile, like glass, suspended in mid-air, only to be shattered into tiny pieces, almost impossible to put back together again.

I'll never return to whole, there will always be pieces of me, too jagged and small to refit together again.

Yet Noah's hug comes a close second to mending some of the broken pieces I've left sitting for too long. His skin is warm, soft, and comforting, a blanket of my favorite kind.

I breathe in his familiar scent, basking in whatever time I have left with him.

"As friends, I refuse to let him harass you."

I look up, catching him staring down at me. "Friends?"

"Are we not?"

Friends. It sounds nice. Sounds less complicated. Sounds... definite.

Is that what I want? Just friends?

Things are complex as it is.

I step out of his embrace, keeping a safe distance, away from any temptations. "I think tonight, we should keep our distance until things wind down."

He rubs the back of his neck. "If that's what you need."

But is it what I want? Is it what he wants?

He's so willing to follow my lead, never batting an eye or thinking twice.

"Is that what you want, too?" I'm way too clammy, my

hands slick with sweat, anxious to hear his answer. It shouldn't matter, because there's nothing more that can come of this.

Noah grabs my face, his palms rough from old callouses, and strokes my cheeks. He leans forward, his lips graze my nose, trailing up to my forward where he kisses the center, breathing deeply. A single kiss to the forehead is enough to solidify what my heart has been trying to tell me this whole time.

He pulls back. "Red, go rest, okay?" It's an order, one I've taken too many times before. Noah's hands slowly leave my face, brown eyes melancholy mirror my own emotions.

He's kicking me out, and it strikes a chord. Embarrassed, I start to back away, tripping on my own two feet, hitting the door with my back. "Shit, sorry."

"Are you okay?" Noah takes a step forward, ready to steady my body.

I wave him off. "Yes, fine." Why am I running out the door? Why can't I stop running until I'm safely in my cabin?

I sink to the floor, trying to stop my heart from bursting through my chest. Closing my eyes, I rock back and forth, keeping a rhythm to slow down my racing thoughts.

But it's no use, I'm spiraling, faster and faster to rock bottom, crashing on jagged rocks, tearing my skin, breaking my bones. All old wounds reopen, spewing dark times and harsh conversations—belittlement of something I can't control. Cornered like prey, whipped with words so degrading I'm left with internal scars, never fully healed, never seen but always under the surface. Taunting me, biding its time until I slip up, let someone in again, only for the cycle to potentially repeat.

Head barely above water, I crawl to my bed, hiding under the covers, hoping the extra barrier will protect me, even though the battle is all in my head.

CHAPTER 56
HANNAH

ONE YEAR AGO...

I slip the black dress over my head, feeling it snugly around my hips. It used to fit. It used to look slim and elegant, now it's a mess of rolls from my body because it prefers to keep the weight and then some.

Disgusted, I'm about to take it off when Liam walks in.

"Please tell me you're not wearing that," he remarks, slipping into the closet, swiping through jackets.

"No, I'm not." Already hit by my own low self-esteem, I try to remove the dress, forcing it over my breasts. I hear a tear, find a rip, and toss the stupid dress aside.

Liam comes up behind, looking at us through the floor-length mirror. "What do you think of this jacket?"

He wears a black blazer, shiny gold cufflinks reflecting in the light. It fits him perfectly.

"Very handsome," I comment, hugging my torso.

He nods. "Go with that blue dress. My parents will be at this event, so we must dress modestly." He returns to the closet, choosing a pair of shoes.

It's my go-to safety dress whenever previous outfits struggle to fit, and I slip it on. Plain, an ugly shade of blue, and modest, as Liam said. Because Mommy and daddy are going, and I must make sure I look like a typical housewife.

But for Liam, I'll do it. Because for Liam, I'll do anything.

He's only looking out for me because he loves me.

Picking my black flats, I'm about to put my hair up when Liam stops me. "Keep it down." I let my hair fall, knowing he wants to keep my neck hidden because of the weight I gained so nobody points out my flaws. Very considerate. Dabbing on some concealer, light eye shadow, and blush, Liam hands me a clear mascara tube. "Don't want you showing up looking too draggy."

"It's just mascara," I remind him.

"Yeah? Black makes it look trashy. My girl isn't trashy."

It's the tipping point, because now I can't wear my favorite mascara. I'm rolling it back to him. "I'll use my own, thanks."

"I was just suggesting, no need to be rude about it." He's defensive because it's my fault.

"I wasn't. I just want to use my own."

"It doesn't look good on you."

"So?"

"Hannah, maybe you should go rest before we leave. And when you wake, make sure the attitude is gone." He slams our bedroom door shut, hard, leaving me staring at the girl in the mirror, who looks depressed and worn out. Bags under her eyes, hair lifeless at the ends, complexion rough and bumpy. Her body betrays her, making it vulnerable to anyone, even to her boyfriend.

That girl is me.

WIND RATTLES THE CABIN WINDOWS, howling from the snowstorm outside. I awake before sunrise, tossing and turning in bed, struggling to fall back to sleep. In tangled sheets, I feel claustrophobic, kicking them completely off so I can breathe. Sweat coats my neck, seeping into my hair.

I stare at the ceiling, debating on staying up until I have no choice but to move and get ready, knowing it'll kill me later. I can blame it on the wind, but I know what haunts my mind.

The text I received before dinner yesterday from my doctor, explaining we need to go over the recent test results of my blood work had landed a blow. Her wording said it all, and I refuse to look at anything until I see her.

But I know. I know instantly that her message means issues ahead.

My PCOS is a constant reminder of how careful I need to be with how I live and what I consume. Right now, it messes with my sleep, it contorts my brain with thick fog, where I can't remember some things, and it brings me closer to the diabetic line, like my mother.

I send her a text, knowing she'll get it sometime in the morning, letting her know I'm okay and I miss her. Still trying to convince her to come down for Christmas, though she keeps dodging the question like it's an Olympic sport.

Go figure.

Then there's Noah.

He's complicated, charming, and frustratingly complicated. It's his attitude toward my body and my imperfections that baffles me. For someone so beautiful in every shape and form, my body is the last thing he's turned off by. Rather, he worships it like he's going to church.

I won't lie, sometimes I miss his sarcastic remarks, and I find a thrill in the tryst we share, even at the beginning.

I wonder if he's awake.

Unplugging my phone off the nightstand, I scroll through our open text thread. We barely text as it is, but I can't sleep, and I wonder if the storm has woken him.

> Me: Hey.

Seconds tick by, then minutes, before my phone chimes. I smile.

> Noah: Surprised to find you awake, Red.

Propping all the pillows behind my back, I send a text back.

> Me: It was a shot in the dark to see if you were awake.

> Noah: I rarely sleep.

Huh, interesting.

> Me: Same. I guess we have that in common.

> Noah: Are you alone?

What an odd question.

> Me: Yes?

Is he worried I'm with someone else? No. No, that's impossible. Noah has flings, and after the travesty of his last relationship, I understand why. There's no way he's thinking that someone like me would have another man in bed. Having two men at the same time... I can barely get one to stay.

> Noah: Just curious. Did you need something?

> Me: Bold of you to assume I need something.

> Noah: I can hear the attitude in your voice from here.

> Me: I hope it slapped you in the face.

> Noah: And what if I like it?

Heat hits my cheeks as his words take effect making my skin flush. Okay, this isn't how I thought the conversation was going to go. Maybe some banter and witty comebacks, but this? I've never done this before. Never...sexted. Is that what we're doing? I'm most likely reading into it, as texts can show zero emotion. I mean, we've seen each other naked, had shower sex for crying out loud, and somehow texting Noah makes it feel more...intimate.

But I have nothing to lose.

> Me: Do you now?

> Noah: Yes, Red. Any mark you leave, I'll happily wear like a badge of honor.

I take a sharp breath, my chest aching in a weird way. It's not the normal despair, where someone gives you bad news or a passing of a relative, no, it's the sense of someone teetering on a line of more than just want on a surface level. And Noah is reaching over that fine line in the snow.

Defensive walls start to take shape, because if he breaches it, I can't handle the repercussions of the downfall that will surely follow after.

Me: That's a bit dramatic.

Noah: Just stating the truth. I see no complaints on your end with the hickies I leave on that pretty skin of yours.

Me: Yes, well, I don't declare my love for them like a poet.

Noah: Is that so wrong? To express what one does to another? How deeply you affect me.

This isn't the Noah I met a couple of weeks ago. He's different, bolder, and his words are like honey, sweet, tangling like a web inside my head.

My hands start to shake, anxiety overtakes my whole nervous system. His confession catches me off guard and I send out my best response to deflect.

Me: It's just sex, Noah.

But I never hear from him again for the rest of the night.

When the early morning hour creeps in, the sun peeking through the blinds, my alarm blares, forcing me to move and get ready.

I check in between my shower and brushing my teeth, even when I call an Uber.

Standing outside the entrance of Snowy Peak, I look over my shoulder, trying to see if I'll catch him strolling along the snow-covered path, the storm leaving behind frosted trees.

But it's radio silence the whole drive back to my apartment in Boston, resting my forehead on the icy window, watching the outside world blur.

It's not just sex. It never was.

IT'S JUST SEX, *Noah.* Her text replays over and over in my head, reminding me where she stands, where I should stand with her.

But it's not just sex anymore, it's more, and whether I admit it or not, it's happening regardless of whatever self-control I have left.

She has taken all of it at this point and set it on fire, and now I only see her through the smoke and ash.

And she cuts me down with one sentence.

Sleep never came, and I've been up ever since, staring at my ceiling, while the wind whistles outside, ignoring my stomach protesting for not eating. I kick off all the blankets, getting overheated, and my legs are restless, too. Fuck, I'm an asshole leaving her on read, but what the hell do you say to a woman who has no idea you've fallen for her?

I'm up before I can talk myself out of going over to her cabin, dressing hastily, almost tripping as I try to shove my legs into my pants. I brush my teeth, apply deodorant, and some cologne.

Because if I don't go now and lay it all out, then I'll regret never being honest with her and myself.

I swing open the door to find Henry's fist in mid air, his eyes squint as he takes me in. "Where are you going?" As the words leave his mouth, a look of recognition crosses his face, and he says, "So I was right?"

"Not now." He's lucky I don't have time for this.

"I'm not here to say told you so, although it would be nice to gloat I was right."

"Then what the fuck do you want then?" My patience is wearing thin, and Henry has five seconds to tell me why he's holding me before I kick him in the dick.

"We handled the rumors, and Liam was removed from the resort. They found camera footage of him stalking you and Hannah the other day on the halfpipe."

My knuckles crack, trying my best to hold in my rage and not punch something. "That slimy son of a bitch!"

"Yeah, I know. I guess he has a secret record not even Hannah knew about. I ran into Maya, and she's going to let her know."

"When did you tell her this?"

"Who? Maya? About ten minutes ago."

I push past him, hearing him grumble, "maniac."

I'm half jogging, half running up to her cabin, ignoring weird stares from other guests, skidding right to the front steps. I'm about to knock when Maya's voice halts me in place.

"She's not there."

I turn, catching sight of her small frame stuffed comfortably in a green puffer jacket, cheeks red and eyes glassy from windchill.

"Is she at the dining hall?" I question, already barreling down the stairs, ready to run again.

"No, she left the resort. Why are you here, Noah?" Maya

crosses her arms, completely within her right to question a man who's acting frantic, trying to find their best friend.

It's the way she poses the question and how she's grilling me that makes it easier to decide to tell the truth. "You know why I'm looking for her, Maya, and if I have to spell it out to you, then I'm wasting more time."

She bites her bottom lip, most likely debating whether to share information. "Is it for real?"

I'm walking up to her now, placing my hands on her shoulders, forcing her to look at me. "Please, Maya, tell me where Hannah went?"

THE NURSE NAMED Amy checks my weight, marking down the results on a clipboard. I'm afraid to look at the scale, afraid to see my lapse in keeping up with my health, and she accuses me with a bony finger. Yelling at me for not sticking with my regimen and failing.

Instead, she smiles and escorts me to room three, going over my vitals, right down to the stupid blood pressure cuff that makes my arm feel like it's going to explode.

Amy gives me a hospital gown and draws back the curtain, letting me know that Dr. Ghoshel will be in shortly.

I strip down to my underwear, leaving the back exposed, and sit on the crinkly paper, swinging my legs back and forth.

My pulse quickens while I wait, letting my thoughts run rampant, my phone hiding under my pile of clothes on the corner chair—the entire ride into the city, not a single response from Noah. I smack my forehead, realizing I never canceled our practice, and I'm about to get my phone, when a light knock stills my movements.

Dr. Ghoshel peeks her head around the curtain, giving me a kind smile. "Hello, Hannah, how are you?"

"Not bad, a little tired," I confess. Okay, more than tired. I'm fucking exhausted.

She takes a seat at the computer and types away, while I give her the rundown of how I'm feeling. When I tell her my period is late, she clicks away on the mouse, most likely finding my recent test results.

She states that my blood pressure is good; however, my weight has fluctuated, putting me closer to the line of pre-diabetic.

It's my test results that raise the most concern. My A1C levels went back up, putting me back at a 6.1, which explains the delay with my menstrual cycle.

My heart sinks in my chest, and I scold myself for going so off script and getting distracted by other things and people—one singular person.

"It would be ideal to put you back on metformin," she says, touching my breasts as I lie there, making sure no unusual lumps have taken form.

Tears sting the backs of my eyes, threatening to fall. How goddamn embarrassing.

She can sense my inner turmoil and continues the full body examination in silence, having me bend over to check my spine, right down to listening to my heart.

Dr. Ghoshel rolls her chair and sits in front of my legs. "Hannah... It's okay to feel discouraged."

Jesus, Doc, must you call me out like that? Tears spill, landing on my exposed knees. "I don't want the medicine."

"Although I can advise you, I can't force you. Hannah, I'm going to recommend a nutritionist, okay? I think if you want to continue on your own, it would be a good idea to get one, at least to steer you toward the right foods to help combat PCOS. Sugar is your biggest enemy, and the nutritionist can help with alternatives."

"They're not going to force me to eat like a rabbit, right?" I hiccup in between tears.

She shakes her head and laughs. "No, Hannah. They'll help with a food plan that better suits your individual needs."

Dr. Ghoshel puts in a referral to a nutritionist; luckily, she's in the same building. I get dressed, then check my messages, finding them stale, and worry that Noah took my "just sex" comment to heart.

I can lie all I want, but it stings, it really does, knowing that I might've hurt his feelings. Heck, I'm pretty sure I hurt my own. Noah is unexpectedly someone I want to lean on, but my walls won't allow it. The higher it's built, the harder it is to climb and take refuge in my heart.

I can't bear another mistake or another heartbreak.

And I think Noah is capable of being both.

I EXIT my doctor's office, trying to wipe away my tears, when I notice Noah sitting in the waiting room, elbows on his knees, legs bouncing.

He takes a good look at me and shoots up from his spot, rushing over. "Red, what's going on?"

Why is he here?! "How did you know I'd be here?" Great, the last place I expect to see anyone, let alone him, has to be at my yearly checkup with my endocrinologist.

"Maya, and before you start shouting, I forced her to tell me."

I dry my face with my jacket sleeve and push past him, ignoring the weird stares the others in the waiting room give me. "Well, it was a wasted effort. I don't need you here, so just go, Noah."

Although my heart is screaming for him to stay, seeing me like this is too much.

He tries to catch my arm, but I dodge his touch, keeping my pace, trying to find the nearest elevator to the parking garage. I know ignoring him is a wasted effort. His footsteps continue to shadow mine, and now we walk in silence, my anger simmering deep, my tears now dry, and my eyes sore.

Being angry is stupid, lashing out is stupid, and yet I can't help it.

I find an elevator and try to sneak in with a group, only for Noah to cut off an old couple, taking the last spot. I drill my eyes into him from behind, watching his back as someone asked him to push the button for ground level.

Noah peeks over his shoulder, his left eye drilling into me. I look away, picking at my nails. We reach the parking garage, the elevator doors open, and we all pile out like sardines. I make haste, weaving through the bodies of strangers, pulling out my parking pass to locate my car.

Noah has no issue matching my frantic stride, trying to get away from him. "I'm just going to force myself in your car."

"If you do, I'll cut your dick off," I threaten.

He chuckles behind me. "Red, we both know cutting my dick off ruins the real fun."

I groan, tucking my jacket closer to my body. "Go away."

Almost running now at this point, I spot my silver Hyundai and dash through the other cars, loud honks sounding in protest from almost getting hit, Noah right on my tail. Clicking the unlock button, I try my hardest to jump inside the driver's seat, only to find Noah already sitting comfortably in the passenger side.

Son of a bitch is too fast.

I bang my hands on the steering wheel. "Please, just leave me alone, Noah."

He stops my hands from hitting the wheel. "Red, stop, you're hurting yourself."

My heart pounds erratically in my chest, the sound pulsating in my eardrums. We stare at each other for a while, and slowly, he removes his hold from my wrists, testing to see if I'll throw hands again at the steering wheel.

He reaches forward, cupping my cheek. "Hey, it's just us, nobody else."

"Noah... I'm...not perfect." Tears sting the back of my eyes, threatening to spill over. Because no matter how much I want Noah, the odds of him accepting me for who I am, right down to my physical health, will always come between us.

Nobody wants tainted goods.

"I looked up your doctor's office. Endocrinologists specialize in hormones, thyroid issues, diabetes... PCOS." He now has both hands cupping my face, forcing me to fully look at him. "Is that why you hesitate when you take off your clothes? Why do you make comments about not feeling good enough?"

I want to turn away, to disappear forever. It's all too raw and real, laying my insecurities all out on the table, or in this case, my car. Apparently, therapy is not the only place for it to happen. "I can't..."

"Can I tell you a story then?" Noah asks, stroking my cheek with his calloused thumb.

His eyes, the color of amber with flecks of gold, warm my chest. Lips lush and pink, slightly parted as his breath mixes with mine.

He's so beautiful. "Yes," I shakily whisper.

"It's about this arrogant son of a bitch who thought he had it all. The girl, the career, everything. He felt so secure and loved that nothing could touch him. At the height of his career, he trusted someone he thought was his anchor, who could ground him and keep his head on straight. It turns out she loved someone else more." He pauses, gauging my reaction, continuing to stroke my cheeks.

"Go on," I whisper.

"When it's his turn to complete the halfpipe, all he could

picture was the girl he thought he knew with the best friend he thought he could trust. He started to lash out and tried to find comfort with other bodies rather than face his own demons. It changed him in ways he wasn't sure he could come back from."

"At the end of the tour, he is told he must help a group of strangers save a family-owned ski resort. Instead, he bitched and complained because he wanted to go home, but he goes anyway so he wouldn't let anyone down. What he wasn't counting on was the fiery red head who would put him in his place, challenge him, and make him see he's worth more than what his past tried to make him think, or at least he believes."

My tears spill down my face, and Noah wipes them away. I swallow, the sound echoing in the silence. This is too much, too much inside my small car. Space, I need space, if only to breathe for some time so I can think straight.

"Noah...please...not yet," I beg, closing my eyes as tears escape from under my lids, my eyelashes catching some of the drops, soaking in the salty tears.

"Don't cry," he whispers.

"It's too much." My words are barely audible, my bottom lip trembles.

"Please wait to drive until you're able to focus, Red. I'll be devastated if something were to happen to you." Noah's warm lips press gently against my forehead, then his hands slip from my face.

The passenger door opens and shuts in a swift motion, and I'm afraid to open my eyes to see him walking away. I cover my face and cry, my shoulders shaking with the rough inhales of every sob that pours from my body.

Eventually, I control myself enough to focus solely on the road. The traffic leaving is brutal, forcing me to remain in this tight space. I refuse to put on music or even call someone to block out the silence, instead drowning in it and accepting my fate.

Home is where I have to parallel park too many times to fit into a tight parking space, cursing my shitty landlords who have oversized trucks.

Heaviness weighs on my chest as I unlock my door, finding my space exactly as I left it weeks ago, how everything remains the same, untouched, yet a reminder of what can change if you let someone new in. Someone you least expect and has you awake at odd hours of the night, wondering if they feel the same.

I slink over to my bedroom, landing face-first on my messy bed, my eyes sore from crying. Maybe if I just lie here, all my problems will go away, and maybe Noah will forget about me.

About...us.

CHAPTER 61

HANNAH

ONE YEAR AGO...

"Are we not going to talk about this?" snipes Liam.

I roll my temples with my pointer fingers. "We already have, those are my options. Until I can get it managed, I don't think we can completely weigh out the bad."

Liam throws a mug in the sink, and the sound of porcelain cracking makes me jump. "Hannah, this is serious. This dictates our future."

Our future, never just mine but ours.

I get up from my place at the table, taking my paper plate to the trash. "I'm aware of how dire the circumstances are, but I'm still young, we're still young. I can reverse it."

Liam leans over the sink, shoulders tense, sighing like I just told him his favorite show got canceled. "Our future is planned, and to have it taken away so easily..." he shakes his head, almost disgusted by the thought that I've become tainted.

Because in the end, it's my fault. He can recover, but I won't. I probably never will.

"You think I wanted this?" I say, anger rising to the surface.

He looks over his shoulder, eyeing me like I just insulted him. "I sure as hell didn't."

"So, it's all my fault for how genetics screwed me over?"

"It's a hell of a good excuse not to try and be healthy."

"Are you serious?"

"You've been lazy, Hannah, more than usual. Yeah, you packed on a few pounds, and I was hoping it would pass, but now this? Don't you care how this affects me, too? My girlfriend threw herself away, looking less put together and seeming more comfortable with her bigger size. Now you're throwing this diagnosis at me, because you chose to let yourself go?"

Liam's words are a cold, hard slap to my face. I grab my keys off the hook by the door. "I'm going out, don't look for me."

"Where the fuck are you—."

I slam the front door before he finishes his sentence, running down the steps from the third-floor apartment we share. Skirting around the corner, I stop, clutching my chest, trying to breathe through the pain. His words slice through my newly healed wounds, forcing them to reopen and bare all to witness the mess it makes. Tears stream silently down my face as I try to control myself before the other tenants start to notice my panic attack.

He loves me...he cares...he's only lashing out because he's upset too...

But why do I feel like he's blaming me?

I SLUMP against the kitchen counter, my body aches, and my shoulders are tense. Everything hits me at once, a heavy weight against my chest, making it hard to breathe. Water, I need water, hoping it helps release some of the pressure or makes me feel better.

With shaky hands, I pour myself a glass, gulping it down like I've been parched for days. Refilling it, I take another big gulp and almost choke, resulting in a coughing fit. Stupid.

I gathered my overflowing mail before coming inside and went through it, coming across the Boston Globe. The front page is a picture of me, bewildered, with Noah standing behind me, trying to get my attention. I stare at it for I don't know how long, examining every detail, right down to my body, how exposed I am. All my imperfections on display for everyone to see and mock. To ridicule. Because their caption, "Noah Hart finds a new type," makes me think whoever wrote the article is looking for a big reaction.

And they got it.

Crying is a common emotion lately, stirring up unwanted past mistakes, past abuse, past hardships.

"Hannah," says Maya outside my door.

Shit, shit, shit. Fuck.

I love her, but I can't face my best friend. She'll demand I tell her what's really going on.

"Hannah, open up; I know you're in there. I already called your mother to confirm you're not at her place," she says.

I crumple the newspaper in both hands, trying to hide any evidence, and toss it into the trash. Wiping my tears on my sweatshirt sleeve, I attempt to hide the evidence of my snotty cries, then unlock the deadbolt and walk away, hearing her turn the knob to let herself in.

"Hannah," she says again, following me into the living room, the door shutting roughly behind her. I grab a blanket and tuck myself in the corner of the couch, wrapping myself up like a human burrito. "What, Maya?"

She tosses her keys on the coffee table and joins me. "Noah came back alone."

"Obviously," I scoff. I pull the blanket up to my chin, avoiding her chilling stare. When she gets serious, I expect her to rip me a new one, but she usually covers my wounds with a Band-Aid after. "Thanks for telling him where I was."

"The man is very persistent when it comes to you."

"But you're my best friend, and I trusted you not to say anything."

"Another person involved to help you out of whatever funk you're in is fine by me."

My tough love bestie.

"It was also the fact that Henry tracked me down to tell me that Noah hasn't been doing well. The man has been sulking since he got back, hiding in his cabin."

I barely look her way, playing with a loose string on the stitch of the blanket. "I don't owe him anything."

Maya grips the blanket and pulls, tossing it on the floor. "Hannah Rose St. Pierre. What is going on with you?"

I cover my face with shaky hands, trying to breathe.

"Hannah, what happened?"

"It's not something I want to talk about."

"You refuse to bring up how you and Liam broke up, and every time I try to ask you about it, you shut down. I'm trying to be a good friend and give you space, but it's been a year! What did that bastard do to you?"

I crumble to the floor, broken, exhausted, emotional. Maya follows me and wraps her arms around my shoulders, squeezing. "What happened, Hannah?"

But words have left me, except for my cries, devastatingly broken. It's like I can't breathe, I'm swallowing too much emotion, and I start to drown. Every box I chained, locked, and threw away its key is now wide open for everyone to gawk at and judge. Maya holds me as I pour out my entire heart, as it twists and tightens from the pressure I kept down for so long.

How do I tell my best friend that my ex had mentally and emotionally abused and controlled me during our year together? How do I tell her that I needed therapy and coping mechanisms to keep myself in check? How do I tell Maya that if she, Noah, and Henry were not there to sit at the same table, I might've collapsed from fear?

The smallest man who ever lived returns, only to shove his engagement in my face.

Because I ruined everything.

CHAPTER 63
HANNAH

ONE YEAR AGO...

All of Liam's suitcases are taking up space in the hallway. I watch from my seat in the kitchen, him running around, looking for anything that belongs to him, right down to the silverware. He's quiet with a permanent scowl for an expression, eyes narrowed whenever our eyes meet. A face I once found handsome is now an ugly reminder of what we shared.

But I'm kicking him out.

Snow falls heavily outside, predicted to drop at least a foot. So, it's only fitting that I make Liam leave during the height of it.

Call it justice, I call it revenge.

I hit my breaking point because I was secretly seeing a therapist, knowing Liam's actions in our relationship were not normal.

It took some time, but I started to see through his facade, once a shiny new toy, now tarnished and rusted. Never the same again.

Arms crossed, I sit comfortably in my chair, which is part of my dining room set; everything down to our bed and living room set all belong to me. Even this apartment, which is in my name, is mine to kick out whoever I damn well please.

He dumps whatever crap he finds in a big, plastic trash bag, throwing it over his shoulder. "Happy, Hannah? Are you happy that I'm getting kicked out in the middle of a snowstorm?"

"I'll be even happier once you stop talking and leave," I snipe, using all my coping skills to create a nice shield from his harsh words.

His hands crinkle the trash bag even more. "You were a waste of time."

Smiling is one perk of keeping your shields up, and in return, it pisses off your abuser. "Right back at ya."

His brother Toby comes and helps him remove his belongings from my hallway, shutting the door so he can't get a final word in.

Instant relief hits, my smile fading to a half frown, eyes and body exhausted from the emotional toll Liam took out on me.

Deciding on a nap, I make my way to my scarce bedroom, walls bare, the top of the dresser empty, even our shared closet, where most of his stuff took up space, is practically empty.

A note is left, taped to the closet door, my name in messy writing. I bring it over to the sink, pull out a lighter from a nearby drawer, and burn it, watching it turn to ash.

Like everything we've ever had, burnt to absolutely nothing.

I tell Maya everything, right down to my therapy sessions, to his degrading comments about my body, trying to hide my imperfections from friends and family, how we stopped having sex after six months into dating, and about his controlling habits of what I put in my body.

It's taken time for me to heal, but seeing him again at the resort with his fiancée and trying to provoke Noah...

"I will kill him," she threatens.

"Is it worth it? He's already trying to sabotage the event. He'll just amp up his antics more." I stir honey into my tea.

"But he got away with it. I don't like it," she protests, blowing on her own tea.

I shrug. "We have to trust Coach Jones and his team of snowboarders to pull this off. Otherwise, our efforts will have been for nothing." I checked a few of the ads I made, and found that many people have been clicking through to Snowy Peak's main website. "Did your parents update on ticket sales?" Crap, I never updated the website with the tree lighting ceremony photos.

"No. I'm sure they will when we...I get back." She looks at me over her steamy mug. "Hannah, I think you should go back. Liam was removed from our resort. They found camera footage of him stalking you and Noah just before the fight."

"Are you serious?" Anxiety prickles my neck.

"Local authorities also discovered he has a record for vandalism. My mom told them she wasn't comfortable with him there, so they removed him."

"What about his fiancée?"

"We didn't kick her out, so who knows? Plus, the sneaky bastard switched the seating that night at dinner. I asked my mom to see the seating chart. He's been trying to sabotage it all since his arrival."

I can't imagine what else he would've got away with if Maya's parents didn't step in. "Did you find out who he paid to get the information about the inn going under?"

She shakes her head. "No, and that's the freaky part. I thought about Cassy, but she's been MIA. I'm thinking she checked out already."

We sip out of our hot mugs, my mind wandering to dark curly hair and haunting brown eyes. I thought about seeing Noah again, and my promise to Jill and Anthony. I'll admit, I'm mentally exhausted, not at all ready to face anybody.

"He hasn't been practicing since you left," she mentions.

"And how do you know that?" Then it hits me. "Are you texting someone?"

She puts her mug down. "Just Henry."

"Ahh, I see. And do you care to tell me why you were so mad at him that night at dinner?"

"Would you believe me if I told you I don't remember?"

"Somehow I don't buy it."

"Listen, whatever you may think, you're wrong." She fiddles with her hair, a tell-tale sign she's hiding something. I'll ask her later about it or wait until she's ready. "But Henry said he barely leaves his cabin. Has he tried texting you?"

My phone has been dead for a couple of days, and I can't locate my spare charger. "It's dead, and I left my charger back at Snowy Peak."

"You can borrow mine." She's about to reach for her bag, but I stop her.

"No, I like having some peace." And not checking social media and seeing any negative comments about my body from the article.

Space, however...space from Noah, I'm not ready for.

MAYA STAYS for a few extra days, most of the time we're on the couch yapping away or completing one of the many puzzles from my collection. Time is fleeting, and Maya tries to convince me to come back, but I need some time. Christmas is in two days, and I've decided to spend it with my mom. Thankfully, she respects my choice and doesn't bring it up again, but I can tell she wants to press the issue further.

We're sitting on my living room couch, the faded brown leather seats making it easier for me to pick at, making more of a mess, but also satisfying my anxiety. Maya takes it upon herself to serve me some hot chocolate, and our mugs sit on dog coasters she got me a couple of years back. She suggests we watch TV, surf countless channels, and end up on a Christmas baking show.

"Oh, sweet, they're making Christmas cookies!" Maya exclaims, reaching for her hot chocolate.

I grab mine as well, blowing on it until it's cool enough to take a sip. "I like it when they do the icing."

"Same! It's so satisfying to watch." She takes a big sip,

sighing in contentment. "Gosh, I really outdid myself with the hot chocolate."

I follow suit, the warmth coating my throat, the sweet, decadent chocolate exploding on my tongue, bringing me back to early Christmas days with my parents, of colorful lights and tilted snowmen in our front yard. "This is definitely your best batch."

She smiles big, scooting closer to me. I throw my blanket over us and settle in, my hands nice and toasty from my hot chocolate mug.

We watch a few episodes of them battling it out with their holiday cookies; some are incredible to watch as we rate our favorites and predict who will win.

Maya's phone rings, she reaches for it, and Henry's name flashes on her screen. She ignores it and tucks it on the side of the couch.

I cock an eyebrow. "You guys call each other?"

Her face turns a bright shade of red. "No, actually, this will be the first time." Maya avoids my eyes by staring intensely at the TV.

Huh, interesting. "Are you going to answer him?"

"Now why would I do that?" She continues to avoid my stare, drinking the last of her hot chocolate. "It's just him asking where you are, honestly."

"Because of Noah?" My heart twists, picturing him sulking in his room. I never wanted to push him away; it's just easier for me to deal with my issues and not rope someone else into all my problems.

He has enough on his plate...

I'm supposed to help him, help Maya and her family to get the two-time gold medal Olympian back on his feet to save my best friend's family ski resort, and I'm letting them both down.

I'm a shit person and a friend. "Maya, I'm so sorry." My eyes well with tears because I'm constantly disappointing someone.

"Whoa, no. This is not your fault." She slams her mug down, removing mine, then takes my hands in hers, looking at me with determination. "My family's resort and its financial issues are not your problem, okay? You've done all you can by just being here for us."

Tears are now spilling down my cheeks, my bottom lip quivering. I've been strong for so long, and my exterior has started to crack from all the pressure, along with my feelings for Noah.

Because deep down, I've fallen for him, and I still can't let him in. "I don't like letting people I care about down, that's all." I'm doing it right now to avoid going back, like a coward.

Maya pulls me into a hug, rubbing my back. "You could never let us down, Hannah. Never."

She lets me cry for however long I need, stroking my hair while I soak her purple sweater with my overflowing tears. It's a relief to let it all out, with the comfort of your best friend.

When I finally calm down, Maya lets me lie on her lap while she plays with my hair. "Can I tell you something?"

"Sure," I say, half asleep.

"All those dates I've been on...never led to anything. Not even a kiss, and not only that..." she pauses, taking a deep breath before she continues. "I'm still a virgin."

Even half asleep, my eyes bugle, but I don't dare move, knowing she's trusting me, her best friend, with her secret.

When I don't respond, she continues. "I denied every chance, every kiss, because I didn't want to take a risk."

"But losing your virginity is important to you," I add, squeezing her knee.

"It's because I don't take risks, which is why I've barely done anything with a guy. It's okay to kiss a few frogs, and I've denied every single one, and at this rate, I'll probably end up alone."

"Maya, you're incredible, you won't end up alone!"

"Agree to disagree."

I adjust myself so I'm looking up at her, her eyes shining bright from the TV light. "Why are you saying this to me?

"Throw everything I said about Noah Hart out the window, Hannah, and take your risk."

MAYA LEAVES BEFORE I WAKE, leaving a note telling me she loves me and she hopes to see me back at the resort for the event. Because she is Maya Gomez, she took the liberty of charging my phone while I slept. She won't push me to go, but I know she's secretly hoping I will. I'm not even sure if my presence is enough.

Days go on, and Christmas arrives. I bought a new charger only to stare at my phone, waiting for a text that will never come. And it won't because I pushed him to go. All my other belongings sit untouched back at Snowy Peak, so I had very little to wear for Christmas Day with Mom.

She makes a wonderful small dinner for us, her classic decor of colored Christmas lights and a Christmas tree reminds me of my early childhood days. Buttery rolls, and later, her famous apple pie, fill my stomach, warming my body and making me sleepy.

I'm sitting on her black, leather couch, reclined and under my newly knitted blanket she made me for Christmas, when she decides now is the perfect time to ask about my love life.

"Anything new?" She eyes me over her coffee mug.

"About?" But I know damn well what she's asking.

"Hannah."

I play dumb. "Maya's good, so are Anthony and Jill."

"And Noah?" My heart nearly stops because there's a good chance she's seen the article.

"Fine."

"He's very handsome."

"Mom."

"What? I can't ask why my daughter is seen with an Olympian? What's he doing for Christmas?"

Where the hell is she going with this? "How would I know?"

"May or may not have spoken to Maya before your arrival."

I am going to kill her. "There's nothing to tell. I helped him get back on the slopes for the event, that's it."

Mom puts her mug down on the coffee table. Her dark brown hair falls over her shoulders when she leans forward, her blue eyes are twins to my own. "Hannah, if you like him, what's holding you back?"

I swallow hard, knowing my own mother has no idea of what my past relationship with Liam is like. Therapy, yes, but not the reason. But she's my mom, and her judgment is far from hurtful. "I'm afraid it's going to end up the same way it did with Liam. He wasn't the best, Mom."

She waves her hand at me like it's old news. "Oh, he was a clown. I spotted that from a mile away."

I blink a few times, realizing what came out of my mom's mouth, then snort a laugh. "That much is true."

"But Noah...?"

"Noah is..." Dangerously addictive, arrogant, and intoxicating. He's a complicated mess, like me. Maybe we are perfect for each other. "He's leaving after the event; nothing can come of it."

"Do you want to be with him?"

Her question is so jarring that it takes me a few minutes to answer. Mom has never been so blunt before. I wonder where it's coming from. "Yes, but..."

"No buts, Hannah, do you want to be with him?"

"Yes! Okay, yes, I want to be with him."

"Then what are you waiting for?"

I've been staring at my phone for the past hour, debating whether to tell Maya if I'm coming back or not. The event is today, and even after my revelation with Mom on Christmas, I still hesitate to go.

Noah's story comes back to me as I'm staring out my window, watching pedestrians go about their day. His vulnerability and honesty about what happened to him must have been a lot, and he didn't have to tell me, but he did. He trusts me to let me inside his head because he knows the root of his twisties and how everyone he thought loved him hurt him in the end.

Except...me. Noah knew somehow, through the arguments and intimate moments, that I truly believed in him.

But if I don't go, he won't perform, and I know Maya says it's not my fault, but if I don't return, Noah will continue to hide out in his cabin and ditch the event. He's the star of the show, the one everyone is dying to see perform in a small town.

I absentmindedly start packing my things, rummaging through my clothes, getting new pairs of underwear, and cuter outfits.

My mind is already made up, I just refuse to acknowledge it

because I'll let myself chicken out. He probably doesn't care about me now, and honestly, I'm most likely the only one madly in love, but if I can get him to listen and perform, then at least it won't be all for nothing.

The clock on my phone reads 9:45 as I pay the cab driver, throw my duffel bag over my shoulder, and quickly exit the vehicle. Snowy Peak is a winter wonderland of colorful wreaths and Christmas decorations. Staff are already ushering in people through ticket lines, clasping colorful bracelets around their wrists.

Traffic delayed my arrival, but thankfully, the event doesn't start until 10:30.

My cabin remains untouched—clothes in disarray, some hanging off of furniture. My camera lies in the middle of my bed, and I grab it to check my storage card. Out of habit, I double-check my gallery—and freeze when my own body fills the screen.

Noah's large hand cups my breast, my love handles, even my chin, forcing me to look directly at the camera. All my nerve endings tingle. My stomach flips; my ears are pulsating from how hard my heart pounds.

"Promise me if you ever doubt yourself, you'll look at them, okay?"

He knew, he sees right through my messed-up mind, that I've been doubting myself, even having sex with him, and wanted to reassure me I am worth it. Regardless of who came after him, I'm not only worth it to someone but to myself.

I am worth it, even before him, and Liam, I am.

Through all the haze and roadblocks, I'm always worth something, even to myself.

I hope I have enough time to remind Noah as well.

Checking the clock, I have exactly fifteen minutes before the boys go set up at the halfpipe and hopefully convince Noah to perform.

Changing out of my dark green coat for my signature pink and blue winter hat, I dash out the door, almost knocking over a couple and their child.

"I'm sorry!" I yell behind me, racing through the cluster of cabins until I spot cabin twenty-four. Taking the steps two at a time, I trip on the last step, almost landing face-first, but I gracefully catch myself.

"Noah!" I knock aggressively, hoping my annoying knocking gets his ass moving. "Open up!"

"He's not in there."

I whip around to see Cassy, arms crossed, a permanent scowl on her face. "Excuse me?" Out of all the people, it's her that gives me an update on his whereabouts.

"I said, he's not in there. He's already up at the halfpipe. Maybe if you paid attention, you would know that. Or did he already dump you?" Cassy flips her hair and leaves, heading in the direction of the event, leaving me standing on his front porch, mouth slightly agape.

But I don't have time to reassess, jumping over the steps and hightailing it straight through the growing crowd of guests.

I'm running, trying to push through; hopefully, I'm not too late. Noah is about to start, and my panic rises when I reach the barrier, catching sight of Henry, waving at him, praying he sees me.

Bodies bump into my back, making me stumble into the barrier, but I won't give up, I can't give up. No matter what, I have to see him before he performs.

Jumping like a mad woman and waving my hands around like I'm trying to direct a freaking plane, Henry finally sees my frantic moves and comes rushing over. "Move, let her through!"

But it's no use, people are trying their hardest to get as close to the barrier as possible to get a great view, some shouting back at me to fuck off. Last time I checked, this is a family resort, but they can't control the hungry fan club.

"Fuck this," mutters Henry and holds out his arms to me. "Do you trust me?"

I nod and get a grip with my snow boots on the barrier as Henry grabs my waist and hoists me over. People start bitching, mostly young teenage fans, about me bypassing security, but I'm already running up the side, my breathing hard and chest tight from the cold.

"Go, Hannah! Go find him!" Henry yells from behind me.

His encouragement drives my legs to run faster, and I thank my lucky stars I bought those expensive snow boots with better grip so I don't fall on my ass.

I spot Mark and Cody warming up, Coach Jones talking with Taylor, but there's no sign of Noah. I hope to God I'm not too late and he's already at his starting point.

Using whatever breath I have left, I start to shout his name. "Noah! Noah, wait!"

My layers are starting to make me sweat with how hard I'm running, but I persevere, calling out his name again, hoping the wind carries my voice to him. "Noah!"

It's as if time stops, snow has stopped falling from the sky, and even the crowd below is in hushed tones when Noah pokes his head around Mark and Cody.

Our eyes lock, and he makes no hesitation to toss his snowboard aside, throw his goggles, and slide down to meet me halfway. He grabs my face, eyes scorching through my very being, lips parted, and his breathing just as heavy as mine, for only sprinting a short distance to me.

"Hannah," he sighs, like his whole world makes sense again.

Time is ticking, and I'm not sure if it's enough for him to conquer whatever demons plague him, but I hope what I say to him is enough to try. "Noah, you were right. I've always believed in you. Since the beginning, when we hated each other, I never doubted you could do it."

"Hannah—"

"No." I stop him before he tries to get a word in. "I need to say this. Please."

He waits, never letting go of my face.

"And you believed in me. You knew from the beginning I was worth it. I am worth it, regardless of what happened in my past; I am always worth it." Tears are threatening to fall, but I hold them steady and deliver my last line to him. "Whatever happens, you'll always make me proud, even when we part ways. I will always be proud of you."

I take his hands and shove him back, using my eyes to tell him he needs to do this, and I'll be right here watching till the very end.

Noah hesitates, lingering, watching my face, but only nods and retrieves his stuff, heading to the starting line.

Henry catches up and pulls me aside. "I'm so glad you made it."

I turn back, watching Noah disappear beyond his teammates. "Let's hope it's enough."

I'M at the starting line, sliding my goggles over my eyes, watching the crowd below cheer. Morning wind picks up, chilling my nose and cheeks. I'm counting backward in my head from ten, inhaling and exhaling in between to keep my nerves in check. So far so good, and even better after seeing Red.

Gosh, she's even more breathtaking when she's all disheveled from running up the hill. Her cheeks the color of red roses, lips pouty and plump, eyes as blue as the fucking Mediterranean Sea. Knowing she's here and back to see this through warms all my muscles. My chest vibrates with a familiar emotion: one of love and trust. It throws all our fights, and she's pushing me out the window. There's nothing to forgive; she's not at fault for how I arrived unexpectedly at her doctor's office and reacted the way she did. I overstepped, big time. And I gave her space, hoping, praying, to see her again and hear her voice one more time.

Now she's by my side and waiting to see this through with me.

Because when I reach the end of my run, I know who I'll be celebrating with at the bottom, who I'll hug and kiss when it's over, and I'm not letting her go, not this time, regardless of what her last words were to me.

I'm going to save her best friend's ski resort. I'm going to save us.

An announcer hushes the crowd, and I roll my shoulders in anticipation as he goes through the roster of each Olympian. Each second that passes is another attempt at psyching myself out, and I refuse to let my insecurities destroy what I've worked so hard to build.

"First up is two-time gold medal Olympian Noah Hart! All the way from Salt Lake City, Utah!"

Cheers roar up the halfpipe, and the crowd goes berserk, waving signs and phones, capturing every second.

I get into my stance, wiggling out the last of my anxiety, and picture the one person who has become my anchor.

A shot is heard, and I'm coasting down, wind whipping past, gaining speed for my first trick. Blue eyes come to mind when I ease into a butter trick, a Nose-Roll 180. It sticks, not a single hiccup when I lift the nose from the snow and pop an airborne spin, turning it into a full 360.

Shouts of excitement and whistles erupt when I land, and I continue, my mind utterly empty of everything except for my image of Red.

My lips are chapped, breathing heavy, preparing for my next move. Air to fakie is my favorite in the lineup, and I'm able to jump, launch from one of the walls, and come back down, but riding backward. It's flawless when I complete it, chasing the high of the adrenaline rush of not only my moves but the crowd as well.

It's everything I've missed these past few weeks, having full control of my brain and how I'm able to move my body without restraint. It's who I am down to my core, a turning point in my childhood that made me the man I am today.

It's Alley-Oop time, and I smile, remembering when I tried to help Red polish it. The way she rolls her eyes and argues, how defiant she is when she believes she's right and someone else is wrong. I barely register my actions when I'm already completing the move, soaring even higher in the clouds.

Chants of my name get louder the further I get to the end, wanting my last move to make history here at Snowy Peak.

Double McTwist 1260 is the move I performed when I lost my last gold medal, and it's the move I'm going to make now.

Only this time, I'm going to stick the landing.

ANXIETY RUNS through my body at a hundred miles per hour, making my hands shake, my legs weak, and even my head. Watching Noah from down here is maddening, worse than when I was trying from the top.

He's been doing incredibly well so far, and I'm still waiting for a mishap or his body to contort in mid-air, sending my heart into overdrive of worry.

Noah has one more move, and if he makes it, he's back and able to perform on his own without my help.

I won't lie and say it doesn't break my heart, knowing he doesn't need me anymore, but at least he's back on track to win more gold medals if he chooses to do so.

Noah starts to get ready, riding down, when he shifts his board, heading toward the vert. Henry came down with me to the bottom barriers. Maya is on his left, leaning over, anticipating what he'll end his run with.

Seconds tick on, but it feels like hours when Noah performs his final move, combining three and a half twists and then two more flips, all in one piece of air, landing perfectly, gliding right down to the finish line.

I don't catch what happens next, news outlets swarm, and even Henry jumps the barrier, pushing through to get to Noah.

Noah managed to battle his twisties and perform an amazing run for Snowy Peak, getting the media attention we need to hopefully garner more revenue to save it.

Maya and I hug tight, jumping up and down like school girls, over the moon at the turnout.

Everyone is still chanting his name, and security comes in to wave the media back to give him some room.

"He's good now. He did it," I say, watching him take off his goggles. He doesn't need me anymore. The realization has set in, and I'm already starting to back away.

Maya is too busy looking for whomever to notice my departure, and I turn to head back to the main building, fighting the current of the crowd coming at me.

When I'm further away, I take one final look back, smiling with tears in my eyes, knowing he's basking in his success.

I'm almost to my cabin to gather my things when I hear heavy footsteps behind me.

"Red!" His voice echoes, halting my movement, but I don't dare turn around. Noah comes into view, putting up his hands to keep me from moving forward. "Where are you going?"

I sigh, my heart sinking further into my stomach. "Home, Noah. It's over. You got over your twisties and performed perfectly at the event."

"So, that's it? You're not going to stay and celebrate?" His eyes dart back and forth from my mouth to my eyes. "You're leaving?"

"Maya understands. Besides, it's over now. You can go home." And never see me again, but I can't say it, the words won't come out. I'm on the precipice of whether I confess my feelings or let them die right then and there.

"You're my cloud nine, Red."

All functions of my heart stop, making it difficult to catch my breath. "What did you just say?"

"You heard me."

Of course, I hear him, I hear him loud and clear. "No, I'm not, I can't be."

Noah shakes his head. "Yes, you are." He grabs my face, forcing me to look at him, his calloused thumbs graze my cheeks, right to my bottom lip. "Hannah." It's like he can't continue, having a hard time breathing.

That makes two of us.

"Noah—"

"No, no. What you feel isn't one-sided. It never was. God, Hannah, I was captivated by you the minute we met."

I can't form words, I can't even process his declaration. I can only stare, a rush of uncertainty, not one hundred percent sure he's telling the truth.

"Hannah, say something, please." Brown eyes search my face, trying to reach inside and cure my fear of rejection.

"How can you want someone who might not be able to give you a future with kids?" I'm shaking now, my secret word-vomiting from my mouth.

"That day...when I waited for you at the doctors..." His eyes search my face, knowing he's piecing everything together.

I make it easier and tell him the truth. "I have PCOS, Noah. It makes it difficult if I can't get it under control."

Noah is shaking his head. "No, Hannah. That doesn't change how I feel about you."

"But kids..." What the hell am I even thinking? Having any future with Noah Hart sounds so ridiculous, let alone having kids with this man.

"Why can't you see how desperate I am to have you? You're my brightest star when I watch the night sky." Noah says.

"Do you love me?" It's the only words I'm able to speak, but

I need to hear him say it out loud, to know if it's even a possibility; otherwise, I have to run as far away with my tattered heart once more.

"Yes. Yes, I love you. I'm so in love with you, Hannah—all of you. Every part of you is my favorite. You're all I think about and wonder how I can make that smart mouth snap back or smile." Warm, brown eyes search my face, his hands move to my waist, pulling me closer. "Our deal we made, that was me trying to get close to you without actually admitting it to myself. Meeting you has flipped my entire world upside down, wanting nothing more than to wake up to you." Noah rubs his nose against mine. "I never want to go another day not knowing where you are or what you're thinking. Not talking to you for these last few days killed me, but I kept my distance because I hurt you, and I know I did. It was never my intention, and for that I am so sorry."

My tears are falling now, and cupping Noah's face, I make sure I'm all he sees. "I shouldn't have reacted that way, and for that, I'm sorry."

He shakes his hand. "No, Red, please don't apologize for something I did wrong."

"But it's no excuse for me to react how I did, Noah."

He shushes me with his hand. "I invaded your privacy by forcing Maya to tell me. I broke your trust, and it's not fair to you." He's trembling now, waiting for me to forgive him.

Little does he know, I already have. "I forgive you, Noah, because I love you, too."

"Really?" He sounds so small, so unsure of my declaration in return. It's cute and heartbreaking. I never want him to feel that way again.

Tilting his face, I kiss him slowly, loving how his lips move against mine, how perfectly in sync it's become between us. His tongue darts out, and I meet him halfway, deepening the kiss, not caring who's around us to see.

All that matters is here, right now, with Noah, and our love for each other.

I break us apart early, our foreheads touch, our labored breaths matching in tempo. "Yes, Noah. I really do."

He sighs like a heavy weight has been lifted off his shoulders, then picks me up and spins me around. I'm laughing uncontrollably, yelling at him to put me down.

When he finally does, his mouth finds mine again, biting my lower lip.

I moan quietly, the sensation trailing down to my toes, wiggling inside my boots.

He lets go. His eyes smolder, half-closed. I know what he wants—because I want it too.

"Make love to me, Noah."

CLOTHES COME FLYING off the minute my cabin door shuts behind us. A hot, desperate need to feel my flushed skin against his is already making me wet. Noah kisses me as if I might disappear forever, that I might take back my declaration, but I'm too far gone, too deep in the trenches of Noah Hart. There are no other arms I would rather be in than his.

All the other times, he took his time, savoring every part of my body to his liking, but now, we're two ravenous fiends, skin on skin, hands finding all the right spots to grab and squeeze. The sounds that come from both of us aren't human, more animalistic.

We're on the floor, the soft carpet on my back, legs intertwined, the fireplace blazing with heat. Kissing Noah is never enough; I'm always wanting more every time his lips touch mine. Tongues fight for dominance as his hands cup the back of my head for more control. His erection presses against my stomach, and I wrap a leg around his hip, moving against him, wanting him to know how soaked he's already made me.

A growl escapes deep in his chest, tugging at my lip with his teeth. "Hannah, baby, you're drenched."

Taking one of his hands, I guide them down to my clit, our breaths hitching at the same time when they find its mark, circling around and around. Arching my back, Noah exchanges his pointer finger with his thumb, teasing my entrance, while his thumb circles around my clit.

"Ahhh!" I'm obnoxiously loud, aware that there's a possibility that Maya is next door in her own cabin, hearing this. "Noah, I need more, please."

And I don't give a shit.

Not anymore.

Not when Noah has me forever.

"I'm going to fuck you into oblivion, Hannah. I want to hear you scream."

I pull at his hair, forcing him to keep eye contact. "It's Red to you."

Our lips collide, breaking only to catch our breath. "Yes, it fucking is."

Because I love that nickname. I loved it when he first touched my hair, tucking it behind my ear, knowing it has affected me ever since.

Noah wastes no time placing hot kisses on my inner thighs, keeping them steady when he blows cool air at my clit, enticing my hips to roll.

He chuckles. "Now, Red, I need you still. Can you do that for me, baby?"

I want to pull the hair out of my head. "Yeah...yeah, sure."

No, no, I can't. Not when he's sucking hard on my inner thigh, leaving his mark.

He pulls back. "Hannah." He uses my real name as a warning. "I'm going to start all over again if you can't stay still."

"Fuck! Fine!" I groan, gripping the carpet for support.

He takes my pussy with his teeth and pulls, almost forcing me to come early.

Then his wicked tongue darts out, stroking over my clit, moaning in appreciation.

I'm about ready to combust when he holds back, laughing.

My nails dig into his shoulders. "If you stop again, I will die, Noah Hart. Now, fuck me properly, or I'll leave."

"Such a dirty mouth on you, Red." He plunges two fingers inside me, pumping. "But your threats are empty, because I'm never leaving you—never again."

He works his fingers, grazing my inner walls until they clench, preparing for what will surely be an earth-shattering orgasm.

But he's Noah, and he doesn't play fair.

Like the teasing bastard he is, he removes his fingers completely, leaving me panting, legs spread wide on the floor.

Brown eyes look upon every inch of my exposed body, licking his lips in hunger. He strokes himself, moaning, head rolling back.

I start to touch myself, mirroring his movements, letting breathy moans match his. He peeks at me through hooded eyes, smirking when he sees I'm pleasuring myself.

"Should I let you come on your own? Should I let you watch me make myself come?" His strokes are moving fast, pre cum oozing from the tip.

I shake my head no, slowing down my movements.

"I'm a selfish man, Red. Although I would enjoy this, I want nothing more than to bury myself inside you and feel you come around my cock."

My breathing escalates. "Stop stalling and get over here."

Noah attacks, lifting me in his arms and tossing me on the bed. "Hold the bars, Red."

The metal headboard rattles when I grip the golden bars, my arms above my head. Noah crawls on top of me, his eyes dark and smoldering. He parts my legs with his knee and helps himself to sucking on my nipples. The air hits my core, and I whimper, eyes rolling to the back of my head.

I'm about to let go and reach for his hair when he forces me to stay, gripping the bar. "Let's see how much self-control you have, Red. I'm dying to know. Otherwise, I'm gonna have to tie you up."

I'm panting now, chest rising and falling, feeling heavy. "This is torture."

He chuckles, nuzzling his face in the crook of my neck. Lips dance along my too-hot skin, and Noah bites my earlobe. I hiss, toes curling.

I want to touch him, hold on, and dig my nails in his perfect skin.

He takes his cock and lightly taps my clit, making me jerk. "Noah!"

"Condom, Red?" he asks, hitting me once again.

"No." My response is quick because I'm dying to know what he feels like without that extra barrier.

"And where would you like me to come?" He's stroking himself again, distracting me.

I lick my lips. Noah is giving me a choice, because my pleasure is what he strives for.

Fuck, can he be any more perfect?

"On me," I say confidently.

He comes closer, teasing my entrance with the head of his cock. We both inhale sharply, like it's the first time all over again.

But Noah pushes all the way in, and I moan so loud with him I can't tell where he begins or where I end.

He's steady with his hips, keeping a medium pace, while I hold on to the headboard bars for dear life as he thrusts into me.

Without a condom, his erection is harder, absolutely

euphoric against my walls. Our eyes lock, lips swollen, breath mixing.

"Noah, let me touch you, please," I beg.

"You want to touch me, Red?" He never lets up, thrusting harder into me. "How bad do you want it?"

"So fucking bad, Noah, please."

He reaches forward and removes my hands from the bars, giving me freedom to snake them around his neck, my fingers tugging his hair.

With each hard thrust comes louder moans from my throat, following incoherent words.

Noah brushes his nose against mine, then lifts my right leg higher, entering deeper inside me.

"I love you," he huskily says, pushing me higher toward the peak. His declaration of love will never not make my heart soar.

"I love you too."

We reach our climax together, mine first, my walls contracting, eyes shut as I scream just as he pulls out and spills himself all over my chest. It's warm, but I don't care, not when his fingers enter me to help me ride out the rest of my climax.

My body shakes when it's over, and the absence of his touch is brief, as he returns with a towel, wiping his cum from my chest.

I open my eyes to find him hovering over me. "Hi." He smiles, it's big and beautiful, making me smile in return.

"Hi."

Noah's lips linger for a second, then he kisses me. It's gentle and slow, intimate and sweet, making my toes curl once again.

He pulls away first, pushing my hair behind my ear, then holds me for a while. The only time we're apart is for a bathroom break, but even then, he's only a few feet from me at all times.

Eventually, we come up for air, hang out with our friends at dinner, and listen to his teammates recount their performance, bitching that we missed it.

Noah holds my hand on the table, squeezing it every so often and winking over at me. My love for him grows by the second, stronger, bigger; it's enough to swallow anyone whole, and I'm glad it's someone like him.

ONE WEEK LATER...

Anthony and Jill make reservations at the local tavern, inviting not only Maya and me but Coach Jones, his daughters, the team, and Henry. Tonight, we find out if all our efforts saved Snowy Peak, and the anticipation is killing me.

My legs are bouncing under the table, and Noah has to keep holding them steady. "You're giving me anxiety."

"Sorry, I'm just nervous." And rightfully so, as Snowy Peak means everything to me, and if what we did, what the team did, doesn't help rejuvenate all that lost revenue, then it's truly over.

Noah leans in, his lips tickling my ear. "After dinner, I can help ease some of it, if you like?"

I shiver. He knows damn well I want nothing more than for him to ease the fuck out of me, but now is not the time. I pinch his side, and he yelps in pain. "Not right now, too many ears."

He tugs at a loose curl and smiles. "Whatever you say." Winking like an idiot, I shut him up with a quick peck to his lips.

Nobody is surprised at our recently changed relationship status. Rather, the guys, even Maya, my own best friend, were taking bets to see when we'd finally stop eye fucking each other and get together. Maya obviously won cause she knew. The girl is super observant when she wants to be.

Henry hasn't been able to keep his eyes off of her ever since we arrived, and I'm starting to think there's something more happening between them, but until Maya is ready, I won't press it any further.

Anthony orders a bottle of an expensive red wine, and the waiter pours each of us a glass, leaving an extra bottle on the table.

Jill taps her glass, signaling everyone to pay attention. "I want to thank you all for joining us this evening, and especially a huge thanks to Coach Jones and his men for helping us put on such a wonderful event here in Vermont."

Glasses all raised in unison, with mumbles of "yes" and "here, heres." I'm already smiling at Maya when she turns to me, her eyes filled with happy tears.

Anthony stands next, glass in hand, looking at all of us around the table. "When we first established our ski resort, it was in hopes of bringing friends and family together to create long-lasting memories and hopefully strangers to cross paths." He gives me and Noah a quick glance, smiling, then continues. "But we never thought it would last for over twenty-five years. When our now ex-accountant came to us, letting us know our revenue was tanking, we all but threw in the towel."

I freeze, catching Maya doing the same. Ex-accountant?

"Dad?" Maya says, a look of uncertainty marks her face.

"Yes, we discovered Dennis has been using our funds to embezzle it all into his own personal accounts. That's why our revenue was tanking. Not because people didn't love Snowy Peak, it's because we trusted someone too much and overlooked any wrongdoings he committed."

Holy shit, Dennis is an absolute piece of shit.

"But, ultimately, it was our daughter Maya and her best friend Hannah who reminded us that just because times get tough, we can't give up. We must strive every day and try our hardest, regardless of the circumstances. It was the reminder we needed to call up a dear friend for help."

Jill is already crying, and Coach Jones is beaming like a proud dad, literally. His daughters, Elise and Ella, hug him on either side, and even Mark with his wife Sophia, Cody, Taylor, and Noah are chanting Coach's name.

"And because of their gracious decision to make Snowy Peak their last stop on their tour, it is with great honor to announce, Snowy Peak is staying open for business!"

In our private room, we all cheer, Noah kisses me, then high-fives the guys. Anthony and Jill hug, tears flowing freely now. Henry awkwardly looks around, watching Maya run over to my side, hugging me tight.

My favorite place in the entire world, a place so close to my heart, is safe to continue for however many years the Gomezes decide to keep it running.

Coach Jones downs his glass of wine, and a cheesy grin spreads across his face. "I think a new tradition has been made."

Anthony downs his glass, smacking Coach on the back. "A tradition indeed."

TWO YEARS LATER...

I'm more nervous than I should be. I've had this planned for months, right down to the minuscule details, courtesy of Maya and her ability to hunt down everything I needed. Time with Hannah over the past year has been everything and more, from romantic dinners in Italy to early sunrises in Hawaii. We've done everything since saving Snowy Peak, and now I sit, nerves on edge, trying to get myself to calm down enough before she comes up to the roof.

The manager of her apartment finally gave me the okay after bribing him with Olympic merchandise and two free tickets to the Olympic Games. He was more than eager to lead me up here himself, where I had Maya help decorate the rooftop.

I spread out a thick white blanket, trickle some loose rose petals on top, and put a bottle of champagne in an ice bucket. Maya arranged an assortment of chocolates and even took the liberty of picking up Hannah's favorite pizza around the corner, Santarpios. Maya finishes the last of the lights she strung around the entrance, telling me it's on a timer and it'll shut off in an hour.

Hannah's only job is to follow the trail of roses I left for her, leading to the very top.

Maya sneaks behind part of the entrance, camera in hand, along with Hannah's mother, Beth.

I asked her weeks ago, barely able to get the words out, thinking I might puke, when she touched my face, smiled, and gave me her blessing.

Now, I wait with bated breath, counting down the seconds in my head, hearing the soft creak on the stairs as Hannah comes closer to the top.

Suddenly the door opens, and I'm turning, ready to greet the love of my life, when Henry strolls right over.

"Who the fuck invited this clown?" snaps Maya.

"You're late," I say, ushering him over to where both ladies are hiding.

"I texted Maya for directions, but she never responded." He gives her a dirty look, kneeling down so he's out of sight.

"Never got it." She rolls her eyes like he's the biggest inconvenience to walk the planet.

"Liar."

I squash their bickering before it gets ugly, and save Beth, Hannah's mom, from having to deal with both idiots on her own.

It's December, but in New England, the weather isn't always true to its season. It's roughly sixty degrees, and a light breeze ruffles some of my hair, and I hold my breath as Hannah makes it through the door.

She's in her usual comfy clothes, black leggings and her favorite cream sweater, the one she wore on Christmas Day a year ago. Her brown boots click when she walks closer, the brightest smile reaching her blue eyes.

"Hey," she says, reaching for my hand.

I take it, knowing she can tell how clammy my palm is. "I thought we could have our two-year anniversary dinner up here."

"Oh really?"

I pull her in, kissing those lips that claimed me a couple of years ago.

I'll never forget the first time we met. Never forget that red hair, so striking, just like her eyes, so blue it takes my breath away, even now. She cares so deeply about the people she loves and places she calls home. Her determination to save Snowy Peak made her even more irresistible to me.

The way she carries herself, her quick whip of her tongue whenever I piss her off, to the sounds she makes when I get her so close to coming undone. How she comes apart at the seams when it's just her and I, tangled together in sheets, exploring our bodies, taking it to new heights.

That's my Hannah.

My cloud nine.

Hannah is a religion I'll gladly worship, day in and day out. I'll kneel for her on jagged rocks if it means I can spend every waking moment and from sunrise to nightfall.

We pull apart, and I watch her take a big sniff, eyes lighting up like fireworks. "You got my favorite pizza, didn't you?"

It's all going to plan, her walking over to the pizza box and opening the lid, I follow closely behind, getting down on one knee behind her.

This is it, this is everything I've wanted and more, to spend the rest of my life with the most selfless, beautiful woman I've been given the privilege to know and love.

"What a perfect pie," she comments, turning back to me, only to find I'm kneeling in front of her.

She gasps, hand covering her mouth, blue eyes glistening. "Noah."

"Hannah Rose St. Pierre, from the minute we met, I knew exactly who I wanted to spend the rest of my life with. It's always been you. My cloud nine. Will you marry me?" Fuck, my hands are clammy, my right leg is trying its best to keep me steady.

Hannah kneels, cupping my face with both hands. "Of course I'll marry you, Noah Hart."

Taking the ring out of the velvet red box, I slip it on her ring finger, watching the 14 karat stone shimmer under the city lights. She kisses me senseless, completely unaware her best friend, Henry, and her mother are hiding nearby.

I break away first. "All right, guys, you can come on out!"

Hannah looks confused, searching around, when she spots Beth first, running over. She meets her mother halfway, crying, then Maya joins, and Henry comes over to me, giving me a hug.

"Gonna be a married man now, huh?" he says, ruffling my hair.

I push him playfully. "Yes, will you be my best man?"

Henry beams, face red as he rubs the back of his neck. "Are you sure?"

"Who else is going to stand by my side while I marry the love of my life?" Honestly, Henry has been through so much shit with me, it's only right he's the one to stand by my side when I marry Hannah.

"And we all know Maya is going to be her maid of honor, so it makes things easier that you both already know each other," I add, watching them hug from where we stand.

Henry's face falls, turning sour. "Great, can't wait."

I laugh, smacking his back. "Lighten up. By the way, we're thinking of doing our reception at a familiar place."

Hannah comes over then, Maya in tow.

"Oh really? Where?" Maya asks.

Hannah catches on, wrapping her arms around my neck. "Some place snowy, I presume?"

I nod. "Snowy, indeed."

THE END

Checked Inn
Coming Soon

The following is an excerpt of the first chapter of book 2 in the Snowy Peak Series.

Be adivised this is an uncorrected proof.

CHAPTER 1

MAYA

"Maya? Maya Gomez?"

I'm mid chew staring at the one person I never thought I would see again. My parents, Jill and Anthony, eager expressions make the once delicious, buttery dinner roll taste bitter.

I have to swallow hard, along with gulping most of my water to get it down my esophagus before I choke to death.

It's been two years since I've been on a date—one date with this man who ruined it all by pulling out a gift card to pay for it. Somehow and some twisted fated way, he's here standing before me.

Gift Card Dude smiles like he's won the lottery. My smile is forced and painful, my insides start to shrivel up.

God forgive me.

He's waiting, for what? I don't know. I blink several times at him like a deer in headlights.

What the hell do I say to him?

I don't even remember the poor bastard's name!

Mom is ready to find out on my behalf. "Hun, who's your friend?"

"Uhh..." I want to crawl under the table and never come out.

"Oh, I'm sorry, where are my manners? I'm Shawn." He extends a hand, shaking Mom's then my dad's.

And here I thought Noah helping me turn him down easy would keep him away. I need a stronger repellent spray.

"Yes, right, sorry," I mumble. Get me the hell out of here.

"It's crazy seeing you here of all places!" He's overly cheerful, reminding me of how easy it was to like him. He is always so confident and upbeat, with shaggy blond hair and puppy dog brown eyes, he expels positivity. You can't help but return the feeling.

No, Maya, do not feel bad.

Because god forbid I stick to my guns and try to let a man down right the first time.

"Do you come here often?" Dad asks.

"Whenever I have a gift card, I like to come here."

Jesus fucking christ.

Cringing so hard internally, I might combust where my blood sprays everywhere like a shitty horror movie.

Shawn laughs, it's loud and weird, almost like he's choking. "My friends call me the king of gift cards, discount hustler if you will." Finally registering his attire, he sports worn-out khakis and a green puffer jacket, his hands moving a mile a minute.

His icks are all starting to come back now.

This is supposed to be a nice, once a month dinner with my parents, Instead, it has turned into a skit on SNL.

Kill me now.

Dad catches a glimpse of my expression and sits up a little straighter. "Well, it was lovely to meet you Shane-."

"Shawn," he corrects politely, his exuberant smile never faltering.

'Right, yes. If you don't mind, we're going to get back to our dinner with our daughter." My dad's smile is easy to mistake as genuine because there's a good chance he's catching my vibes of how I really feel about gift card dude.

"Oh, of course! Enjoy! Maya, it was great seeing you again! Maybe we can catch up sometime?"

His request makes it hard to keep eye contact, my eyes wander over to my half eaten dinner roll, picking at it when I say, "Ah maybe, I travel a lot."

"Totally understandable! And it was lovely to meet you all. Have a wonderful dinner!" His buoyant goodbye makes me sad, mainly because he has no idea how I struggled internally to hide away.

He's a nice guy, he just has too many...attributes that don't fit my vibe. It's a very polite way to say he is weird, and I don't have the heart to tell him to leave me alone. So, I had Noah do it for me, and clearly that didn't fucking work!

He's getting a lengthy text from me later tonight.

I have no problem defending my friends and family from asshats who inconvenience them or break their hearts. I'm the first one swinging and the last to get a word in. But when it comes to my failed dates and rejecting them, it's a hit-and-run situation.

There's no in between, I wasn't wired that way.

"Sorry about that," I apologize, resuming with stuffing my face with my now cold dinner roll.

"It's not your fault. I mean, he seemed like a nice young man," Mom says, taking a sip of her wine.

Dad, however, rolls his eyes. "Once I got a good look at Maya's face, I knew she wanted him gone. Did he hurt you?" His voice drops, Papa Bear activated.

"No! No, oh god no. He's just...someone I didn't mesh well with on our date." I like a man who knows how to woo a woman with his cash flow.

"Wait..." Mom pauses, I catch each gear working overtime in her head. "Was that Gift Card Dude?" Totally forgot she knew the lore behind this man.

Curse myself for being so open to dear old mom.

"You named him gift card dude?" Dad's chuckle begins, until he's in hysterics, face red, tears streaming down his face, the entire table starts to shake from how hard he is laughing.

Mom tries to get him to relax, patting his back as he coughs through his laughter.

"Ugh, all right, changing the subject now, please!" Thankfully, our waiter returns with our entrees, filet and steamed broccoli with a garlic mash.

Dad catches his breath and manages not to choke to death on his own saliva. "Sorry, I just can't help but laugh at the nicknames you give them."

I stab aggressively at my filet, with a steak knife, and cut it into uneven pieces. "It was an accident." One I will *never* make again.

Dad snorts, but Mom hits his shoulder playfully. "Anthony, enough. Our daughter is already traumatized as it is."

He holds up his hands. "Hey, you gotta kiss a frog or two."

Luckily, my lips were nowhere near him.

We continue our conversation before *his* unexpected interruption, chatting about my job as a social media manager for Owen Sanders and his incredible journey as a five-star Michelin chef in New York City. I've only been at it for a few months, and it's fun, not my ideal position, but it helps pay my bills.

And my shoe box apartment in the city.

Dad dabs at his mouth with a maroon napkin and clears his throat. "I love our once-a-month dinners and your mother, and I am so happy to share some exciting news with you."

I raise my eyebrows. "Exciting news, you say?" Pushing my

plate aside, I link my fingers, elbows on the table, and rest my chin, waiting. "Do tell."

"We think it's time your father and I enter a more relaxed venture. One where it's not so leader-based." Mom clasps hands with Dad, both grinning.

Either they're waiting for me to catch on or to ask a follow-up question. I choose the latter. "Oh, and what venture would that be?"

"Retirement," they say in unison.

"What?" I rub my ears, making sure nothing is blocking them. "Come again?"

"Your father and I are not getting any younger, and we believe it's time we hand down the resort...that's if you still want it?" Mom says.

Yeah, I want it... But now? I'm only twenty-six, and it's been two years since we saved it from going under because their shitty ex-accountant, Dennis, stole almost all the funds. I'm banking on my late thirties to hopefully receive it... I just got a new job to...

I can't let my parents sell it either. That's a hell fucking no from me.

They're watching me, probably guessing correctly about my internal freak out. I need to tell them yes, I have too. Snowy Peak is my second home.

I'm...not one hundred percent ready, but for my parents to enjoy early retirement, then I'm going to have to be.

"Yes! Omg, of course! Are you sure?" I exclaim, reaching for their hands.

They squeeze mine back, tears in their eyes. "Oh, Honey, I'm so happy to keep it in the family. Don't worry, we'll make sure everything is transferred over and in good standing before we leave you to it." Mom pats my cheek, then she's so proud of me.

My face starts to get hot, and my anxiety makes my fingers tingle. "Um, I gotta use the bathroom, I'll be right back."

I'm almost running like I'm getting chased by a serial killer to the ladies' room, almost knocking into a waitress carrying a tray full of food and slipping inside.

Not bothering to check under the stalls, I lean over the sink, trying to breathe through my nose. "Holy shit." I look in the mirror, my face is crimson, even more so against my pink blouse.

It's only natural that I grab my phone, searching for Hannah in my contacts but remembering she's on vacation with her fiancee Noah. I hit back and snort when Henry's name is under hers. He's Noah's assistant and a pain in my ass.

Clicking on it, I'm half tempted to delete. We haven't spoken in awhile and whenever we're in the same place, the ski resort to be exact, we somehow miss each other.

I only have his number because he needed info on Hannah's return to the resort a couple years back.

My thumb hovers over the call button, like he would answer me. I never forgot his comment from two years ago either.

The woman's bathroom door swings open, making me jump, as a mother helps her daughter choose the furthest stall. I'm trying to stop my heart from pounding so hard when I hear a sound coming through my phone's speaker.

"Maya? Are you there?"

I stick my ear to my phone. "Who's this?"

"You called me."

Shit.

His voice is smooth, velvety... I hate it.

Henry.

Preorder Checked Inn here:
https://a.co/d/o1QnjmwT

ACKNOWLEDGMENTS

Where do I begin? I ask myself constantly when I write out my acknowledgements but it has to start somewhere.

So here it goes.

I want to thank my agent, Angie, for being my cheerleader and encouraging me to write my very first rom com. For letting me give her crazy ideas and still willing to work with how chaotic my brain can be sometimes. I know more amazing opportunities our coming for us!

For Marni my editor, you've been with me for over 8 years and read every story. Our journey will forever continue until you get sick of me. Thank you.

Thank you Liz Parkes, my fabulous cover designer! You truly knocked it out of the park and captured Hannah and Noah so perfectly I sobbed when the final image delivered to my inbox. I can't wait to work with you again!

I want to thank my alpha and beta readers, Kelsey, Christine, Morgan, and Elena. For taking the time out of your busy lives to champion for this book and making sure it's the best it can be!

Thank you to Erika for believing in this story and letting Cloud Nine have its first foreign translation with Brazil! You're truly a wonderful human who cares so deeply about books and the authors. Everyone needs an Erika in their lives.

My family and close friends, thank you for letting me live my dreams and supported me through some rough months. Your constant support and love was what got me through most of my hardships with this project.

To my sidekick, someone who has become my best friend and anchor, Elizabeth. Thank you for being by my side while I navigated a new project, and let me cry, complain, and laugh for months about dumb stuff because it's what we do. Life would be so dull without you.

Finally, to my readers. I cannot thank you all enough for sticking with me this long and watching me hop from genre to genre and still willing to read every crazy story I make. You guys are the real MVPs.

ABOUT THE AUTHOR

Amanda is a Netflix binge watcher, Buffy and Gilmore Girls fanatic, and bagel enthusiast. Residing in the suburbs of Massachusetts, she lives with her black lab named Jack.

www.amandasinatra.net